THE UNRAVELING MAN

DAVID HOWARD

COPYRIGHT

ISBN: 9781976761973

❀ Created with Vellum

For Vicki
What a team we make

1

"The bed is not going, that much we know," Kat Nolan said definitively as she looked around Joe Brandt's apartment. His three rooms were filled with moving boxes, disassembled bookcases and the art from his walls now stacked by the door. Joe and Kat had spent months arriving at a decision to live together and then, with greater difficulty, scheduling his move into her apartment on Mississippi River Boulevard. Now that winter was on St. Paul's doorstep, they knew they'd better relocate him soon or it would drag on into spring. This was one of the last Sunday afternoons they'd have available to move his stuff before snow fell.

Despite her modest salary from the county as a psychological therapist in Family Services and her considerable grad school tuition at the University of Minnesota, Kat owned a two bedroom apartment overlooking the lusciously wooded parkway perched above the steep bank along the Mississippi River. The area was among the most desirable neighborhoods in the city and her home was on the classiest street, with the loveliest setting. It was the sort of place most people can only dream of calling home. It had oak floors, a four season sun porch, high quality period details, a remodeled chef's kitchen, spacious rooms, high ceilings and meticulous built-ins. She actually owned the whole 1920s six-unit brick apartment building and the other five rents more than paid the upkeep, so she made a monthly profit. This meant Joe wouldn't even have to contribute rent to live with his lovely girlfriend in a place that was far better than any home he'd ever known. He'd soon be moving half way across the city and to the other end of the quality-of-life spectrum.

Kat had decorated each room of her home with style and taste at costs she couldn't bring herself to reveal to him, knowing that the expense would horrify him. Her place had come together perfectly so it was chic but livable. Kat loved her home. Joe loved her place. Kat loved Joe and Joe loved Kat. 'So what's the problem?' he asked himself.

In Joe's apartment, Kat surveyed his things and said, "We could donate it all to the Salvation Army." Her eyes landed on such eyesores as his frayed easy chair, the couch with a plaid throw covering exposed springs, a coffee table that had come from the Salvation Army in the first place, the Formica kitchen table, the dishes which almost seemed intentionally mismatched. Other than his framed diplomas from the University of Minnesota undergrad and law school and a handful of basketball trophies, her eyes could not find anything that she could imagine seeing in her home.

She was having a hard time transitioning from it being hers to it being theirs. She loved the idea of Joe living with her, just as she loved all the nights he had spent in her home and bed already, the Sunday mornings doing the crossword, the Sunday afternoon hikes down through the river bluff park to the bank of the Mississippi right below her place, sex in the sun porch in broad daylight because no one could see into the third floor. The trouble was, she wanted Joe living in her apartment without changing it at all. 'Is that too much to ask,' she kept asking herself without wanting to admit she knew the answer: it was.

"Some of this stuff will go to my mother," Joe said. "That furnished place of hers has a lot of crap in it."

'What in here would improve that?' Kat said to herself but she succeeded in leaving it unspoken. "Have you decided what goes to her yet?" she asked tactfully.

"That's why you're here," he said with a grin and a squeeze. He didn't seem to be picking up her body language.

"And the stuff that doesn't go to your mom?" Kat said. 'Free rent, a beautiful place and an eager woman in your bed don't make a good enough offer?' she asked herself.

"There are a few things I could donate, I suppose," Joe admitted. He wasn't actually as dense and unaware as Kat supposed. He knew he was making her suffer, but they were negotiating and he was accustomed to wrangling the best deal possible in plea bargains with criminals and their clever attorneys. As an assistant district attorney for Ramsey County Joe was used to demanding more than his adversary wanted to give. In her work Kat was used to giving – so their starting points created an inequality in their strategies, just as his moving into her home was an imbalance. They'd yet to find a means of making him feel like he would be both contributing and belonging.

He knew exactly what she wanted. She hoped for no sign of his presence except the dent in his pillow which she would fluff out before she left for work. Her immaculate home would remain perfect as long as his multitude of imperfections did not mar it. Not only could he not conceive of living with such perfection, in a weird way he worried it might drive him away. He wanted this move to be permanent, but for that he needed more of himself in the place – warts, faux-cherry laminate and all. It was better to stake out some territory for himself now than try to claim a few square inches later. Better but not easier.

Joe gestured across the unworthy vestiges of his life and said, "Let's designate a corner of the living room to put the stuff that I'll donate and a corner of the bedroom for stuff we'll give my mom. The rest we'll put by the door to take to our place and figure out how to rearrange."

'Rearrange!' reverberated through Kat's mind. 'But it's perfect now,' she thought. "A reasonable start," she said as she picked up the faux-cherry laminate coffee table and carried it to the far end of the living room.

"Don't think my mom could use that?"

"Not really," she said and put it down in such a way that Joe knew this piece was not within the negotiable realm. He didn't much care for that table anyway and added a lamp he disliked. That encouraged her; maybe he was willing to part with nearly everything, she dared to hope. Then she'd chip away at what little remained.

And so an unspoken war began. They worked in parallel, almost entirely in silence and always warily watching the other's choices. She bodily slid the couch into the 'donate' area and he set one of his mismatched floor lamps beside it. But soon their cooperation ended. She slid the easy chair into the same area while he stacked boxes of books – his only non-controversial possessions – near the door. Together they dragged the mattress and box spring over with the donations and while he was taking apart the bed frame, she added the two remaining non-matching floor lamps. She went after both the tall white and the short brown nightstands, but then he attacked her discards by putting a couple lamps atop the easy chair and pushing it over by the door. He was keeping them; these things had gotten him through college and law school and were among his longest-running relationships. She noticed of course but she retreated.

When she saw all the furniture together, it was even more distasteful. No two pieces shared design, color, wood or any recurring element. The only common thread was that they had fit in a limited physical space and performed some basic function. Aesthetics had never entered into the equation. As she passed the damn easy chair and lamps he'd rescued from donation, she asked herself, 'Where the hell could they go?' Then she realized he was watching her and reading her mind.

"That chair fits my butt perfectly," he explained.

"It's never looked like a non-standard butt," she said and hurried out of the room. He followed and watched from the bedroom doorway as she looked askance at his dresser.

"I have to exist somewhere, Kat," Joe said.

"I know."

"Face it, I'm ratty, old and broken in."

"I suppose I could just throw a chenille cloth over you, put you in the corner and you'd blend in a bit," she said and finally let her eyes fall on him. They had to laugh. "I know I'm being unreasonable."

He shook his head as he slid his arms around her.

"I care how things look and, well, you don't."

"Obviously," he agreed.

"So can't I just make it look nice for both of us?"

"I'd feel like a guest."

That hit her. "You would?"

"What would reveal I lived there if you had your way?" he said. "Be honest."

"The inside of your dresser drawers."

"And my ten percent of the closet."

"Yeah."

"Think that's enough?"

"No."

"Think I should just stay here?"

"Absolutely not," she said with a flash of anger. "I guess we both have to give something up."

She grabbed his hand, dragged him to the living room and pointed to the end where most of his collected worldly possessions sat conflicting with each other. "What do you see?" she demanded.

He understood, but he couldn't give up his image of himself as a tough negotiator. A plea bargain felt right only when it was deemed completely lopsided by the other guys but they had to accept it anyway. "A poster for the aestheti-cally challenged?" he suggested.

"So I have a point?"

"Of course you do. I'm an aesthetically challenged oaf who needs a coffee table I can put my feet on."

"You've never put your feet on my coffee table."

"See?"

"Because you always feel like a guest?"

"It's your very nice and shiny coffee table.

———

SUNDAY WAS USUALLY a busy time for Cory Trammell because most of the day-slaves in St. Paul had the day off to think about the homes they foolishly believed they owned. As an arborist he had to deal with people whose lives he could see but could never actually fathom – their unques-tioning devotion to a society which systematically cheated them. But his thoughts on their misfortunes were forgotten as he scrambled upward in a hundred and fifty year old elm with the spryness of a man in his mid-thirties. He would have an assortment of handsaws dangling on ropes beneath him, along with one ancient Stihl chainsaw that had cut the equivalent of a forest in his strong grip.

It was a marvel to his customers to watch this big, solid, broad-shouldered man belt up, put on his boot spikes and clamber up the trunk of their beloved shade trees to disappear into the changing fall foliage like a squirrel in its natural habitat. They would watch as he worked his way to the top, bending branches with his two hundred pounds. They all asked why he didn't use a cherry picker to hoist him up like the utility company used and he would just grunt, "Don't need it" and scramble skyward.

The real reason he didn't use a cherry picker, besides the expense cutting into his income, was that the use of large industrial equipment required a county permit. As a truly free man who adamantly exercised every shred of his precious independence, he would never deign to ask permission from any government. Instead, he did his job entirely under the county's radar. Every job he did went undetected, though his daily work efforts took him to the tops of Ramsey County's tallest trees and along all the roads the government struggled to keep useable despite enduring pot holes and a winter that lasts half the year.

Tree trimming season was only a few months in the fall before winter fell like an anvil in a single afternoon, generally between Halloween and Thanksgiving. By then it was too late to trim trees and Cory switched to selling Christmas trees and firewood from his truck and trailer. When the snows began to blanket Minnesota, he'd put chains on the tires of his Ford pickup, load the truck bed half with firewood – you never knew when someone wanted a home fire

– and half with heavy bags of sand and salt with the weight distributed over the rear wheels for traction. He would mount the plow on the front and sell his services, clearing driveways and parking lots. The chain-driven snow blower worked for walkways and he'd have the kids do the stairs. The one constant, besides how hard Cory worked, was that he only accepted cash. Period.

He had learned years ago not to try to argue with his customers about accepting checks or credit cards. At one time he had attempted to reason with the slavish fools who didn't even realize they were owned by their government masters. Those discussions had inevitably become heated and ended with no payment or without a future customer or with flying fists, an ambulance for the other guy and dodging the police for him. It wasn't worth having to disappear all over again, uprooting the family and finding new customers. If those fools believed the lies, that was their right.

Now he merely stated 'cash only' before he climbed an inch or plowed a foot. He no longer tried correcting the misconceptions of lifelong government-owned fools and reserved his teaching for his children. He let the guileless masses discover in their own pathetic ways just how thoroughly they had been sabotaged by the overlords who had sold their future on the day of their birth. They weren't his problem, they were just how he fed his family.

————————

KURT MESSNER WAS A REPEAT CUSTOMER. Cory plowed his drive and walkways in winter and two falls ago had artfully trimmed both the majestic elms on his boulevard. This year it was the oak in the back. Cory had tried to convince him the oak needed trimming two years ago, but, like most living the life of the oppressed, the man had to watch the expenses because his taxes always went up, his health insurance paid less each year, public school was supposedly free but cost him thousands anyway and the company where he crunched numbers kept telling him they could replace him with a younger, cheaper guy.

Kurt lived scared and Cory actually felt sorry for him. Even so, he didn't offer insight into the enslavements of the society he embraced, because he'd feel threatened. It was better to clear the snow, take the cash and trim the man's trees as he could afford it after watching the lion's share of his hard-fought income go to government leeches.

Kurt liked to watch Cory toiling in the tree and, like so many of his ilk, he tried to convince himself he could do it too if only he owned the right tools. Cory knew it was his inability to climb, his absence of knowledge, his failure of courage and his laziness which kept Kurt on the ground only dreaming of being able to do what he did. He didn't mind being watched at work as long as his customer stayed out from under the falling branches while he cut his way toward the top of the tree, letting each trimmed limb fall onto the thick tarp his son spread under the tree.

"What year are you in school?" Kurt asked the boy.

"He's home schooled," Cory said.

"He getting a good enough education that way?" Kurt asked as Cory topped off the gas in his chainsaw.

"What's seventeen times thirty-nine, Patrick Henry?" Cory called to his son as he continued unfolding the tarp.

Nine year old Patrick Henry Trammell smiled for less than a second and said, "Six sixty-three, Dad."

Cory grinned at Kurt and got ready to climb.

"You two had that one set up."

"You ask him one."

"Patrick Henry's his name, like from the American Revolution?" Kurt asked and Cory nodded. "Okay, I'll play along. How much is forty-seven times eight?"

"Three seventy-six," Patrick Henry said without hesitation, then waited as Kurt did it in his head.

"Your boy's a math genius, Cory," Kurt said.

"Just well schooled."

"What is he, like, twelve?"

"Nine. Big for his age," Cory said as he stepped onto the wide trunk of the tree and started on his way up. "Stay clear of the falling branches, okay?"

As Cory clambered up the tree, both Patrick Henry and Kurt watched him with admiration and envy.

Kurt moved out from under the tree and edged over toward the boy who was tall for nine and already showed the broad shoulders he'd gotten from his father. The way he wrestled the huge tarp, Kurt figured he also had the man's muscles. The boy grew uncomfortable under the watchful eyes of what he and his dad called 'their kind.' He was trained not to talk much to their kind. Dad said it was dangerous.

"Best to stay well back, mister," the boy said.

Kurt backed away and watched Patrick Henry haul a few fallen branches to the corner of the tarp. Kurt uncovered a patio chair that was already under plastic for the coming winter and took a seat to watch as the boy ran to his father's pickup truck and returned with a small electric chainsaw and a long extension cord.

"You got a plug I can use?" the boy asked.

Kurt flipped open the weather plate over an outdoor outlet and plugged the cord in, but when Patrick Henry powered up the chainsaw to check it, he panicked and unplugged the cord, stopping the saw. "You better leave that for your dad, son," he said.

"I gotta trim the branches," the boy protested as more large branches fell to earth.

"Cory," Kurt yelled up into the tree. "Your boy's trying to use a chainsaw."

"He's got to trim the branches," Cory yelled back.

"But he's only nine."

Cory backed halfway down and, flipping the long belt around the trunk so he could maneuver, he skirted around so he could look at them. "He's been doing it since last year and still got all his fingers and toes."

"But man," Kurt protested, looking down at the boy.

"I taught him and he's rock solid," Cory said in a tone that silenced Kurt.

Patrick Henry snapped his safety goggles on, then yanked on his big leather work gloves and stood over the nearest branch, his chainsaw poised and ready to fire up. Kurt muttered under his breath, "My kid uses a plastic hammer on a plastic nail at a plastic workbench and still bangs his thumb," as he finally plugged the cord in. He could barely stand to watch and sat there with the power cord in hand ready to yank out. But the boy was adept. He trimmed the small branches off the large branches which he then cut into foot and a half sections like fire logs. The boy was efficient, careful and downright professional.

2

It was only the middle of the afternoon, but already it looked like the sun was about to set. Joe was driving his old Toyota, Kat rode shotgun with nested lampshades on her lap. The back seat was overstuffed with boxes, the lamp bases and an ottoman he wanted to keep for some reason that defied common sense and good taste. She tried not to look at any of it – since it all represented defeat. The frilly edge of one lampshade was beyond the pale and she was determined that it would land in a dumpster before she let it into the apartment.

"I'm really excited about carrying only one apartment key from now on," Joe said.

"Unloading all that extra weight," she said with an attempt at humor as she watched the gray sky rather than focus on the squalid nature of the neighborhood they were leaving. She wouldn't miss coming over to this part of town and wondered if Joe actually might. There was something about his psychological make-up that attracted him to undesirable places. Joe seemed to be right at home in locations that made her feel, if not outright scared, at least a bit squeamish. The therapist in her knew why. Joe had endured a horrific childhood of poverty, crime and, most especially, physical beatings alongside his equally abused mother, all thanks to his father and uncle. Those years had left scars – both physical and emotional – and altered the way he perceived the world. It occurred to her he might actually feel uncomfortable in more overtly safe places – as if deep down he felt he didn't belong. As always, Joe presented her with a case study as well as a lover, friend, partner and ongoing challenge.

They drove south across 94, the interstate freeway that cut across St. Paul, and headed toward Summit Avenue. The transition was always astonishing to Kat who had spent far more time around Summit than in the downscale environs north of it. Mansions from the 1880s and 90s lined the wide boulevard revealing the considerable wealth that had developed during the rapid growth of the city. It seemed strange to her to think that such a comfortable and stately area might make anyone uncomfortable.

They caught each others' eye, flashed bright and enthusiastic smiles and returned to their solo thoughts. Both worried, yet neither could admit it, now or earlier during the packing of the car. That stress didn't look like it was going to fade very fast. She felt just like all those nearly naked trees that lined Summit – stripped of their protective leaves, their skeletons standing there vulnerable to the assault of a long, cold winter.

"Want me to oversee the donation to Salvation Army so you don't have to watch it all hauled away?" she asked.

"I'm not going to go into mourning over it," Joe said. "It's just stuff."

"Stuff that you're comfortable with."

"I'm comfortable with you."

"Let's keep it that way. I'll meet the workmen."

Joe grinned disarmingly. "I think it would be more satisfying for you if the farewell involved matches," he said and she realized he picked up more than he let on. "That lampshade is hideous, isn't it?" he added.

"Which one?" she said, her hopes leaping.

"With the frilly edge. Want to toss it?"

"Dying to," she said and they both laughed.

CORY CARRIED an armload of the thicker branches cut to length and stacked them in the bed of his dirty beige and rust-spotted pickup while Patrick Henry hauled a huge bundle of smaller branches and loaded them into the home-built trailer. Soon the trailer was brimming over and Cory was putting the tarp and his tools in the truck as the boy stretched netting over the trailer to contain its load.

Kurt stepped out to admire the day's work. "If I hadn't seen how great the elms grew back out after you trimmed them, I'd say you cut off too much," Kurt said.

"Gotta think what the tree needs next spring, not what it looks like this winter," Cory said.

Kurt pulled out the cash he had ready to pay and offered it to Cory, who winked and pointed to his son.

"Better give it to the treasurer."

Kurt handed the boy more money than his older son had ever held and watched him count it without affect. "You just study math or you getting more in your schooling?"

The boy looked to his father as he stashed the money in a zippered pocket and got a nod. "Know much about Patrick Henry, the American patriot?" he asked.

"'Give me liberty or give me death,'" Kurt said.

"Know any of the rest of the speech?" the boy asked. When Kurt shook his head, the boy began to proclaim, "'It is natural to man to indulge in the illusions of hope. We are apt to shut our eyes against a painful truth and listen to the song of that siren till she transforms us into beasts. Is this the part of wise men, engaged in a great and arduous struggle for liberty? Are we disposed to be of the number of those who, having eyes, see not, and, having ears, hear not, the things for which so nearly concern their temporal salvation? For my part, whatever anguish of spirit it may cost, I am willing to know the whole truth; to know the worst and to provide for it.'"

Kurt watched with amazement and caught the pride in Cory's face as his son delivered his speech flawlessly. At the end, Kurt clapped in genuine appreciation. "That's very impressive. You know what it means?"

Again the boy looked to his father's nod, "A smart person doesn't fool himself. He looks at the real world and sees it for what it is instead of what he wishes it was."

"Very perceptive. Can you give me a for-instance?"

"Santa Claus is a nice story but you're fooling yourself if you believe it. No one brings you gifts except people who love you or people who want something from you."

"You don't believe in Santa?" Kurt said with alarm.

"If you do, you should sit up Christmas night and watch. Eyes that see and ears that hear," the boy said too tartly for Cory's taste.

"That's enough," Cory said. Then he turned to Kurt and stuck out a hand to shake. "See you first snowfall." Kurt made a point of shaking the boy's hand as well then watched them drive off, wondering to himself if he was maybe doing something wrong in his life. By the time he got inside, that fleeting thought was already gone.

JOE WATCHED Kat pay the two guys who had hauled over his surviving furniture and many loads of boxes from the apartment and was a bit appalled by the tip she gave them. After she shut the door behind them, she girded herself to turn back to look at her apartment strewn with his things and it was a lot more than either of them thought he owned.

She tried unsuccessfully to hide her shock at her once-beautiful rooms crammed with a hodgepodge of glaringly inappropriate things. She smiled and knew it didn't hide her feelings. Her wonderful apartment was a messy jumble and even her possessions looked shabby now.

"You look like you need a drink."

"Make it a double, no, triple," she said and pulled him into a fervent hug.

They both needed reassurance because, even to Joe's eye, the place now looked nearly uninhabitable. Just as the embrace was getting interesting, his cell phone rang.

Joe saw on the display it was Byron Enright calling him. The Chief Investigator and police liaison for the district attorney's office, Enright had become quite fond of Joe during a major murder case they pursued together. The respect and affection had been mutual as Enright had helped the young prosecutor learn how cases were really handled. "Byron," Joe said, "what's got you calling on a cold Sunday afternoon?"

"You busy?" Enright asked.

Joe looked at Kat as she scrunched up hard against him. "Yeah."

"Good, then this is as inconvenient for you as it is for me. We got a murder."

"Then the body isn't going anywhere," Joe said. "I can

hear the wind whistling outside and just thinking about going out there makes me shiver."

"The dead guy is indoors, Joe. In a nice warm bed."

"Lucky him," Joe said. Kat broke the embrace and walked among the newly arrived things, pushing them around trying to make manageable pathways. It wasn't a comforting sight. "I don't know why you need a prosecutor for a fresh body so close to dinner time."

"I'd like a law mandating all murders be discovered during regularly scheduled business hours, but that's like pissing up a rope. Easy to envision, impossible to do."

"Not sure I want to envision it, Byron."

"So the victim is a friend of Bittinger's and he's begging us to have our best people on it. Hence the call."

"You cleared it with Stacy?" Joe asked, referring to the Chief of Prosecution who assigned all cases in the DA's office. She was Joe's boss and her approval was crucial.

"I might be alone in my belief that I'm devilishly handsome, madly witty and impossibly good at my job, but that don't make me a fool."

"So do we have any initial thoughts?"

"Looks like maybe the kid brother did it."

"We got a suspect already?"

"I'm handing you an easy conviction here, Joe."

"Heard that before. So where I gotta get to?"

"Out front of your place...Kat's place."

"You're already on your way to pick me up?"

"Stopping for coffee will slow me down."

Joe closed his phone and looked at Kat, who had heard it all. She was now sitting in his arm chair. "Comfy?"

"Trying to get there," she said, then joined him at the door. She affectionately wrapped his chic wool scarf twice around his neck as he bundled up. "Who's dead?"

"A friend of Bittinger's."

Byron Enright had the heat cranked up in the SUV and a steaming coffee in the cup holder as he and Joe drove out of the city. Joe cupped his hands around his coffee and grinned. "You'd make a helluva wife, Byron."

"I can be bitchy," Enright said, "but at least I'm usually horny."

Enright was a formidable man slouching toward fifty who had gone a bit to belly. Even so, Joe suspected he could still be as hard as necessary for an investigator who rarely had to run down a suspect or win a fist fight. And the former cop seemed to have insight into – and an opinion about – every subject Joe had ever seen arise; he was still waiting to see the man stumped.

"So how you like living with lady-love?" Enright said.

"Today's our first official day."

"Best day of your life..." Enright said with a smile. "Of course, it goes straight downhill from there."

From everything Joe had seen, Enright seemed to be a happily married father of three boys. But as always, Joe wasn't entirely sure what to take seriously from him.

"So the victim is a friend of Bitt's?"

"He'll run it down for us when we get there," Enright said. "Sounded upset."

They drove out of the City of St. Paul proper and into one of its oldest suburbs, Little Canada. Founded by a Canadian by the name of Gervais, the township named a beautiful lake after him and then proceeded, to the horror of Canadians and French speakers alike, to pronounce it 'Jarvas.' Solid and respectable, it was mostly working class as well as mostly peaceful and safe. The township averaged one murder every few years. This was its year.

Once they were off the freeway, Joe was disoriented, as he always was outside the city itself. What he noticed most was the sparkle on the streets. Humidity from the warmer day had frozen to the pavement as the temperature plummeted and the tiny ice crystals caught all the lights in their prisms. It was a pretty precursor to the first snowfall – something nearly everyone in Minnesota loved. That admiration usually disappeared before the second snow.

"Doesn't it feel like it's a bit early this year?" Joe said as they drove along deserted residential streets.

"Real winter arrives just about the same time every year and each time, we all say the same thing," Enright said. "Isn't it a bit early this year?"

"Selective memory, I guess," Joe said.

"Same explanation for having a second child."

"That go for a third child, too?"

"No, that's Stockholm Syndrome," Enright said. "Over time you become enamored of your captors."

They turned onto a street where red and blue flashing lights joined the white lights from the houses and the many Christmas decorations which had already gone up. Together all the lights made a wondrous display in the ice crystals on the sidewalks. Somewhere at the end of the parade of colored lights was a corpse.

S t. Paul Police Detective Ed Bittinger recognized the SUV Enright drove, which belonged to the District Attorney's Office, as it parked and stepped out of his Crown Victoria. He was slim, wore a pencil thin mustache and was the veteran of countless murder scenes in St. Paul itself. But this was Little Canada, which had its own police force and he had been obliged to wait in his car.

Bittinger solemnly shook hands with both of them and guided them toward the one-story house where all the activity was. It was a quiet residential street, mostly ramblers built in the 1950s, and nearly every one of them had bundled-up people standing outside watching or staring out their identical picture windows. "Thanks for coming out. They don't like me hanging around inside, but they got no choice about letting you county guys in. I'm hoping to tag along." A gust of wind raced through them, making them all shiver. "Earlier than usual this year," Bittinger said. Joe and Enright exchanged a knowing look.

"So who's this guy to us?" Enright asked.

"Ice fishing buddy of mine. Him and his dad got me

started ice fishing back when he was still a boy. After his dad cashed it in too early, we continued to go fishing half a dozen times a winter," Bitt said. "He ushered at my wedding in his dad's place when he was just a teen and I probably got drunk more times with Jordan than anyone I know. A great guy."

"Drinking buddy. They're precious. Sorry, Bitt."

"What do we know so far?" Joe asked.

"A 30-aught six up from the chin through the top of his head...with his thumb still on the trigger," the detective said bitterly. "Lying on his bed. Meant to look like suicide. Fortunately his wife's out of town."

"But you don't think it's suicide?" Joe continued. "I'm sorry, but that situation sounds pretty definitive."

"Thumb's still on the trigger?" Enright asked.

"A 30-aught six is a rifle?" Joe asked.

"With a very powerful bullet," Enright said.

"Korean-era Springfield bolt action sniper's rifle," Bittinger said. "Belonged to his grandfather."

"To fire a rifle at yourself...wouldn't you have to use your thumb?" Joe said, stretching his arm out.

"Ever fired a gun, Joe?" Enright asked.

Joe was desperate not to reveal that truth.

"I gotta get you out to the range," Enright said. "Guns have a kick. The bigger the bullet, the bigger the kick. You fire a rifle with your thumb, you don't have much of a grip on the weapon. The gun will jump straight back – Isaac Newton and I worked that one out."

"And his thumb is still on the trigger right now," Joe said, "defying you and your buddy Newton?"

"Now you get it," Bittinger said. "Poor Jordan."

"So it was fired up under his chin, then put in his hands with his thumb on the trigger to fool us?" Joe said.

"By a stupid guy who thinks he's smart," Enright said.

"And you think the stupid guy is a brother?" Joe said.

"His baby brother, Sonny Sherwood." Bitt spat it out.

"Sounds like a sidewalk solution to me," Joe said.

Bittinger just scowled at him and shook his head. "He's not pissed off enough, he should be outraged."

"I like him for it," Enright said.

"Whoa. We haven't seen the body, the crime scene or either brother yet," Joe objected.

"Never let the facts get in the way of a good theory." Enright said, then pointed toward the house. "Shall we go gather up a few stray facts just in case we need them?"

Just then, the front door opened and Jamie Volante, Chief of the Little Canada Police stood in their path. He was late fifties, short, round and unhappy.

———

THEY DIDN'T GET home until way past dark because Cory had to drive an extra thirteen miles to drop the tree cuttings at a commercial dump which had no security cameras. Patrick Henry spent the entire drive spotting and counting security cameras at every store, gas station and intersection they passed. As always, they kept their baseball caps low, the license plates artfully dirtied and drove under the speed limit. Cory signaled every turn and kept an eye open for pickups he might steal the license plates from. It was time he put on fresh ones even though there'd never been even so much as a parking ticket. Cory was world-class at keeping a low profile.

By the time their circuitous route through St. Paul and the further reaches of Ramsey County finally brought them past Bald Eagle Lake to the county's edge Cory's son announced, "Seven hundred twenty-one."

"Big Brother just keeps expanding," Cory said.

"Bastards," Patrick Henry said. He'd learned ages ago it was usually safe to swear at the government and, at nine, he already knew what Big Brother meant.

"The state has turned on mankind," Cory said.

"Trying to tear our minds apart and put them together their way," the boy added enthusiastically. He knew this by heart. "But we know our own minds, don't we, Dad?"

"They'll never control us, but they'll never stop trying either," Cory said as he turned off the remote and narrow paved road, then headed up a dirt drive past an unused mailbox until he pulled up to a chain across the road. No house or building was visible in any direction.

The boy hopped out and went to the rusty chain which looked like it hadn't been touched in years. He didn't touch it either; he just pulled up the post with the chain still padlocked in place and walked it across as Cory drove the pickup and trailer past. The boy replaced the post and they bumped ahead up the overgrown road into a rather dense forest, leaving the entrance looking untouched.

The house was little more than a cabin which hadn't seen new paint in thirty years. It also hadn't seen it's owners in a decade, Cory had discovered when he'd first scouted it. Perfect. House, barn, a place for the trailer, lots of hiding places for things best not found and a big propane tank that had begun nearly half full. The fuel had run out last winter and now he had to bring in portable tanks. He couldn't have a propane truck bring a delivery and document that they were living there. Instead he had a rig with tubes and valves that a friend had made for him so he could upload the portable tanks into the big one and run the heat and stove in the house. It worked great.

He pulled the truck up past the barn, unhitched the trailer and wheeled it by hand through the large doors. The boy went right to his mother when she came outside and offered her the day's take. Abby Trammell fit the cabin-in-the-woods. She had a rugged, homebody look about her; handsome face and sturdy figure but she looked older than her thirty-one years. She kissed the boy and he didn't object as he figured out the 40-40-20 split of the day's gains in his head. By now Abby trusted his figures; she used to double check his numbers, but now she simply handed Cory the forty percent for business expenses, pocketed the forty for the household and then went into the woods with the boy to stash the savings.

She gave him a leg up at the third pine after the oak and he scrambled up into the low branches. Dad had chosen the tree because it kept its density all winter and the hidey-hole wouldn't be exposed. Patrick Henry pulled out the triple-bagged cache and unwrapped the layers of plastic so he could add the day's savings share. He didn't count it, but he'd kept track in his head. They had $2740 in savings. That would get them through a long dry spell, he figured as he wrapped up and hid the money. After he wedged the pine cones atop the bags in the hole, totally hiding the contents, he leapt back down to his mother's feet.

Cory watched from the barn door as Abby and their son headed toward the house. The boy became more boyish when he was with his mother and she still resembled that young, lost girl he'd met and taken under his wing. She'd been so lucky he found her in time – what with her open, believing eyes. There had been men at the bus station sizing her up, calculating what she would earn them until they'd used her up. The world would have devoured her and she hadn't even had a clue they were eyeing her. He had saved her and she'd thrived under his care and guidance. Just watching those two chasing about like kids – not even adding his beautiful Betsy into the mix – was all the empirical proof Cory ever needed to confirm the absolute truth of his approach to life. He was doing everything right.

After Patrick Henry darted inside, Abby turned back, spotted Cory watching and smiled to him. 'Everything will be just fine,' is what that smile usually declared. And the truth was, Abby believed it the day she and Cory married without the benefit of family, clergy or legal papers and she had believed it most days since she'd begun calling herself Abby Trammell. Small next to him but just as willing to work as her man, Abby was generally able to convince herself everything would indeed be fine, even when they had to move at a moment's notice or when he just disappeared for days, as he sometimes did. In almost all things, she trusted that Cory had everything under control.

As she went inside, Abby knew that this day would test them both, but first she had to feed the kids and get the heat going now that they were all home. Then she'd break the news and hope he'd keep his cool and also that he had a good plan ready to go. She didn't try to reason through everything he understood, but she had long ago recognized he just simply 'knew' things about the world she would never be able to comprehend. That alone was a comforting thought – that he had all the tough issues covered for them, that she was safe in trusting his wisdom and insight.

"Son, go see to the truck and tools," Cory said as he entered. The boy raced out before Cory could tell him to take Betsy. He went to look for his daughter who was somewhere back inside the house and still working her way through that huge stack of books he'd picked up at a garage sale a few weeks ago. It always amazed Cory what people would sell for a quarter after spending forty times that to buy it. Betsy was a voracious reader of novels, curled up under a blanket and in a world of someone's making. It always looked to Cory like those were her happiest moments when he'd sometimes watch from the doorway, unseen by the girl so immersed in her imagined world.

She had her mom's good looks and long, sandy hair; she had her dad's piercing blue eyes and, it seemed to him, his intellect. She 'had ideas' and that worried him because he knew those notions came from the same kind of defiance that had led her mother to run away years ago into a dangerous world without adequate preparation. Abby had been lucky he'd saved her and he'd done everything he could to give Betsy far better preparation for the dangers of the world. So he tolerated her teenage rebellion when she didn't challenge him directly.

"Go help your brother," he said. "You can pull the truck in."

Without reading another word, she leapt up, shrugged out from the hug he tried to give her and raced off. He watched her go and realized she would soon really be the girl her mother had been when she'd run away. Next year she'd be fifteen.

———————

Betsy climbed into the truck, then adjusted the seat forward and the mirrors to her angle as Patrick Henry watched, envious. "Let me do it. He don't have to know."

"Get us both in trouble? No thank you, Fool."

There was no key to the truck – it had been stolen of

course, they all knew that. Betsy had known since she was little older than her brother how to start a car without a key and now it was so routine, she could do it with her eyes shut. Patrick Henry leaned in the window and watched her find the wires, touch them and start it up. He pulled back out as she let off the emergency brake and shifted into reverse. She'd practiced on every drivable inch of their land, up and back the drive to the county road; Dad teaching and shouting to ensure she would know how to take care of herself in this world. That included driving in an emergency, which had never happened. She'd mastered the clutch in all that practicing and now slowly reversed the pickup toward the open barn doors. She made the turn while ignoring the hand signals her brother gave her and got the pickup in place on the first try. Damn near parallel to the trailer, right where it was supposed to be.

She climbed in the bed of the truck and started handing her brother the tools their father hauled each work day. Soon they wrestled the big tarp onto its shelf near the snow plow attachment for the front of the pickup. Betsy hung up the heavy tool belt with all its saws and clippers on ropes. Patrick Henry loved the chainsaws and laid them out on the workbench to oil just as Dad had taught him. Meanwhile Betsy stacked the branches that had been cut for firewood to dry in the curing racks along the side of the barn and made quick work of it.

"Take your time," she told him as she headed away.

"What are you gonna do?"

"Go for a walk," she said. "Don't you go back inside until I come fetch you, okay?"

"Can I play in here after I'm done with the saws?"

"Don't be stupid, Fool," she said and stomped out. They both knew the barn was solely a place of work.

The boy liked being outside the house just like his sister, so he would take his time with the saws, then he'd clean and sharpen the boot spikes used for tree-climbing.

Betsy walked quickly and without hesitation straight away from the small house which had only one light on in the kitchen. The woods were dense; the remoteness was what Dad had liked when he found the place. Betsy knew her way even in the dark evening and once she was not in view of the house, she headed for the tree her brother had just climbed. With a wary look to be sure she was unseen and alone, she skittered up the tree, pulled aside the pine cones and took a modest share of the latest deposit for herself. She was saving up, because there was going to come a day when she'd need to finance her own way out of all this. She was going to go into that world, no matter how dangerous both her parents said it was. Half of what they said wasn't true anyway; it didn't match the books and she knew those were telling the truth.

She scrambled down, returned to her regular route and kicked up enough fallen leaves that Dad couldn't see her path. It was the same place she always went when she said she was going for a walk and her mother admonished her not to leave the property.

Like her brother, Betsy was big for her age. Fourteen, she was tall and really 'starting to fill out,' she kept telling herself. Not that anyone would notice. There was no one to notice. When not stuck at home, she'd go out and work with Dad and wear a big old jacket and work gloves and be watched by old men who owned trees.

She crossed the property line without even slowing, as she did almost every day, and headed right for her favorite spot in the world, a tree. It was an oak from which most of the leaves had now fallen. There was an easy, comfortable perch about halfway up where she could sit for an hour without any part of her butt going to sleep. She had her own hidey hole in the tree branches and she added the recent cash to her secret plastic-wrapped savings.

Then she settled into that perch and raised the binoculars she kept hidden in the tree. She'd stolen them a year ago so she could see out of her tiny, isolated world. Her roost gave her a perfect view of the school. It was Sunday so there weren't buses and kids and all the daily business, but she knew the schedule. It was a combined middle and high school and there were activities on Sunday evenings. Parents dropped kids off and the older teens drove with friends. Some cars held boy-girl couples and they took their own sweet time in the cars before heading inside. They were fooling around like the kids in the stories she'd read. With each other. They were being normal. It all seemed impossibly far away.

ABBY HAD ALREADY PUT the house fund into the can on the shelf and she had the dinner started. There wasn't much of any way to keep avoiding it, but she still couldn't bring herself to volunteer the information to Cory.

"What'n hell you thinking about so hard," he asked.

She guessed it was time. "A man walked up the drive today," she said as off-handedly as she could manage.

Cory bolted out of his chair with alarm, on his feet and fists clenched. "You talk to him?"

She shook her head and looked him in the eye as the rage welled up inside him even as he forced his fists to uncurl. He didn't hit anyone anymore. Not at all.

"He didn't come to the door or nothing. Betsy and me

hid and watched. I figured he thought our road led to that park or something. He just turned around and left."

"Did he see you?"

"'Course not!"

"How long did he stay? Was he alone?"

"Looked like he was surprised to see the house and I didn't have nothing outside, there was no sign of us."

"So he just walked up and looked around?" Cory said as he stared out the window at the drive, then over at the barn where their son cheerfully worked. "Anything official-looking? A badge or gun?"

"Just an ordinary guy holding a map," she said.

Cory slumped back into the chair. "Could have been a cop or an agent maybe, half a dozen different government agencies. They use ploys like that."

"Betsy and me agreed he just looked lost."

"If the government is going to come looking for us, you don't think they'd know enough to pretend to be lost?"

"I really don't think it was anything more than a guy looking for a back way into that wilderness park maybe."

"Guy goes looking for a wilderness park in winter after walking over a chain and up a deserted drive?"

Cory seethed as he shook his head, thinking deep and hard and unhappily. "I haven't even scouted another place. Thought we'd get another winter out of this one."

"This house has been good for us. I'd like to stay."

"Don't see how we can," Cory said, stewing. Things had recently started to feel good for everyone in the family and then someone walks right up to the house. 'Just goes to show,' he thought, 'you can never get complacent. They're relentless in their pursuit of free people.'

4

Credentials had been flashed, scowls had been exchanged and Enright had seemed to shrink his formidable presence down as he befriended Chief Volante with contrite apologies and reassuring promises of 'merely technical assistance.' Joe was impressed. This routine had to have been practiced over the past decade, because Enright's domain was the entire county. Most townships in it had their own police forces, which led to territorial disputes and inter-departmental distrust, but Enright was obviously an old hand at smoothing ruffled feathers because all three of them were finally ushered into the house.

Sonny Sherwood sat on the living room couch staring blankly into space like the stoner he was. In his early thirties with straggly, thinning hair, he sported an inadequate mustache and mangy goatee. He wore engineer boots and had his wallet on a chain looped from his wide black belt, but he was no biker. If he had muscles or tattoos or a massive attitude, they were well hidden.

"He been Mirandized?" Joe asked Bittinger.

Bittinger glanced at the nearest officer who shook his head, so they just stayed back.

"What do you know about him, Bitt?"

"Came ice fishing with us once and lit up a joint, so I kicked him out of the shack. He never came again."

"He done time?"

"I kinda remember Jordan saying he did a short stint for intentionally ramming another guy's car. Over a girl."

"Isn't it always?" Joe said as Enright approached.

"We can go in if we behave."

They put on the booties they were required to wear in the site and Enright tried to get Bittinger to wait outside rather than see his friend's body, suggesting a last image of them ice fishing would be better. Bitt just ignored the warning and insisted on joining them in the bedroom. All three of them pulled on latex gloves as they entered.

Blood spattered on the white painted headboard of the bed where two officers were collecting forensic evidence. There was a silver dollar size hole in the headboard and it was surrounded with hair, bone and brain matter, along with a large corona of blood. A lot more blood had seeped onto the bedspread Jordan Sherwood's head was on. His feet, still in work boots, were on the floor and it looked as if he'd been sitting on the edge of the bed, but fallen backward. The most disturbing detail was that his face had not been touched so he was still recognizable; he was in his late thirties and had a three day beard. He wore jeans and a flannel shirt and there was a rifle laying upside down on his belly with his thumb on the trigger. The gun was bigger and longer than Joe had imagined, which seemed to confirm Bitt's doubts that this was suicide.

One of the officers was dusting the rifle as Enright leaned over to inspect more closely. "Getting anything?"

"Not even a partial," the officer said.

"He wiped the rifle down before shooting himself?" Bittinger said angrily.

Joe watched Enright work, but was already growing impatient. He didn't know why he was needed at all and felt they should just let the local police run with the case. He sidled up to Enright and whispered, "We shouldn't be here."

Without glancing at him, Enright said, "I know, but we gotta give Bitt a good show and then drag him away."

Joe saw the need to help their good friend and started to take an in-depth look at the crime scene. The bed under the body hadn't been made, yet otherwise, it was a very neat bedroom. There were hair brushes and perfumes lined up on the vanity and the room had a female sensibility.

"Where did the bullet end up?" Enright asked.

The two local officers looked at each other, glanced anxiously over the headboard where they spied a hole blown in the wall and rushed out of the room.

"This was his own rifle? Do we know where it was kept?" Joe asked, but Bittinger shook his head.

"His old man showed it to me once years ago. Only time I ever saw it before. I didn't know Jordan still had it."

"The wife was out of town a couple days, I'd say," Joe said, pointing at dirty socks and underwear kicked partly under the frilly bed skirt on one side.

"Good catch," Enright said as the two cops returned.

"Bullet's lodged in the chimney two doors down. You oughta come see," the returning officer said and led the parade out the front.

Volante and his men were inspecting both sides of the house next door to the crime scene, then the chief was beckoned from the next house over. Enright had Bitt and Joe hold back, went to join the locals who were all gathered around the chimney of the house two doors down where the bullet had lodged in the brick. Light shone through a hole in the side of the house between the rifle and the final resting place of the bullet. Enright shook hands all around, patted Volante on the back and returned to Joe and Bittinger. He never slowed his pace as he led them away.

"Good thing no one was hit inside the house in the middle," Enright said. "Went clear through."

"We ain't one tenth done, Byron," Bitt complained.

"We don't belong here, not now. Not like this."

"We all know it's the brother."

"You're probably right, but let them figure it out."

Bittinger seethed, but got into his car and finally drove off. Joe guessed he was planning to have several drinks in his friend's honor. It would be a better path for him. "He's too emotional about the case, blinds him."

"Good thing that never happens to you," Enright said as he unlocked the black SUV.

———

THE TEMPERATURE HAD PLUMMETED INSIDE AS WELL as outside, so Abby had distributed extra blankets to the beds in the two heated rooms. The news they were going to have to move again was unsettling for all of them and Betsy stomped about in outrage. "Even their kind don't make teenaged girls sleep in the same room with their brothers."

Patrick Henry studied the floor of the room they generally shared on cold nights not wanting to join her.

"Want to sleep with your mom and me tonight?"

The boy looked up and saw his mother's hand beckoning him to the bed his father sat on. Abby was already snug under three blankets as he happily climbed into the middle.

Cory had to remind himself the boy was still only nine, but as he shut out the light and lay back, his mind was racing. He'd have to research potential houses and that meant time in the library, anonymously using their computers, and then skulking about in unknown places. Moving in a hurry was always expensive. They'd lose a lot of the curing wood, maybe some of his tools and equipment and he'd have to get Travis' stash safely moved and away from the reach of narcs. And tomorrow he'd have to remain invisible while he was among all those enslaved outsiders.

All this confirmed that it was so much better to raise people who didn't have that dependence in the first place. Betsy and Patrick Henry were lucky. They would never have to know the helpless feeling of realizing their freedom had been systematically stolen from them by a world that relentlessly taught them it was their duty to be victims.

Cory finally fell asleep, but it was the sleep of a man who lived in an occupied land. It was the fitful slumber of a man who feared every representative of the outside world, they were the people who hunted his kind.

Cory Trammell was an insurgent in his own country.

ENRIGHT DROPPED Joe off on Mississippi River Boulevard and it looked like every light in their apartment was on. He let himself into the building and hurried upstairs worrying about what he might find.

Every light was indeed ablaze as Joe entered, yet there was no sign of Kat. He had never seen the place so messy, it was even worse than when left. It was now a hideous jumble, with his chair sandwiched between her couch and easy chairs looking as fitting as a cactus in a pastry shop. Then Kat appeared from the bedroom, sweaty and – surprise of surprises – messy herself. She carried a heavy box of Joe's books which she plopped down on a stack of boxes in the corner of the living room. She brushed her hair out of her eyes and gave him a perfunctory kiss.

"Blends in well, don't you think?" Joe said.

She didn't see the humor as she looked at the clutter of their combined furniture, the stacks of his junk in the sun porch, piles of boxes and god-awful lamps wherever she turned. She headed back into the bedroom.

"It'll get better," he said, following her.

Her bed – their bed, he reminded himself – was pushed far to one side and stacks of his belongings were along one wall. She'd moved them there and was now moving them back to the living room. He picked a box up and followed her.

He dropped his box on top of a growing stack and finally managed to stop her from turning away again.

"For a guy who never buys anything, you sure have a lot of stuff." She forced a smile and finally returned the hug he was desperately trying to wrap her in.

"I'm not sorry for moving in."

"You damn well better not be," she said with a laugh.

"Sorry I own so much crap."

She pulled him down by the scarf around his neck – a present she'd given him. "You'll get better." Then she took him by the hand and led him to the bedroom. "This will go faster with you helping." She picked up another box from the stack. "Take your coat off, this'll take a while."

He threw his coat on the bed, picked up a box of books

and followed. "What's wrong with leaving them against the bedroom wall until we settle it all in?"

They started another stack of boxes in the living room and made quick work of what she'd moved into the bedroom.

Finally, with the bedroom emptied of boxes and Joe's stuff, they pushed the bed back in place, readjusted the night stands and she stood back to look with satisfaction at the one unmolested room in her apartment. It was once again looking the way she'd originally put it together.

"We need one room that actually works."

"Then definitely it needs to be the bedroom," he said.

She looked him over with a smirk. "Think it's that easy to get lucky?"

"I'm already lucky just being here at all."

"Smooth talker."

"How'm I doing?"

"Getting warmer."

He looked around at the beautiful bedroom all put back together, then noticed the chaos of their possessions still clashing out in the living room. He grinned at her and shoved the door shut, blocking the mess out of their lives. Before he could turn back, he found her wrapping around him from behind, nuzzling his neck.

5

A t the end of the drive, Cory put the post back in place, leaving their entry road looking unused. He caught a brief glimpse of Betsy walking through the forest and hoped he'd be able to find another home as suitable to all their needs. She would dearly miss her days in the woods if he couldn't find something so well situated.

Cory was as dressed-up as he ever got. Dockers shoes and pants – thanks to Salvation Army – a button-down shirt and a well-worn down jacket. Doing his best to blend in.

As he pulled onto the small and generally deserted county road, he couldn't help but wonder what had prompted that man to walk up their drive. He had to admit there were no signs of a surveillance van or any other dead giveaways. Still, this was too dangerous to ignore and he knew the outside world was nothing if not relentless. By limiting his complete withdrawal from society to his immediate family, he had hoped his life off the grid would not bring the full frontal assault he'd seen destroy more than one free man. David Koresh, and guys like him, had unwisely chosen to recruit followers and that's what led the government to destroy them. Cory had found a smarter way.

Stay small, remain free.

Six miles of turns, lane changes and driving through parking lots with front and back exits finally convinced him he was not being followed. He pulled up to a Ramsey County Library that was just over a mile from home, parked on the side street and was walking to the entrance when a police car turned and drove right toward him. He played it cool, patted his pockets as if he'd forgotten something and headed back to the truck, head low and hat way down. After he got in and shut the door, he could see his hands were trembling, even after the cops drove right by.

When he entered, he had a feeling that the younger librarian with the frizzy hair remembered him. She smiled right at him and he contemplated going to another library, but this place had an easy system with the free computers, you didn't need a library card to use them and there was a back row where no one could look over your shoulder.

THERE HAD BEEN frost during the night, but it had already melted on the windshield of Joe's car on the street. The engine would take a minute to warm but before he drove off, he spotted Kat racing right toward him. No jacket. He rolled down the window thinking there was a problem or he'd forgotten something, but she just leaned in and planted such a kiss on him that a passing car honked. She raised a leg up in parody and kept right on kissing.

"Remind me to start my car more often," Joe said as she leaned back out and realized her front was wet from the thawed frost on the car. Unfortunately, he sensed she had lingering doubts – like he did – and needed reassurance they hadn't jumped the gun with the move. Worry had plagued them both and remained unspoken throughout the night in the perfect bedroom, sequestered from the mess he'd brought.

With a huge shiver up her spine from the cold, she waved, spun about and raced back to the building.

He raised the window as the heat finally kicked on. 'How did my life ever get so good?' he asked himself as he watched her all the way inside. Before he even got the car in gear, his cell phone rang, it was Kat.

"Miss me?" She was waving from the front entry. "I promise not to hector you insufferably, it's just that I've never lived with a man before."

"I guess I should have told you sooner – I did live with a woman before."

"You did?" she said with surprise.

"When I graduated from high school, I moved out."

"You're not half as funny as you think you are."

"I'm scared and excited. It comes out as lame jokes."

"Honest? You're scared and excited?" she said, now waving from between the boxes in the sun porch. "We are gonna do great," she said, trying to convince herself and him in the same moment.

"That we are. So how about lunch?"

"I've got evaluations at St. John's Hospital this morning, that's why I've got the late start," she said. "Besides I'm almost ready to jump in the shower."

"Okay, I'll be right up."

She laughed and hung up.

LIKE MOST EVERYTHING in the outside world, computers were quite foreign to Cory, but unfortunately he sometimes needed one. He was well aware that every keystroke was recorded, every request was logged and every moment he dallied over a computer left him more vulnerable. He'd taken a sticky note from the librarian's desk and put it over the camera, but every minute was still nerve-wracking. Nevertheless, it used to take days of driving around and startling hermits and retirees when he'd suddenly appear at their homes. Now he'd learned to search for places that had been for sale for years and then he discovered county tax sites. They were gold to a man in his situation; he just had to copy down the information.

"You know you can just print the page from here and get it at the front desk," Joyce Pond said to him. She was well past eighty and sat a couple computers down from Cory. She smiled as he looked up from his hand-written list.

"What's that ma'am?" he said, snugging his cap down.

"For a dime you can print a page from these computers. I do it with all the recipes I copy," Joyce said. She held up a sheaf of printed pages to show him.

"I applied for a library card, but it hasn't been delivered yet. But thanks, ma'am. I'll do that next time," he said, vowing never to return to this library. Two women had noticed him and had looked at his face. Too memorable.

Joyce was already at his side, leaning over his keyboard, pressing keys. "Don't even need a card, just give them the dime a page." Before he could stop her, the page was sent and the screen told him it was printing.

'Damn,' he thought. Now they had a copy of the last page he'd identified to look into. He'd have to start over.

"Thanks so much, ma'am," Cory said and wiped his screen – as if that made a difference. He took his list and inched past the lady. He stopped at the desk and it was the frizzy-haired librarian he gave the dime for his page. She smiled too. Damn. The last thing he wanted was to be remembered.

BETSY WAS up in her tree of course. She'd brought a blanket, the book she was finishing and the book she was going to read next. And the binoculars for spying on the school, but classes were in session so no one was outside. She wrapped herself up against the cold damned universe her dad made them live in and regretted that she was going to have to leave the world of her book in another forty-some pages. She was happy when the boy and girl in the book finally kissed. Normal people got to do normal things and all she could do was read about it.

Patrick Henry was seriously conflicted. For months he had harbored a secret goal he could only pursue while they lived here. He'd kept his ambition hidden and wished there was more time to prepare himself, but last night he'd heard the news that they were moving again. So he had to do it now or he might never get a chance.

Even at the tightest hole, Dad's tool belt slipped right off his waist so he wouldn't be able to wear it. The boot spikes were a different story, their nylon straps could be snugged to any size foot. He slipped the spikes under his jacket along with the adjustable waist strap Dad used to climb up trees. He'd closely watched how to flip the strap up on the other side of the trunk, move up a couple steps, then flip the strap and climb more steps. Dad had said that once you could see over the roofs of the houses, you were at the top of the world. He couldn't wait, he had to see that before they moved away.

With the climbing stuff hidden, he strolled out of the barn, past the house where he knew his mother would be watching and headed into the woods. He didn't follow the path his sister so obviously left, but walked right toward the tallest pine. It was a red pine, his dad had taught him, and it had to be seventy feet to the crown. Very tall, but not so big around he couldn't use the strap on his way up and then he'd see over the whole world from up there. Just like Dad, he'd experience the wonder.

With the boot spikes nicely snug, with the climbing strap around his waist and around the tree in a single loop, he measured the distance between his stomach and the trunk with his hand just like Dad did. He looked up the long bare trunk to the lowest branches so high up above, then he dug a spike in. He got the angle wrong and the spike beneath his boot just took off a piece of bark, but on his second try, it was good. The other spike went in perfectly and he had both feet off the ground. When he went to flip the strap up, it wasn't as easy as Dad made it look but finally it traveled up a foot and he followed after it.

The boy now completely understood why climbing a big old tree always made Dad happy. You were the most powerful guy around, up there over everyone's head. Such simple things holding you up as you left earth entirely on your own power. Alone, free and under your own control. Higher now than the trees that were losing their leaves, he wondered if Betsy had any idea how visible she was in that barren tree he'd known about for months. He waved, but of course with her nose in a book and her attention on the fools over at that school, she didn't notice him. He could see several balls that had been kicked onto the school's roof. And he was mastering the spikes and the flip of the strap the farther up he went. He was dying to touch the bottom of that lowest branch way the hell up there.

There it was, that lowest branch, the kind Dad would scramble up onto. The crown of the tree spread out so nice right over his head and forty feet of conquered trunk stretched below him. He wanted more than anything to stand up there like he'd seen his dad do, top man in the world, but he was no fool. He would touch the branch, take a good gander all around, then climb down.

But as he reached up, he slipped out of the strap.

Skittering down, trying to grasp the trunk.

Then as he fell, a spike caught the dense bark.

Sending him flying right off the tree into thin air.

OLD STAN EVERETT always told anyone from that day on 'it looked like the boy was flying like Superman.' The little boy's arms were stretched out in front of him and his body was horizontal, not even that close to the tree. The old man had seen him careening down toward the cold hard ground just off the little back county road. Stan screeched on his brakes and left the car in the road as he ran into the underbrush, scratching the hell out of his own face as he struggled to find the boy.

Blood spurted from the boy's arm and he writhed and screamed as Stan got to him. He could see bone protruding from his arm and out through his jacket. Stan stripped his coat off and fumbled out his cell phone at the same time. He wrapped the boy up and called 9-1-1 all at once.

Betsy hadn't heard her brother's screams, but the siren sure got her attention. Dropping her books and blanket, she clambered down when the ambulance stopped so close to home. She scrambled through the woods and hid nearby as the men from the ambulance lifted her brother onto a stretcher. 'Stop!' she wanted to shout, but she knew better than to let anyone see her.

Instead, she did what she'd been trained to do – the only safe thing in her family – she ran to get Mom.

6

K at had to pull over to the side of the road outside St. John's Hospital to the let the wailing ambulance race to the emergency entrance. The EMTs opened the rear of the ambulance as she parked in the nearby employee lot, then, while she walked toward the emergency entrance, she noticed a hysterical woman climb out and seem to fight against the EMTs as they pulled the gurney out. Kat was grateful it wasn't her battle as she bypassed the fracas and went inside to meet with her first psych client.

She was well known around St. John's Hospital, first from having a residency there during her psychology training at the University of Minnesota. Then, after she started working for Ramsey County, Kat spent Monday mornings in the emergency medical unit, seeing both in-patient and out-patient clients.

She picked up the report on her first consultation as she entered to meet him; his situation was commonplace. Mr. Williams had walked away from the treatment center, he'd missed his latest parole meeting, he'd been picked up on the street 'acting crazy' – as the police report put it – and his parole officer wanted help deciding if he should be put into an overcrowded jail, an overcrowded halfway house or on the waiting list for an ankle bracelet tracker.

She thought Mr. Williams was rattling his handcuffs where the cop had secured him across the table from her, but then shouting overpowered the tenuous quiet of the drab little conference room where they met. It was a stone's throw from the emergency admitting center and whatever the commotion was, the noise was so loud Kat felt the need to peek out to investigate. Even for an emergency room, this was out of the ordinary. A nurse and a couple orderlies frantically beckoned her to follow as they ran toward the receiving area. She left the attending cop with Mr. Williams and hurried after the other staff.

The decibel level only increased as she neared the entry door where a boy howled and a woman screamed "Leave him alone!" and "Don't touch my boy!" while a growing cadre of medical, emergency and police personnel all said some variation on "Calm down, Lady, we're trying to help him." It was the same hysterical woman Kat had seen outside fighting against the EMTs.

Abby was struggling urgently to keep their kind from touching Patrick Henry despite his serious injuries.

The doctor had trouble getting near the boy who had thrown off Stan's blood-soaked coat and was kicking ferociously with feet that had very sharp boot spikes on them. Abby had hopped into the ambulance to stay with her son when she couldn't get the emergency techs to leave him beside the road. She desperately wished that Cory was there, he'd know what to do, how to make them stop.

Among Kat and the hospital personnel, no one could begin to understand their resistance to treatment.

The ER doctor begged Kat to reason with them, to

emphasize that they needed to help the boy, to set the compound fracture and to see if he had internal injuries from the fall. The boy was losing blood rapidly and could go into shock any second. Kat tried to de-escalate the situation by getting everyone to back away, but even with a bit of breathing space, Patrick Henry and Abby looked like cornered animals whose panic kept escalating. Kat spoke calmly as the boy writhed in pain and whimpered, "Mommy."

She tried to get the woman to acknowledge how injured her son was and understand the dire consequences of not treating him. When that failed, she tried a different tactic and asked their names, which only added to their hysteria. It was clear Abby did not want her son to be treated and Kat tried to determine if it was a religious objection, but quickly became convinced it wasn't. Insanity was becoming the only plausible reason she could imagine.

While Kat had been trying to talk rationally with them, Abby was relentlessly struggling to pull Patrick Henry off the gurney, even though a bone protruded from his arm. The EMTs at the door turned to Kat. "Do we have the right to stop them?" one asked and everyone shrugged.

This was a new – the refusal of emergency treatment for a child with a guardian present. While the boy's blood drained and his youthful reserves started to fade, they were all unsure what to do.

So Kat thought to call Joe for a legal opinion.

WHEN HIS CELL RANG, Joe was outside a courtroom in St. Paul's downtown City Hall and Courthouse Building. He was first chair in a trial that had begun the previous week and was conferring with Liza Upman, who was his second chair in prosecuting the case. The Ramsey County District Attorney had the two of them specializing in domestic abuse cases, especially if a child had been involved. Joe was renowned in the DA's office for his rapport with children and the rumors had grown until he was thought to have some sort of mystical connection with abused kids. His own past as a victim had become known and had been an easy explanation for his ability to connect with endangered children. He had his own doubts that he was such a wondrous specialist, but Liza was a big believer in his perceived powers.

In truth, she was a big believer in Joe in general, but had learned to sublimate most of her feelings after he'd revealed his relationship with Kat. So she worked hand-in-glove with him and had to settle for 'good friend.' Sadly, her sentiments about Joe were freshened all over again when he had rather giddily described his moving into Kat's apartment over the weekend. He didn't mention the debate over his worldly goods and Liza had not asked for details. He was unaware of her feelings and she was determined to keep it that way.

They were about to go into the courtroom to hear the defense witnesses, since they'd finished the state's case on Friday. They were prosecuting a wife for shooting and wounding her husband because she'd believed he had molested her daughter from her first marriage. The pre-teen girl had been their star witness on Friday.

On the phone, Kat urgently explained the situation with the severely injured boy and his mother refusing treatment. He told her the kid was not legally competent, so all care decisions were entirely up to the mother. She could have refused treatment legitimately before any care had been initiated, but once the EMTs had begun medical treatment, it became much more difficult for her to stop urgent and possibly lifesaving care. If she refused care now, Joe considered it depraved indifference unless she had previously established religious reasons that she could prove. Kat thought that was unlikely and said the woman had insisted that the laws did not apply to her or the boy.

"They're not our laws and you can't force us," Abby had screamed. Their kind were every bit as stupid as Cory had always claimed.

While Kat and Joe spoke, Abby tried to drag him off the gurney, he screamed again and the doctor warned that the kid was now definitely going into shock, so Kat stepped in to stop them. Abby lashed out with a ferocious shove that sent Kat sailing into a fire extinguisher. She tried to catch herself with an outstretched hand, then howled with pain as she grasped her injured wrist. That was enough for the staff, who all dove into action, helping both Kat and the boy at the same time. In a panic, Abby pushed past an EMT and scampered away before anyone could follow.

"Hey! What's happening?" Joe shouted into the phone that had fallen onto the floor. At the same time, half the medical team wheeled the nearly unconscious boy into the ER as the doctor shouted demands. A nurse and an EMT helped Kat into an ER bay and Joe heard an urgent request for a doctor and an X-ray technician. Then he heard Kat say, "Do you think it's broken?" before they were out of range.

"Kat's been hurt," Joe said to Liza just as the bailiff called for them to the courtroom. "I gotta go."

Joe had gone so ashen just listening to whatever he'd heard on the phone Liza wanted to console him, but instead she took the sheaf of papers they'd been going through and pushed him to go. And truth be told, she wanted to get as much lead time in court as she could, so it wasn't a hardship to take over during the defense's presentation.

BETSY WAS sweat-soaked from running the whole way and, because she didn't leave their property very often – and then only with Dad – she had gotten lost. But finally she found the library and, looking a bit wild, sprinted with her last strength for the computers. Cory was not there and she collapsed in despair as a librarian approached with concern. One look and Betsy raced away.

Abby arrived at home in much the same state: beyond distraught, covered in sweat from the escape and her very long run all the way from the hospital. Nearly as much as she worried about having lost her son, she was in a panic about telling Cory and what he might do.

She was matted with Patrick Henry's blood, so she dressed in clean clothes. But as she buttoned up, Abby realized every fear her family lived with was coming true. The government had taken their boy. Cory wouldn't listen when she explained how hard she fought, how many of them it took to take him away and how impossible it now seemed to get him back. What would they do? What would Cory do? Where was Betsy? Did they get her too?

7

Joe had driven fast to the hospital and repeatedly tried to reconnect with Kat's cell phone, but it was not being answered. Unfortunately he had far too much life experience of physical injuries to convince himself he was merely overreacting. When he arrived and got through the gauntlet of an ER now on high alert, he found Kat having her wrist wrapped in a bandage to support it. It was a sprain, not a break and, though painful enough for her to take three Advil, she was smiling – for him.

After he hugged her and inspected the bandaged wrist, he said, "I thought psychology was a non-contact sport."

"Just like law," she said. "You really didn't have to come down here. Aren't you in court?"

"Liza's got it."

"Good, so you can go back now. I've got clients to see and I'm way behind. At least I packed a lunch."

He helped her off the exam table and held her close as they inched out of the bay. "Thanks for coming," she said with a big kiss to his cheek. A nurse came in and handed her the banged-up phone. It had four messages and missed calls on it, all from Joe. "Missed me that much already?"

"Nobody warned us the first day of living together would involve a murder and an assault," Joe said.

"Plus a compound fracture and a bat-shit crazy mom."

"Our life on the wild side. So, how's the boy?"

"Good question," Kat said and went to the nurse's stand to ask.

"The boy's in surgery and the guy who called the ambulance for him is in exam room seven," the nurse said.

"What happened to the guy?" Joe asked.

"Face and hands all scratched up from going through bushes to find the boy. He actually saw the kid fall."

Kat went back to Mr. Williams to catch up on her backlog of clients, but Joe wanted to know more about this boy and his mother. Child endangerment and assault were possible charges, but first he needed the full story.

The scratches on Old Stan's face and hands were being cleaned and dressed as Joe interviewed him and he related his tale of the boy flying like Superman for the eighth time since arriving at the ER. Stan described how the mother had come running out of nowhere when the boy was being loaded into the ambulance. She screamed at the EMTs, demanded they stop and even physically fought against them. At the last second, she climbed in with the boy just before the doors closed. Stan had never seen her before, had no idea where she came from or who she or the boy was. He didn't usually drive that little county road, but he was looking for a new place to go for his morning walk. He asked about the boy and Joe told him he was in surgery, then patted Stan on the back for being a Good Samaritan.

Stan gave Joe a detailed description of where he'd found the boy, what the tree was like and what bushes he'd pushed through. On his way to the car, Joe texted Liza that Kat was all right but he had to make a stop on his way back to court. He promised to join her after the lunch recess.

HIS PHONE NAVIGATED for him and soon enough he was in a remote part of the county he'd never seen before. It was only a couple miles from the city hospital, but it was a lot more rural than he'd thought Ramsey County ever got. He drove through dense forest with only the occasional house nestled in the woods as the road became narrower until it was only a lane and a half wide. There was little evidence of use, yet it wasn't more than twenty miles from downtown and the courtroom where he was supposed to be. It felt like another world and the idea of being alone in the woods made him a bit uneasy, as if he'd be somehow more vulnerable.

It wasn't difficult to find where the ambulance had pulled over. The thick undergrowth that lined the narrow road was heavily matted down and there was a pool of blood on the edge of the road. He hadn't seen the boy but from the descriptions and now this blood, it seemed like a distressingly similar break to his own injury when he was a boy. His was thanks to his father, not a fall from a tree. This appeared to have begun innocently enough, but it was the mother abandoning her son in such distress that was most alarming. It seemed unimaginable to Joe. His mother had plenty of failings, but efforts to protect her son had been the focus of her entire life. She would not have left him in agony or tried to stop emergency care for him – even under a threat to her own life. She'd proven it.

In this case, he couldn't help but think there was some kind of abuse or neglect involved here.

The thicket between the road and the tree was tall and dense. Beyond the bushes Joe spotted a singular tall pine and marveled not only that the boy had climbed it, but also that he'd ascended high enough to be spotted as he fell. If the old man hadn't seen him and stopped, the kid could have died from blood loss and shock, alone in the woods.

Joe buttoned up and pulled on a hat and gloves to protect himself as he pushed through the underbrush. He was still visible struggling against the wild overgrowth as a pickup truck passed along the road. Joe never noticed it, but Cory certainly saw him as he was driving home from the library. He had simply planned to change clothes and go out again, but he was instantly alarmed by this invasion. It was the second time in two days someone had forced his way onto his property. All doubt was erased – Cory's family was under attack.

Stilling his panic, he drove past, parked well away from his property and slipped stealthily through the woods until he was within view of the tall red pine where the government agent was looking around. The man didn't seem interested in Cory's house today, which was not visible from there, but he had to know it was nearby from his reconnaissance the day before. He wondered if this agent had listening devices out here. The man kept looking up the trunk of the seventy-foot tree and Cory followed his gaze until he saw a climber's belt way up near the lowest branch, about forty feet up. It looked just like his own belt. Did the government put something up there to keep tabs on him? Had that been the purpose of the visit the day before? No wonder there was no surveillance van; they probably had some kind of relay installed in the tree.

Cory studied the guy's face after he took his hat off. He looked like he was built; not a big guy, but solid and decidedly self-confident. Cory knew he could take him down man-to-man, but he probably had backup. That was how the oppressive government always worked.

Joe's eyes trailed down the tree trunk from the height the boy had been when he fell and came to rest on a matted area a good ten feet away. Where the boy hit there was a pool of blood with a lot of footprints around it. Staring down at the boy's blood on the ground was a nasty reminder of one of Joe's personal ghosts: a growing puddle of blood as the result of his father's fists. But his mother had acted completely different from this kid's mom.

She had fought to protect him.

It started with a baseball rifled by his father into the back of Joe's head when he was seven or eight, sending him face down into the dirt of the back yard. As lights flashed and his ears rang, Joe was plucked aloft by his collar, his feet dangling off the ground as his mother's screams cut through the fog in his head. Suddenly he was dropped and, as he fell back to the ground, he could see that his mother had bashed his father's head with the baseball. It stunned the man, but also increased his frenzy. His wrath was taken out on his wife, driving her down right on top of Joe. His fury was unleashed on her and blood flowed from her wounds onto the dirt below him while she successfully shielded her son.

Joe stared down at a very similar pool of blood and wondered what had prompted this boy to climb the tree and what had driven his mother to try to refuse medical care and then abandon him in the midst of a crisis. He felt certain that the answers led back to the father. It was fear that had prompted such strange behavior from the mother.

The boy's dad had driven it all, just as Joe's father had propelled the horrors of his own childhood. Maybe it was just his own perspective, but he couldn't believe it originated with the mother. She had fled out of fear, Joe felt certain.

He had to find out what evil lay behind this so he could put a stop to it.

———

Cory watched the motionless agent until the man suddenly pushed his way back through the overgrowth to his car on the road. Far worse than his anxiety about the agent's actions and his visit yesterday was the urgent need to move his family, because Cory now knew the government would bring a frontal assault on them.

He was agitated as he stepped into his house and didn't want any resistance from Abby about moving today before the sun set. This was as urgent as any move they'd ever made and he couldn't stomach her fighting him on it.

Through her tears and fear, Abby was already packing everything she could grab. Cory was surprised by the tied-up yard bags by the door as he entered and called out to her. She shrieked at the sound of him and he found her on the far side of the bed, unable to speak. He saw her bloody clothes on the floor as he wrestled her into a bear hug. Finally she said, "They got Patrick Henry. His arm's broke and they took him from us."

He pushed her away. Both knew his rage all too well, they'd been here before, but he'd learned and somehow diverted his wrath onto a kitchen chair. It shattered into pieces while the little house shook with the force.

"Stop that Daddy!" Betsy screamed as she came into the house. Startled, he looked guiltily at her.

After a moment they sat on the three remaining chairs while Betsy and Abby anxiously explained what happened and that all they saw was Patrick Henry already strapped to a gurney and bleeding all over the place. He was loaded into the ambulance and Abby had forced herself to go with him. At the hospital there had been at least ten cops and nurses who fought against her as she tried to free their son. But she lost the battle and barely escaped them herself.

Everything he ever said about the government was true. Even Betsy now found herself believing it as they talked more calmly about the abduction. If they had ever harbored doubts about Cory's views before today, those uncertainties were now long gone. Abby stared out the window toward that big, frightening world Cory had always protected them from as she railed on about how he had to get their boy back. His dilemma was that they needed a suitable new place to move and, at the same time, he had to figure out how to counter these aggressive actions against him and his family. If they wanted to capture him, why did they go after his family? He needed to understand the government's motives, but first he had to find his son.

He hurried back to the pine to try to reconstruct the story Abby had told. If that was his climbing belt up there, then Patrick Henry had climbed that tree. She'd said the boy was wearing climbing spikes in the ambulance so maybe he'd seen a transmitter and had gone to take it out.

Cory had no idea what to do. His son was hurt, he couldn't do anything for him and he didn't know where he'd been taken. All he knew was he had to find him and get him away from the government, no matter what it took.

Liza had done an admirable job representing the state as the defense presented its case during the morning court session he'd missed. Joe was happy to let her stay in first chair for the afternoon while the defense continued to question their witnesses and she was delighted. He needed to think.

His plans included a grocery list: Kool-Aid packets, white bread, baloney, macaroni and cheese, Oreos. He needed to see his mother and never went to visit without shopping for her. He needed to ask about what could drive a mother to abandon a child. His own upbringing convinced him that the father was at fault. Joe had no better resource than his own mother for the many ways a creatively evil man could threaten and intimidate those closest to him.

Joe's thoughts returned to the courtroom as the defense rested and the judge adjourned the trial for the day. Liza wanted to work on their closing argument, but he begged off and hurried away.

On his way to his car, he texted Kat to tell her he'd be visiting his mother and to ask how the boy's surgery had gone. She texted back, 'Don't eat anything that will shorten your life. I'll check on the boy. I'm still dealing with backlog.' Joe knew she must be perturbed that she was still at the hospital when she was supposed to be done already. She was probably in pain from the sprain too.

8

C ory looked over his tools in the barn. Both his climbing strap and his boot spikes were missing, so Patrick Henry had taken them. He must have had a good reason, but it was the government's actions that had his mind racing. Was it plausible an ambulance arrived as fast as Abby and Betsy said? They just hauled him off and ignored Abby's righteous fight to stop them. For all he could tell, the government broke his son's arm when he uncovered their surveillance.

He pushed through the hanging plastic, which kept the kids out of the drying area, and worried if he'd have enough time to clear the barn for Travis before they escaped. Some of the plants were dry enough to deliver, but the bulk of the marijuana hanging from the rafters was in the middle of the crowded barn and still too moist to pack up. He fretted about what Travis would do if he lost his crop. He'd be royally pissed and Cory couldn't blame him, but his son being abducted was bigger than a couple acres of locally grown weed. He'd have Abby and Betsy keep packing and they'd all move soon, but first he had to find a way to get his boy away from that hospital.

He wound his way through the hanging weed to the cupboard at the back of the barn and dialed in 5-2-9 on the padlock. Patrick Henry's birthday in 1736. Inside were his two hunting rifles, boxes of bullets and the envelope with a couple grand in it that the family didn't know about.

He wiped down the Winchester 94 because the 30-30 had gun oil all over it from the cleaning last summer. With its short barrel, the rifle could be hidden under his coat and he was about to load it when he realized he couldn't take it with him. They had sensors in hospitals that would pick it up and police would come running before he even got close to Patrick Henry. He slammed the rifle back into the cupboard, grabbed a couple hundred bucks and locked up.

Without a word to the women, he drove off, sullen, beyond angry and more scared than he dared admit. He was filled with growing panic at the thought of walking into the heart of Big Brother, trying to find his son in a warren of hallways and machines that look through you. Once he got the boy back, they'd all have to evade a manhunt and there wasn't a thing he could do to avoid it.

AILEEN FELCHER WAS MAKING red Kool-Aid. Joe's mother had never changed her name nor applied to have her long-missing, never-missed husband declared dead. Joe's first legal action when he came of age had been to change his name to her maiden name. He'd offered to do the same for her, but that was a sleeping dog she never wanted to rouse. So she kept the bastard's name and never thought about him.

Joe reached for an Oreo on the plate Aileen had set out

for him so that she could admonish him to wait until after he'd eaten the macaroni and cheese she was making. It was their ritual. He had long ago quit eating the way he did when he was eight, but they carried on this tradition and he dutifully consumed foods that would make Kat cringe.

Just then, she called. "The boy is out of surgery and there's evidence of abuse. A couple more minor bone breaks plus scars and some bruises from the last month or so."

"He awake?"

"Not yet. I had to make up a name for the chart. How do you like John Doe Junior?"

"As long as I can put Mr. and Mrs. Doe in jail, I like it just fine," Joe said as Aileen laid out a heaping plate of macaroni and cheese for him.

"That Kat?" Aileen said. "Send her my love."

"Ma sends her love," Joe said and marveled that his mother could simultaneously serve him a meal as if he were still a boy and acknowledge the adult woman he loved.

After he hung up, he watched her serve herself a small plate of macaroni and cheese. The move to this apartment from their ramshackle family home had allowed her to leave frightening old ghosts behind. She seemed to have relaxed a bit and actually put a couple pounds on her slim, frail body. There were scars around her face and elsewhere from the years of beatings, but Kat had done wonders with Aileen's hair to frame her face and hide some of that past. She could now look in the mirror and not be accosted with those vestiges. But the scars were still there – just as they were for Joe, whose misaligned upper lip had once been the talk of the town decades after his father had split it with a fist and his mother had sewn it up at home.

They were survivors.

Still looking older than her years, despite Kat's efforts

with day-spa trips and clothes shopping, Aileen was never more content than when fixing her son's favorite foods and watching him eat across the Formica kitchen table. Her apartment was a step up from their old house that had been plowed under. That had helped them both bury the horrors of the past, but she'd only been comfortable with a well-worn, working class place, with old furniture and a noisy city park outside the window. It was a lot more like where Joe grew up than his present living conditions in Kat's part of town.

He sipped his Kool-Aid and finally asked his question. He'd been waiting because they had only recently begun to talk about their past in anything like a realistic way. "Did you ever leave me overnight at the hospital, Ma?"

"Why would I have done that?"

"When he broke my arm...did they send me home the same day or did they keep me overnight?" Joe and his mother only referred to his father as 'he,' never by name or 'Dad.'

"We stayed there. He was home so it was safer," she said and looked him right in the eye across the table. "We don't have to go into any of this. He ran out."

"I know, Ma." Another one of their rituals. Their family mantra had long been that George Felcher ran off and they never wanted to look for him. Good riddance.

"So you stayed in the hospital room they had me in after the surgery?"

"Of course."

"What if they'd sent you home?"

"I'm your mother. I stayed with you, gave you the ice water and propped up the pillows under your cast. You didn't sleep very well."

"You remember it all?" he said. Because of the beatings,

the head traumas and the years of abuse, there were whole areas of the universe that were entirely missing or vague in her mind. Yet there were others that she could tap into as if they were yesterday.

"The gown they had you in had teddy bears and they changed the bag of liquid on the pole every hour and they brought you Jello, it was about the only thing you'd eat."

"Orange?"

"See? You remember too."

"Only that and the trial."

Aileen stood up and took Joe's empty plate, then pushed the Oreos toward him. "Tell me about Kat," she said as she refilled his Kool-Aid.

"Well, Kat and I have a client whose mother abandoned him at the emergency room."

"She couldn't have done that."

"She did. Kat was there when she ran off," Joe said. "I'm asking because it seems hard to believe."

Aileen sat heavily across from him and took a cookie as she studied him.

"I wouldn'ta done that, Joey. Not ever."

"I know you wouldn't, Ma," Joe said. "That's what confuses me. How did any kid's mother abandon him when he was really badly injured?"

"Met the father?"

"That was my thought."

Aileen nodded as if it was now a settled issue and they would never have to return to it. Joe knew there were bad mothers; there were drug addicts who needed their next fix more than they needed to stay with an injured child. He knew there were many reasons, just as it was conceivable there was no man in the picture at all. But even a drug addict wouldn't fight against care for her child. And Kat had described a level of terror in the woman that suggested there was someone – the father in Joe's reasoning – and he was the source of her fear as well as the boy's abuse.

"What if he'd demanded you come home and leave me in the hospital? Could he have scared you into it?"

"I'da stayed with you," Aileen said and plopped the whole Oreo into her mouth. She was done talking.

Joe wondered what could have spurred that kind of fear in the mother and kept coming back to the boy's father.

AFTER SCOPING OUT THE AREA, Cory parked his pickup two blocks away from the hospital. The Dockers and everything he'd worn all day helped him go unnoticed as he approached the emergency entrance. With the hat down low, no one paid any attention to him when he walked in the emergency entrance, noticing the security cameras in every direction and working to avoid looking directly at them. He couldn't feel the scans that were going through him, but he knew they were blasting him with x-rays, microwaves and a few other things only his friend Simon would understand.

He kept his gloves on and followed a gurney entering the emergency center to slip past the automatic doors. Since it was busy and everyone was distracted, no one noticed him. Most of the bays had curtains drawn and he had no idea if his boy would still be there. He looked over the nursing station in hopes there would be a listing of patients, but didn't spot one. So he peered into individual bays as doctors, nurses and technicians came and went from them. He lifted curtains aside and saw no sign of his son. That's when a male nurse spotted him.

Cory backed away, trying to avoid a confrontation.

"Who'd you come in with, sir?" the nurse said as Cory stepped back farther and pretended he hadn't heard the man. He tried to look like he was supposed to be there.

When the nurse continued to follow him, he darted out of the ER and headed down a hall that led toward the hospital lobby. He saw a bunch of people sitting in the hallway as if they belonged and he took an empty chair. He wanted to stick around to watch the place, but he needed that damned male nurse to forget about him. As he sat he noticed a couple of people nearby were handcuffed to the chairs. He wasn't the only one the government abused.

He studied the ongoing activities at the entrance to the emergency room, watching gurneys with patients in them pushed one way and another, listening to announcements on the PA and worrying about his exposure. It was probably shortening his life, but what could he do, he had to find out where they'd taken his son, then figure out how to get him back. A woman came out of the room across from the chairs and he was about to hurry away, but she paid him no heed. She beckoned a cop who unlocked the handcuffs on a man near him and led him into the room she'd just been in. Cory watched as that man was exchanged with another man in handcuffs, then without a glance back out to the people in the hall, Kat nodded to the cop and shut the door.

Cory watched the poor sucker just released from the room as he was led away by the cop. But as he marveled at how widespread government abuse really was, he caught sight of something that sent a sudden panic flooding through him. The agent who had been on his property looking at the tree was walking right toward him. He felt cornered. The cop was at one end of the hall and the agent was coming from the other direction. Maybe if he could hit him before he got his gun out, he might be able to get away.

Sitting up in the chair and getting his feet under him, Cory was ready to spring, but Joe just sauntered past without a glance. He knocked on the door, Kat opened it and smiled while neither paid any attention to Cory. Trying to listen in, he got up and pretended to scan a bulletin board near the open door. He was out of Joe's line of sight, but he caught a good look at Kat.

"I can't right now, Joe. I still haven't caught up after that battle earlier," Kat said, then held up her wrapped wrist and smiled. "You should see the other guy."

"This is serious," Joe said. "I have to get the boy to talk while we still have some control."

Kat sighed, signaled to her client locked to the table and then went over to the nearby cop a moment. Cory was ready to run, but the two agents just walked past him. He followed, but kept a distance so he wasn't conspicuous.

"I had another memory about my mother," Joe said.

"How bad?" Kat said as she made an instantaneous shift into therapist mode. But she was secretly pleased. It hadn't been that long ago that he would have hidden from her any association with his troubled past.

"The ones I've repressed are never good ones."

"Your dad too?"

"Of course. Blood and a baseball."

"I'm sorry. Let's talk about it later tonight."

"She would have died rather than abandon me," Joe said. "That's what bugs me about this mother and her son. That she ran when he was so badly injured."

"She could have thought he was better off with us."

"Clearly he is, but..." Joe stopped when his neck hair bristled. He looked around, but chalked the sensation up to allowing his father to enter his conscious thoughts.

"She was terrified of us and so was the boy, but why is he a concern of ours at all? He's being taken care of."

"I filed to make him a temporary ward of the state," Joe said. "Someone in that family is a serious abuser."

Kat shifted back to being a county employee. "Assign him to my friend Marlo at Children and Family Services."

He nodded in agreement as he handed her a custody order he'd written up on his way to the hospital. "I had to put a few words in your mouth to file this on my way over. I can amend it if you object," Joe said as she read through the fairly standard custody form. "He's a ward of the state until we settle things with his mother. The order needs to be put in his chart in case she wanders back for him."

Seeing their names both on the court order, Kat said, "Can we get guardianship transferred to Marlo by the end of the day? He's really not my case."

"Sure, I can amend it this afternoon."

They entered the elevator and didn't notice Cory slipping in behind them, his hat so low he could only see the floor. He was grateful he'd been smart enough to leave the rifle at home, but desperately wished he had some way to protect himself. He was far too deep inside the lion's den, but these two might lead him to his son.

On the eighth floor, Kat led Joe to room 807 and then went to the nursing station to have the court order inserted in the boy's file. She also asked for a copy of the evaluation of the boy's earlier injuries, knowing that both Joe and her friend Marlo would need that information.

Cory watched Kat talking with staff at the main nursing desk where they opened a manila folder and inserted a sheet of paper. Then he saw Joe entering room 807 and was certain Patrick Henry was in there, probably terrified. Had he talked? He would, they had ways of making anyone talk.

INSIDE THE ROOM Joe found the boy awake, but looking haggard and groggy, his arm in a big inflatable tube that immobilized it. He had an IV and monitor and surgical scrub still visible around his hospital gown. A nurse was there checking his vitals and hook-ups. Joe wanted him to remain as a possible witness, but he needed it to seem casual as he questioned the boy. Joe remembered that Kat had named him 'John Doe, Junior' and was surprised to find it even listed on the identifying armband on his wrist.

"Should I call you John?" he said pointing to the boy's plastic wrist name tag.

The boy opened his eyes and shook his head groggily.

"What should I call you?"

"Nothing," he said, scowling from under droopy eyes.

"Okay, Nothing. How did you fall out of a tree?"

The boy just shut his eyes and ignored him.

"Do you often try to fly, Nothing?"

"I'm not nothing!" he hissed at Joe, not being able to find much of a voice after being intubated in surgery.

"What are you then?"

"I'm somebody," the boy said, but the energy to refute his accuser seemed to exhaust him.

The nurse was about to leave and said quietly, "That's probably enough for now."

"Okay." Joe looked at the boy and headed to the door. "I'll have the chart changed to Mr. Nothing Somebody."

"I'm a great American revolutionary."

"Really? Okay. George Washington?" Joe said. "Maybe Paul Revere? Nathan Hale? Patrick Henry?" He noticed a sudden stirring in the boy at the last suggestion.

In half a second he was asleep again just as Kat and the head nurse entered.

"Do me a favor," Joe said to the nurses, "have everyone call him Patrick Henry and see if he denies it."

The nurse nodded and went to the marker board across from the boy, crossed out 'John Doe Junior' and wrote in 'Patrick Henry.'

In the hall Joe and Kat spoke in whispers outside the boy's door while the nurses returned to the station. Nearby and still unnoticed, Cory was watching but didn't dare go close enough to listen in. Every damn fear of his was true. Cops, these two agents, files, visits to his property by the government. Patrick Henry must really have seen something that sent him up the tree and maybe he attacked the agents. Neither Abby nor Betsy saw the actual fall.

Just then an alarm sounded at the nurse's station. The nurses sprinted to 807 and were followed by Joe and Kat. There was no way he was getting in there to carry his boy away, there were too many of them. But now the nursing station was deserted and he could see his son's medical file on the desk. He leaned over the counter, contemplated taking the whole thing and realized they would miss it too quickly that way. Instead, he pulled a couple loose sheets out from inside it, crumpled them into his pocket and backed away before anyone saw him.

He peeked in the slightly open door to 807 where people surrounded the bed and it took all of his will power to keep from charging in. He'd never get away with his son and then they would both be captive. He knew Abby and Betsy couldn't survive without him.

Cory slipped away and found the stairway down.

INSIDE THE ROOM, the nurses were reattaching the monitor electrodes which the boy had unplugged. Plus they reinserted his IV line, since he'd pulled that out as well. Joe watched them work on the boy, his color didn't look too good and his pain level had clearly risen from all the activity. He stepped out of the room and called Enright asking him to search for children born eight to ten years ago named Patrick Henry. He didn't know if that was the full name, but believed a search would bring a relatively limited batch of children for them to check.

Enright thanked him for the opportunity to look for dead patriots. "The guy might or might not have gotten his liberty, but by now he's certainly gotten his death," Enright said as he hung up.

"What makes you think that's his name?" Kat asked. She'd been listening in.

"He said he's a great patriot, then he reacted when I said Patrick Henry," Joe said. "It's a long shot."

"I wish someone would come for him," Kat said. "Then we could settle this and get it off our plates."

Joe nodded, but he didn't actually agree. At every step this was becoming exactly what he was designed for.

9

C ory sat stewing in his truck. He spread out the papers he'd stolen from the folder and found three names. John Doe Junior – his son had given them nothing. Katherine Nolan – the woman who had men handcuffed while she interrogated them; in the document she claimed concern for the boy's welfare while insisting on absolute state dominance over his life. And Joseph Brandt – he had to be the agent who had come to his property; he insinuated the boy had been abused and neglected by his mother. This would be their ploy to keep his son and he needed to come up with a viable plan of his own. He needed help.

BY THE TIME Joe got back to the DA's office, Liza already had a draft of their closing argument ready and watched him closely as he read through it. To make it worse, he had to keep rereading because his mind drifted to that boy. Broken bones, bruises and defiance to the point of disconnecting the IV drip that brought him pain relief. There was a story behind this kid and Joe was entirely too certain where it led.

He finally told Liza the arguments were great and it was fine by him if she did the closing for them. Once he was alone, he called Enright wanting to ask for police to canvass the area around where the boy had fallen. The sooner he could get a line on that mother, and hopefully the abusive father, the sooner he could charge them and get a smidgen of justice. Enright said he couldn't talk long because he was with Bitt and was still trying to wean him from the case of his friend's murder. They agreed that Bitt was jumping to conclusions, but he was like a hunting dog – once he got the scent, he wasn't going to stop. Joe wondered if he was doing the same thing, if he could be wrong about this boy's situation. Maybe the mother was just a really bad seed, the opposite of his own mother.

He needed to be told he wasn't crazy, so he went to Stacy and explained the situation with the boy, the fight at the hospital, the run-away mother, even Kat's injury.

"You're crazy," Stacy said. Chief of Prosecution and Joe's immediate boss, she was a seasoned prosecutor, one who knew the difference between a winnable case, a hopeless case and a crusade. "You're on a crusade."

"There's evidence of abuse. Broken bones, bruises."

"Kids get hurt. Especially boys who climb trees," Stacy said. "Between them, my two sons have five broken bones. My daughter has none."

"So you think I should drop it?"

"I didn't say that," Stacy said with a warm smile. "I was just weighing in on your mental health."

"I'd like to dig into this farther. The boy's a ward of the state for a couple days and he's in no shape to leave the hospital. That'll give me some time..."

"To use county resources on top of the medical bills we taxpayers are paying?" Stacy said. "I realize this is dear to your heart." She had heard firsthand about many of the horrendous abuses Joe had suffered from his father.

She knew he wasn't going to stop, so she figured she'd get out ahead of it. "No commitment of our decidedly limited resources, just your time – preferably after hours. Two days, you see what you can find on this woman, but I want you to stay firmly in first chair in your trial and I don't want you to give short shrift to your other cases." Stacy stood and walked with him to her door. "Either parent shows up in the next two days and, unless there's more to it, they get a stern warning and generous help from Family Services. Am I clear?"

When he got back to his office, Joe filed an amended custody order citing Marlo Kerwin of Children and Family Services as the state's lead custodian of care for John Doe Junior. Then he attacked the closing statement with a new focus and a red pen that alarmed Liza. But as she read over his shoulder, she couldn't disagree – he was right.

CORY PULLED the pickup over and sat. It had seemed like his best alternative an hour ago because there was no one else he absolutely trusted. Now that he was within view of Travis' place, he had his doubts. Under the tarp in the back of his truck were eight yard and garden bags stuffed with the driest of the weed he'd been curing for his old friend – maybe a quarter of the crop. He hoped his buddy would be happy to see it before he told him the rest of the crop was in jeopardy and that the government had taken his son. Travis was known to get agitated and Cory needed his help, not another problem in his life.

Finally he drove toward the battered but sturdy old gate which had a modern voice box mounted beside it. It was the only way to enter Travis' compound. It didn't look it, but the place was like a fortress.

"Hey, Travis there? Tell him it's Cory," he said and found himself wondering how often they swept the connection between the house and the controls to the gate for bugs. He figured Travis was at least as cautious as he was; they were both extremely wary of the government.

"Cory-man, that you?" came over the box.

"Got an early Christmas present for you, man."

The gate rattled slowly to the side. As he drove in, Cory caught sight of a bundled-up guy in the woods back from the drive that led from the gate toward the old house. When he'd found their current home, he had thought of it as his version of Travis' well-guarded world and now wished he'd actually had his buddy's level of protection. It might have kept his family together.

He pulled up past several anonymous-looking cars, nothing fancy or expensive. The main house was old and unpainted and its history as a big farm house was still in evidence. But money had been put where it was needed. That was something Travis always seemed to have, money.

The original farmhouse front door with a cut-glass window in it opened as Cory parked. Travis stood there in a plaid shirt, camouflage cargo pants tucked into combat boots and a low slung holster on his hip like a cowboy might wear. He secured the Velcro strap around his leg like a true gunslinger and the pistol itself was an HK VP9 with the 15 round clip – not a gun that could be drawn fast.

Framed in the door, Travis looked big, but as he

descended the stairs to Cory and they gave each other a
man-hug, he became half a head shorter and considerably
narrower than Cory, who had those big shoulders and arms.
A few months older than Cory, he had a well-practiced look
of menace only partially hidden behind a generally insin-
cere smile. But for Cory, the smile was the real deal. These
two went way back; some of their best times ever. If either of
them cared to admit it, some of their worst times too.

"I was just thinking about that Anoka crop the other
day," Travis said after Cory threw back the tarp revealing the
bags. Each had about twenty pounds dry.

"This is just the cured stuff, a course," Cory assured him.
"Crisp and nice."

"Sweet. Tried it yet?"

"Without my compadre? No way, man."

"Sweeter still," Travis said. When he made a motion, a
guy in a jean jacket appeared from nowhere to fetch the
bags. "Bring us a few tops," he said as he led Cory up the
stairs. Cory watched the guy heft two of the bags and hurry
toward an out-building near the main house. It was a mini-
barn, sturdy and reasonably new.

In the entryway just inside the front door was an open
gun rack. Rifles and assault weapons above, handguns in
the middle and a perfectionist's assortment of ammunition
labeled on shelves at the bottom. Cory knew there was a
gun range built into the basement because he'd been
dragged there on numerous occasions. Since owning his
first gun – together with Cory – Travis had really gotten
into it.

In the living room several guys sat around a huge
matched set of couches and chairs. Every time Cory visited
there were guys in those seats, but it was a revolving door.
They were the kinds of guys he didn't bother to know.

Various underlings in Travis' drug business, he assumed. He'd never asked too many questions, an admirable quality in Travis' mind. The men, all in their twenties and on the unpolished end of the spectrum, nodded hello to Cory as Travis threw himself into the central couch where he always sat. Cory stood out among the lackluster bunch who all assumed he must be another lackey like them, only older.

Cory dropped his jacket on a chair mounded with coats, then took a seat near Travis. Every man there noticed that he wasn't carrying. Usually that didn't make him feel naked, but he was the only man without a gun.

The guy in the jean jacket, Leo Stacker, came in with a tray and left his coat on as he sat. He pulled a stocking cap off his nearly shaved head and grinned all around at the men watching. "Primo looking buds," Stacker said then went to work cleaning several tops on the tray with well-practiced skill. He was totally into it and soon was rolling a Dutch joint with a zigzag tip that looked perfect enough to be machine-rolled. He was a wizard.

Cory was dying to talk alone with Travis, to ask for his help getting the boy back, but with all those guys around, he had to be patient. He accepted the first joint making the rounds, which Travis lit with a mini-blowtorch he'd been flicking on and off. Everyone enjoyed that first taste, but deferred judgment until the obvious expert weighed in. Stacker inhaled deep, held for an eternity and exhaled an endless stream through his nose before smiling, bowing to Cory and proclaiming, "Minnesota grown – the land of ten thousand tokes." He took another deep draw before passing along the first joint and rolling a second. "You grew yourself a winner here, Travis."

Now they all patted each other on the back and passed both joints around. Cory took the shallowest tokes he dared

and noticed that Travis did the same. He was laying his head
back on the chair, watching the crowd gathered around him
and smiling as if stoned, but he'd barely partaken. Travis
liked the feel of the room, the camaraderie and laughter, as
he watched Stacker rolling up a third joint.

Cory couldn't bring himself to disturb that feeling with
bad news, so he bided his time.

Travis looked over at him and smiled, "Great to see you,
man. Family good?"

IN THE KITCHEN, out of sight of the crowded living room and
the men he generally avoided, Simon Pritchard listened in
as Travis explained to the guys that he and Cory went all the
way back to juvie, saying they had been sixteen years old
back then, two guys who knew everything.

'And knew nothing,' Simon thought, remembering who
those two really had been.

Nearly a decade older than Travis and Cory, Simon had
been a science teacher in the school in juvie when the two
boys had been forced into trying to get their G.E.D.s. He was
the first adult to pay attention to Cory's outraged anti-
government passion. A big, strong and angry-as-hell kid
who desperately wanted to think of himself as smart. As a
result, he was easily led and offered a great opportunity for
Simon, who gave the boy's rage a focus and a wealth of ratio-
nales which seemed unassailable – the American Revolution and its quotable leaders. Cory became an avid student
of angry men and words of rebellion.

The two friends had gelled perfectly with a plan Simon
had harbored since the moment he joined the staff at juvie.
Cory's rage and unmatched physical power, in combination

with Travis' gift for gathering boys around him, meant those two could run the entire population, while he would exercise complete control over them covertly. It was exactly what he wanted – to be in charge of a willing and expendable army, all from behind the curtain. No one would know who actually ruled, not even the apparent leaders.

Simon smiled at the memory and how oblivious they had been – and remained – to the influence he'd wielded. These days Travis usually admitted to Simon's genius for business operations and they made surprisingly good business partners – with Travis running the crew and Simon creating the ideas and capitalizing on opportunities. Still, Travis always thought of himself as the boss and Simon was happy to allow him to believe it.

It had actually been Cory's life that was altered more by Simon's attention, though he was less inclined to admit it. While Travis already was a leader, Cory had been nothing but unfocussed rage. With Simon's careful guidance, he had discovered the ideas of revolution and been handed a structure for his hatred that played perfectly into Simon's love of anarchy. Cory had never really seen the bigger picture – largely because Simon had always kept it from him – but what they built was a far cry from the war the boy had declared on the world without a plan or a hope for success. In the end, Simon knew Cory genuinely believed he'd achieved all his notions of revolution on his own. His own triumph was the invisibility of the power he wielded.

ENRIGHT STEPPED into Joe's tiny office and said, "There aren't many hits on the name Patrick Henry."

"We re-fighting the American Revolution?" Liza asked.

"We think that's John Doe Junior's name. How many?"

"Four sets of parents: two who gave them as first and middle names and two wayward couples with the last name of Henry who decided to name their boy Patrick instead of Hank like any normal person would."

"Any of them eight to ten?"

"Nope."

"So Junior's not locally born or that's not his name."

"Can't say which I hope for more," Enright said. "I'll widen to the state database to try to find the poor kid."

"I hope the mom shows up," Liza said. "We still have a trial to win." She took the revised closing argument from Joe, nodded as she read through it and gave him the finger on her way out the door.

Enright watched her leave, then said, "You have such a way with the women. What did you do to her?"

"Corrected our closing argument."

"That's prickish of you. So you get Stacy's go-ahead to pursue the boy's mom?"

"On my own time," Joe said and looked at his watch. "Look at that, it's quitting time."

Enright glanced at his watch and headed for the door.

"Hey, where you going?"

"Home, just like you should," Enright said. "You get an actual crime, we can revisit Nathan Hale Revere."

"Patrick Henry," Joe shouted after him. Then to himself, he muttered, "Abandoning a child IS a crime."

10

When Stacker left the kitchen with another armload of beers to take to the stoned group in the living room, Simon stepped back out of hiding in the pantry. He'd been listening to the guys chatter and all the tales that Travis told of his past exploits with Cory. To hear him tell it, Simon wasn't even there, much less instigating it all. Perfect as far as he was concerned.

Cory had come into juvie hating every kind of organization – the court system which he knew as its victim, the foster care system which had made him its casualty, the schools which tormented him, the police who'd acted as enforcers, social services which he saw as the rationalizers of all the abuse that they helped cover up. In Simon's confident hands all of Cory's unfocused rage at the powers-that-be had been sharpened and given voice.

As Cory became more conversant in the American Revolution and the men who rose up against the despots of their day, he questioned how Simon could work for the oppressors. After all, he was worked directly for the Minnesota Department of Corrections which specialized in the systematic subjugation of citizens. Simon explained he was fomenting revolution from inside the home of the overlords and insisted he was secretly working to liberate the most tyrannized class of people anywhere: children in jail. He pretended to teach while he subverted the institution from within. Cory had believed it all and became an enthusiastic instrument of Simon's insurrection.

All these years later, nothing much had changed.

———

KAT WATCHED the two guys from Salvation Army turn the old couch on its side to get it through the doorway and was looking forward to her last view of it. Most of the junk from Joe's apartment was already carried off and the guys had maybe one more trip.

"It looks bigger," Joe said from the doorway as he scanned the cleared-out apartment.

"I was sparing you from seeing it all go."

They watched in silence as the movers took the last things away and she handed a tip to the the men that, as always, surprised Joe. The things he never thought about.

As they got ready to clean up the final remnants of Joe's former life, he said, "Children's and Family Services still hasn't taken over custody of our boy, Patrick Henry."

"So you're still his guardian of record?"

She turned to him with big yellow kitchen gloves, her hair in a scarf and her rather chic version of old clothes.

"The gloves are clearly what make the outfit, that much I have learned," he said and gave her a hug. Then he stripped off his jacket, shirt and tie to start cleaning.

"I'll bug Marlo tomorrow about guardianship."

"You think the boy was abused?" Joe asked.

"A report came in that there's no evidence of any vaccinations at all," Kat said.

"The anti-vaccination movement is one thing," Joe said, "but what kind of people would refuse treatment while he's bleeding half to death? Even my old man...well, he might have, actually."

"You should have seen her, Joe. She was terrified of us. If I hadn't heard her speak, I'd have thought they were undocumented and fearing deportation back to a war zone."

"Afraid of what, you think?"

"Us. Nurses, doctors, the hospital itself, the cops, the EMTs. All of us. It was almost like our just touching him was contamination."

Kat opened the empty refrigerator, took a quick look and gestured Joe toward it. He looked inside and realized how effectively cartons of milk and eggs had hidden mysterious growths. "I'll get this," he said.

"Damn right," she said with a laugh.

Joe watched her cleaning up after his messy life and thought they both preferred to be here rectifying the squalor of his former life to going home to the impasse of trying to shoehorn his life into her apartment.

"So what was it you remembered your dad doing?" Kat said as casually as she could manage. She knew he was onto her; he realized she was digging just like she did with the children and families she helped. Fortunately, he was more than half okay with that. Not totally, it was still agony for him to wade about in that swamp, but he was willing.

"A pool of blood forming mud on the ground. My mom's blood, not mine."

"Sounds awful, I'm sorry," Kat said as she stopped cleaning. "How was she when you visited her?"

"Red Kool-Aid plus macaroni and cheese, but she said

84 DAVID HOWARD

under no circumstances could she have been driven to leave
me alone at a hospital."

"You were loved," Kat said thoughtfully.

"Which is maybe more than John Doe Junior can say."

Kat paused, kitchen gloves on, a wisp of hair across her
eyes as she studied Joe. Finally she went where she wanted
to go. "You have to get away from this boy's case, Joe. It's too
close for you."

"Yeah, well..."

"Marlo can take it over. Let Family Services take care of
them and forget about prosecuting the mother."

"Child endangerment is a serious crime."

"Yeah...and prosecuting her puts the boy with his father
or foster care. Is that a good alternative?"

Joe's thoughts drifted as he cleaned. What if someone
had interfered when he was a boy? When his mother was
essentially a hostage of his father. What if someone had
misunderstood and had taken his mother away, he
wondered. He'd be dead, he realized. Kat was right and he
had to try to extract himself from his obsession with
this boy.

———————

CORY WOKE up with a start and found himself alone on the
couch in the living room of Travis' house. The huge television on the wall played news clips of Cliven Bundy riding
the range in Arizona on horseback wearing a thick sheepskin coat. The news footage was on a loop with Ammon
Bundy's stand-off in Oregon, his acquittal and even old news
footage of the fire and deaths at the Waco, Texas standoff
with the FBI. Cory couldn't process all these anti-government battles somehow spliced end to end.

On the coffee table were a couple dozen empty beer bottles. The ashtray had the ends of half a dozen joints and Cory remembered Stacker continuing to roll them up. Unintentionally he'd gotten higher than he'd been in years, then dozed off after noticing Travis sitting back and watching the guys all laughing. The feeling in the room resembled the calmer times in juvie, except there was beer and weed. As always, Travis was at the center of a group of underdeveloped guys with low prospects, but now he watched the pack from outside rather than in the middle. He was still controlling it but now slightly above it.

The sun had set. He dragged himself off the couch and followed the sounds of two voices. He headed farther into the rambling old house which seemed to have been decorated in grunge. The only things looking well-tended were the television and the guns. Centerfolds of automatic rifles that looked as sexed-up as Playmates were taped to the walls. The voices were coming out of the expansive kitchen in the back and he stopped just outside the spill of light as he heard Simon Pritchard. That took him back.

He leaned against the wall, listening to that familiar voice and remembering the fervor of his beliefs back then. Simon still spoke about the same old themes he always had. "McVeigh was just plain fucking stupid about it," Simon said. "You got to admire his ambition, but to leave a trail and then volunteer for execution...a true revolutionary stays alive, keeps it going, fights the righteous fight and doesn't let the shitheads find him on the first try."

It was a favorite topic of Simon's. He always knew better than the guys who actually acted on their passions. It reminded Cory how Simon talked up rebellion, instigated chaos and then managed to keep his head down when the authorities arrived. He knew Simon had put the news footage on the television while Cory slept: the Bundy family, David Koresh and Ruby Ridge. According to Simon, insurrection was always justified, but had almost always been pursued in the wrong way. He was endlessly figuring out better ways.

"Simon Pritchard, you old revolutionary," Cory said as he strode into the room, holding out a hand.

He got a man-hug instead from Simon, who was tall and still skinny, even well into his forties. His hair was thinning and graying and he had a nose like a hawk.

"You were sleeping like an innocent in there," Simon said, chiding. "So you finally gave up the revolution and let that woman tame you into submission?"

"I've never taken a penny off the man since Trav and me left juvie and you got your ass fired in absentia."

Simon noticed with satisfaction that Cory was still trying to sound smarter than he was, then said, "It was the big day, I had to express how I felt."

As they stood in awkward silence, Cory wondered how these two worked as business partners, it had never been clear. Travis and he had remained good friends and could still find common ground in the present, but Simon was odd man out. There had been an unspoken and slow-moving schism between Cory and Simon that none of them wanted to acknowledge, preferring to pretend it didn't exist.

Simon studied the two friends and the bond between them that he could never fully fathom. He didn't form bonds, he made useful relationships, alliances. If there was nothing practical he wanted from someone, there was nothing at all. He tolerated Travis' reminiscences and knew it had been hard for him when Cory left for Abby. Even now, years later, it was always a bright day for Travis when Cory strolled back into his world. Maybe it was the same for Cory;

he had certainly always stepped in to help when Travis needed him, which he often did.

At one point when Travis and Cory ran the show in juvie, there had been a rival gang forming that Simon saw as a challenge to his power. Larner was a smart-ass who disrespected him and had a certain charisma of his own that drew in the weaker boys. This rival needed to be tamed.

Because he had the toughest guy in Redwing behind him, Travis loved to swagger, so it was easy for Simon to convince him to start a fight with Larner – they both knew Cory would finish it. What was supposed to be a minor brawl ended up revealing the extent of Cory's rage and that uncontrolled frenzy of his almost ruined their army. By the time the guards stepped in, Larner had been savagely beaten and Cory was facing adult charges. In order to save their power trio, Simon had to swear that Larner was beating a smaller boy and Cory had only broken up the fight. Simon's written statement did the trick and Cory was allowed to stay in Redwing while Simon retained his power structure.

At first Cory had been grateful for Simon's help, but came to suspect he had somehow provoked the whole thing. After that, Cory began to march to his own drummer while Travis continued to see Simon as the smartest guy he'd ever known and remained oblivious to his manipulations. He still believed he was the boss and in control.

"You still letting this boy boss you around?" Cory said to Simon, nodding toward Travis with a smile.

"Him I don't boss," Travis said as he pulled three beers from a full refrigerator. "The dopers and the drop outs, them I boss." He opened the beers one after the other on the edge of the chipped counter and handed them out. "Simon's a great thinker, Cor, you know that."

"Just kidding. What you been thinking up?" Cory said.

Simon and Travis exchanged a look as they both lifted their bottles to half-toast and didn't answer the question.

"Say, did that gas rig work out for you? That propane adapter I built," Simon said.

"Like a charm. As if there was any doubt," Cory said patting him on the back. "Simon-built never fails."

"How many kids you up to now?" Simon asked.

"Just the two," Cory said and his heart sank when he realized it was just one at home. He still couldn't bring up his dilemma to Travis with Simon in the room any more than he could with his crew around. He wanted Travis to volunteer to help, but they had to talk alone to get there.

"Where'd everyone go?" Cory asked, gesturing back toward the living room.

"Getting the weed off the property," Travis said. "Can't have distributable quantities here where we live. Just in case the man accidentally stumbles onto us."

"Right, of course," Cory said. "Someone once taught me, 'You gotta know the system to use the system.' Who was that?" It made Simon grin, just as it was meant to do.

"Look, I got some calculations to catch up on. Good to see you, Cory," Simon said, then slipped into the dark, back recesses of the big house.

"So he's still living here?"

"Almost permanent. You know Simon, he'll disappear for a while, but he's mostly here thinking up a storm for me, for our businesses. The things that guy can dream up..."

"Cool."

"Business has been going gangbusters with him around more," Travis said as he studied Cory. "You'd be welcome a lot more than you realize. I always need a guy with a brain. Someone I've trusted forever, ya know?"

"Thanks, Trav," Cory said. "Means a lot to me. So anyhow, you got a minute?"

Travis nodded, opened the refrigerator to pull out a couple more beers to bring along and led the way back to the living room. "So what's up? Why the early delivery?"

"That's what I need to talk to you about, Trav."

11

"Acting on an invalid assumption," Liza said, barely looking at the revised script of their closing argument. She'd been practicing and was now rehearsing it with Joe outside the courtroom. They both held coffees and watched the personnel of their trial gather nearby. "Should it be 'taking action based on an invalid assumption?'"

"We want to get 'drastic action' and 'invalid assumption' into the first two lines, but let's not cram everything together," Joe said. "Her motivation turned out to be wrong, but that simply doesn't mean what she did wasn't a serious crime."

"We'd be holding this trial for the shooting whether he molested the girl or not. Just because she jumped to a conclusion..." Liza said. "Something like that?"

"'Jumped to a conclusion' is good."

"What's this note you put in the margin?" Liza said, pointing to his red amendments on the page she'd originally written. "'Motivation is in the eye of the beholder...'"

"It doesn't matter what the truth behind the motive is, it only matters what the person believes to be true. If they believe it and act on it, then for all intents and purposes, it IS true for them."

"I like that," Liza said and handed Joe her coffee so she could scribble in the margin of the revised copy she'd worked on during the night. "Where'd you get that?"

"A gift from my father. He'd jump to any conclusion that would allow him to hit someone," Joe said. "He felt he was constantly being victimized, wherever he went, whatever he did. Especially by my mother and me."

She was studying his eyes and knew she was going to have to give the closing back to him. Not only would it please Stacy, but he brought veracity to what he said that she couldn't begin to match. When she tried to mimic it, it seemed like a bad carbon copy. "Only thing my dad ever hit was 'the books.' I never realized how lucky I was."

As they were called into the courtroom, she handed the revised closing statement to him. For her sake, he really wanted to refuse it, but he knew it was in their best interest, just as it was for the state. She was right.

CORY WAS STILL WAITING to open the door as he looked out the fancy cut glass window at the blustery morning. That left him standing next to the open gun rack where he looked over the array of semi-automatic assault rifles that had been modified to make them fully automatic. He was anxious to lead Travis out of the house and he'd already extracted a promise from him to come unarmed.

Simon had collared Travis before he could leave and was watching him unstrap the HK from his waist and hang up the whole holster – like he was Shane retiring.

He pulled Travis out of ear-shot of the door and said, "What are you doing, Travis?"

"They kidnapped his goddamn son."

"And put our crop in jeopardy," Simon said, angrily.

"Who gives a shit about half the crop in his barn? It can't be traced to us and weed's such a small part of the gig we're rolling now."

Simon knew what Travis meant – they could get rid of weed and it wouldn't impact their business beyond how they kept their working grunts happy. Plus weed helped keep the traffic at the sites steady; one-stop shopping for the self-numbing classes.

"Listen, this is an unnecessary risk that you should not be taking," Simon said. "You don't owe him this."

Travis shook his head. There were a few things Simon didn't know – and never would – about him and Cory. There was a personal reason he kept the farm and paid Cory to cure the Anoka crop. He owed his friend big time, so he funneled a little capital his way without making it seem like charity, which he knew the righteous idiot would reject. Travis often called him "the Boy Scout" because he had such a rigid code of honor. It held him back. They all knew he'd gotten his world view from Simon, but others had grown out of it. In Cory those ideas had metastasized.

"Send one of the guys to back him up. This is a huge distraction and the last thing we need is to raise our profile. I got something cooking and..."

"Nothing's changed. I'm totally aboard your next brilliant idea, Simon. I'm focused and I'll be with you every step as it builds up to mind-blowing proportions."

Simon didn't like it, but he knew he wasn't going to talk Travis out of it at this point.

Travis chose his Cliven Bundy sheepskin coat. With the collar up, it looked great on him. He loved the image.

As Cory led the way out the front door toward his pickup, he looked Travis over and said, "No gun, right?"

Travis pulled open the coat and showed his waist without the holster. He felt naked without it. As they sat in the truck, Travis pulled out a wad of bills and counted off a few too many hundreds and offered them to Cory, who wouldn't take them. "For the early delivery. Take it." Cory looked askance but finally accepted it and pocketed the cash. "We got a plan? Hospitals are big places."

"I know the room number, the layout inside, the stairs and where to park. What I don't know is who they got with him, but they don't know his name. Good soldier. He's John Doe Junior to them."

As Cory started up, Travis grinned and felt his blood pumping. It was just like way back: riding shotgun, Cory driving, jacked. 'Man those were the times,' he thought.

After they left the compound, Travis wanted him to take the interstate, but of course Cory refused. He said they had sensors and cameras, but claimed he knew the safe routes. It was all that Big Brother stuff Simon had filled him with that he never let go. The drive was going to take forever, but Travis had long ago quit trying to convince Cory the government wasn't half as competent as he gave them credit for. The Boy Scout had even taken the radio out of his truck, thinking they could track him through it. So Travis just went with it, because it felt great not making business decisions or being responsible for his crew for a while. It'd been too long and he really missed being a man of action with the likes of Cory at his side.

As he took all the side roads, Cory thought maybe they'd pull the fire alarm to create enough chaos to allow them to snatch Patrick Henry. He hoped the feds wouldn't have mounted a major presence, thinking 'it's just a boy.' Having the agencies all underestimating Patrick Henry could be to their advantage. It was those two damn agents that bothered him: Nolan and Brandt. They worried him.

ABRAHAM LASHWAY MOVED with surprising speed for such a large and not-quite-in-shape man in his mid-thirties. In scrubs and sneakers the cold cut right through him from the moment he ran out the door. He could only imagine how cold that damned boy must be, barefoot, in a hospital gown and an arm braced in plastic. The kid had managed to escape the hospital despite his recently mended arm and even more recently detached IV drip. But now the rush of adrenaline was starting to wane and exhaustion was already flooding over him. Yet he refused to stop as he staggered toward the speeding traffic at the county highway.

The orderly lifted the boy right off the ground and headed immediately back toward the hospital. He should be getting time and half for catching escaped patients he thought as he struggled the kicking and screaming boy back.

"So where we going to put him now?" Abraham asked the nurse who had followed them down from the eighth floor.

"It's illegal to lock his room," the nurse said, "but there's no way he can stay here. You'd better sit on him until we get through to the temporary guardian."

JOE DIDN'T PICK up that call until after he completed his summation and listened to the defense's specious claims. The judge sent everyone on a recess before he would give his directions to the jury and they would all be done for the day. He checked his phone and was angry to discover he was still considered temporary guardian of the boy. He shouldn't be the person overseeing this kid's welfare.

"We're still Patrick Henry's guardians?" he said to Kat when he called.

"Not as of ten minutes ago," she said. "They called me after they got your voice mail. I brought in Marlo...she's sitting here right now and says hi. We did an end-around through the red tape and she's signed the papers which are on their way through the system. We're off the hook."

"A big thank you to Marlo," Joe said, about to hang up as they were being beckoned back toward the courtroom.

"He tried to escape from the hospital," Kat said.

"Who did? The boy?" Joe said as he sent Liza on ahead and stayed in the hall to talk.

"Ripped out his IV lines, got all the way to the street in his gown and bare feet and was trying to cross the highway when he was picked up and brought back."

"Damn."

"They now refuse to have him in the hospital. They can't afford to assign someone to watch him every minute."

"What will happen with him then?"

"I'm not happy about it or proud of it, but I've written up a three-day psychiatric watch order on him. I use the escape, saying he's a danger to himself, but you need to get a judge to sign it. There's a locked children's psych ward with a bed being held for him."

"I'm about to go back into the courtroom."

He knew damn well judges were reluctant to put chil-

dren in psych wards without physical injury to self or
others. Joe's instinct was on the side of the boy, figuring that
deeper incarceration was only going to make things worse
for him, but there seemed to be little alternative.

"I emailed the Observation Request to you."

"I'll get it done this afternoon," he finally said.

"Good, because I already promised you would."

12

M arlo Kerwin, as a veteran of the continual war of attrition that was Children and Family Services, was always prepared. From her car's trunk she handed Kat a selection of boy's clothes that she pulled from boxes, guessing sizes and bringing a few spares to choose among. Assembled from Salvation Army and donations, her stash was frequently being tapped into to help clothe her temporary wards. This boy was a more unusual story than most who were abused or neglected by what passed as their families. She had encountered plenty of run-away teens, but a nine-year-old with a broken arm trying to escape was a first.

Kat had assured the hospital staff the court order would be coming so they were prepping the boy for transfer. To make it work, she had to show up in person since guardianship was still being processed for Marlo. At least this would be the end of it, she and Joe would be out of the mix and her comrade-in-arms could take John Doe Junior to a place he'd be safe.

Marlo had the right impulses for Family Services and had yet to be made numb to the impossible task they had, despite her dozen years of fighting the good fight. The best they ever got was a draw. And when they lost, it was always the kids who paid. But this was new: her possible adversary was the child himself. She'd had a ten-year-old murderer, so she wasn't naïve about kids; she knew damage was done that could make them as monstrous as adults.

"Patrick Henry, this is Marlo Kerwin," Kat said in room 807 as they laid out clothes for him to try on. She insisted on continuing to test the name, but the boy gave no response. Abraham was still with him, serving more as a guard – despite the green scrubs – than a caretaker. He was happy to stay because he was instantly smitten with Marlo. She had no ring on her finger and she didn't look away from his eyes as they consulted about their shared obstacle. While Kat went to see about the discharge papers, Abraham watched Marlo hold up clothes to the boy for sizing. Divorced, he figured.

"Got any of his kind back home?" he asked her.

"My day is filled with kids, my house with cats."

"I'm not allergic to cats," he said, giving her a look. She knew what he meant and didn't mind.

Patrick Henry refused to engage with them or the clothes. He was trying to figure out another escape.

"You going to put these on yourself or you going to make Marlo and me dress you, Patrick Henry?" Abraham asked.

"Just you try it, Fat Man."

"He's not fat," Marlo said, giving Abraham a look. He knew what she meant and didn't mind.

"You are getting dressed and you are leaving this room," he said. "The only question is how, Patrick Henry."

The boy tried to hide that 'leaving this room' was the best news he'd heard since he climbed that tree. "Quit calling me that and I won't do it with her here."

"I think we can live with that, Ms. Marlo."

"Yes, indeed we can," Marlo said to Abraham with a smile, then stepped out and found Kat just finishing with all the paperwork. She looked at the nurse and said, "So, what can you tell me about Abraham?" She got a big, encouraging smile in return and it all made Kat laugh. Those days of flirting and hoping were over for her. She had her partner and he was the one, no doubt about it.

"I'll go pull up my car," Kat said, taking leave.

"Be sure to put the child safety locks on in the backseat or this kid will bolt at the first stop light," Marlo said, thinking more about the challenge she and Abraham had ahead of them – getting the boy into the car.

———————

CORY DROVE past the hospital looking to see if there was any sign of the agents. He told Travis they needed to do another drive by to see that it was safe and pulled into a handicapped parking spot to turn around.

On the other side of the same parking lot, Kat drove away with Patrick Henry belted into the back seat. Marlo sat with him and they had filled the front seat with boxes of clothing to block any potential exit for the boy. Even in his weakened state, he'd tried to bolt as they put him in the car, but Abraham had secured him with the belt and closed the door. He'd waved to Marlo and then hurried back inside, freezing for the second time in one shift.

As Kat drove out of the employee parking area, the boy was engaged in trying to undo his seat belt, with his head down and Marlo crawling half on top of him to keep him from escaping. They drove right past Cory and Travis who were studying the hospital entrance.

Cory parked the pickup within a decent run from the hospital but not in a direct line of sight. As he and Travis tugged their coats tight against the wind and walked toward the main entrance, he pulled out an extra baseball cap for his friend and explained the layout of the ward on the eighth floor where Patrick Henry was being kept. He slipped on gloves while he described all the security cameras he'd already spotted and expounded on the hidden sensors and x-rays he was certain were placed everywhere inside. Travis had quit listening, he just wanted to know the room number and which way the elevator was. Cory of course insisted on using the stairs, even though it was the damned eighth floor. Jesus.

Cory already knew there were no security cameras in the stairwells as they trudged up. Then he left Travis on the landing as he went to scout ahead to see if there were any guards at the room. Travis caught his breath because he hadn't done eight flights of stairs since...ever. His debt to Cory felt like it was shrinking by the step, but in truth, it was the institutional atmosphere that put him on edge. The wall color, the cement stairs, the fluorescent lights, the utter blandness. It all created an old and awful feeling.

When Cory returned to the stairway landing, Travis was repelled by the smell that came through the door. "Don't the stink remind you of juvie?"

"What? Here?"

"All of it...man. Like it's taking us back there."

Cory had been too distracted earlier to pay attention, but now that Travis mentioned it, the place brought back ugly memories. It left them both keyed-up.

"Let's just get through it," Cory said and led the way as they made a beeline for the ward. Like commandos, they threaded their way through fire doors, passing pathetic people and weird equipment in the hallway.

"I got no spit," Travis said. He'd been in a hundred situations more dangerous, but he hadn't been inside a place like this since they'd escaped juvie. It all made him feel like a rat in a maze.

At room 808 they stopped to assess the situation. Cory was surprised no one was looking at them since he felt so visible and his heart was thundering. But they had their caps snugged down so they'd not be easily recognized by the agents who were no doubt watching monitors. He hoped they'd have his son in hand before anyone raised the alarm. They crept toward 807 just as Abraham came out of the room with an armload of bed linens and the boy's hospital gown.

Cory leaned around Abraham, peered into the empty room and said, "Where in fuck you got him?"

Travis didn't like the look of Abraham; the short sleeve scrubs were horribly familiar and a powerful trigger. Goddamned green hospital scrubs and hiding behind an armload of bedding. Travis blocked the orderly's way as Cory became more frantic, darting into the room and back out, shoving past the guy and taking another look.

A nurse at the desk saw the two men confronting Abraham and hurried over, anxious to talk with them. "Children and Family Services was just here. They need to talk to you if you're looking for Patrick Henry."

Cory spun toward her and said, "He told you his name?"

Abraham felt Travis grab his bare arm and didn't like the look in the short guy's eye. "Back off, sir."

"You been touching the boy, you fucking bastard?" Travis sneered.

Abraham pushed back, trying to step past the two men at the door.

That was when Travis lost it.

The pistol came out of the back of his waistband and slammed up against Abraham's head in an instant – before Cory even knew it was there. Blood poured down the big man's face and spilled all over the bed linens he held. As bloodied sheets fell to the floor, Abraham took a swing at Travis that sent him reeling backward, off balance.

Seeing Travis attacked propelled Cory into savage retaliation. His fist smashed into Abraham's bloody head before either of them realized he was joining the battle. Cory's strength made every punch overpowering and once he started, Cory could not stop. Travis nearly leapt out of his big coat with excitement as he watched Cory's fists pummel with all the rage he could never fully escape.

Abraham was blinded by the blood, dazed by the pistol and was no match for Cory's ferocity. The nearby nurse screamed and a crowd formed. A visitor to the ward pulled a fire extinguisher from the wall and headed toward the men.

That's when Travis shot into the ceiling.

Stunned, everyone stopped, even Cory. Travis' gun was aimed at the man with the fire extinguisher and there seemed little doubt he might use it. Sprawled on the floor, Abraham was bloody, but still breathing. Travis dragged Cory away and they started to run.

As they darted into the stairwell, Travis felt fantastic and whooped as they sailed down the stairs.

By the time they crashed through the exit door, Cory was distraught, while Travis had a glow like he'd almost forgotten was possible. He felt great.

ENRIGHT WAS WAITING for Joe as he came out of the courtroom. The jury had only been out a couple hours and had already voted to convict. Liza and Joe were happy until they saw the big investigator's grim look.

"Looks like Patrick Henry really is the boy's name and now there's a real crime," Enright said. "Several felonies for starters."

"The boy?" Joe said in surprise.

"Two men came for him, beat a man and fired a gun."

"They got the boy?" Joe said as he found Enright ushering him away from Liza.

"Kat and Family Services had just taken him, so no."

"Kat was there?" Joe said with serious alarm.

———

CORY WAS SO angry he couldn't speak. He had just wanted to grab his son and then go back underground, but that was now an impossibility. Firing a gun in a hospital, bashing that big black guy, then beating the shit out of him. He'd flown out of control and still had no idea how to find his son. Whatever shred of anonymity he had an hour ago was long gone. The government had already been pulling out all the stops and now their pursuit of him was only going to intensify. 'Manhunt' kept going through his mind.

"He looked like him...down at Redwing," Travis said.

'Garmon?' immediately went through Cory's mind, but he wasn't about to say it out loud. They never, ever said that name aloud. "Nah. That what set you off?"

"What'choo mean, set me off?" Travis said indignantly. "He'd had your boy alone in that room, the big faggot." In the glove box he found a rag and started obsessively cleaning blood off his handgun. "Thanks for stepping in."

Both of them thought back to that night with Garmon. Cory had stepped in and lost control then too, just the way Travis had expected.

Cory hadn't thought about Garmon in a long time. They'd made a pact never to discuss that man and they'd stuck to it. Other than talking about funny moments and fist fights from their days in juvie, they had driven that part of their past far underground. These days they talked about their old times as if they started after the escape from juvie when they'd teamed up professionally. The eighteen months in juvie had just been their training camp – Travis for a life of crime and Cory, he told himself, for a life of thoughtful insurrection.

Cory hated himself for believing Travis' promise not to bring a gun. He should have known better, but he'd had no choice, there was no one else he could trust. Abby would have screwed it up, like she did getting Patrick Henry captured in the first place. And there was no one beyond those two; Betsy was too much like her mother. He had been training Patrick Henry to become the partner he'd been missing since he and Travis had gone different directions. He and Travis had remained best of friends – as close to brothers as either would ever have – but the partnership had disappeared for reasons that Travis had just proven all over again. He was too volatile for thoughtful insurrection – he craved action, confrontation, violence.

"How we going to find him?" Travis asked as he threw the blood-stained rag out the window. He noticed a spot of blood on his coat and it pissed him off.

———

"I NEVER SAW IT COMING," Abraham said as he lay on an

ER gurney. They'd already pumped morphine into him, so he was feeling no pain, but was still mystified. "No idea why he took such a dislike to me," he said to Joe and Enright.

Along with the two responding cops, they were all in a crowded bay of the ER. Blood has spattered all down Abraham's face, neck and the front of his scrubs, but being one of the hospital's own, he was the center of an amazing amount of attention and eager help.

"The Marlboro Man's little brother, the one wearing a sheepskin coat...he was the one who hit me first with the gun. When I tried to fight back, the other one jumped in."

"So the big guy we think is the father. He's the one who confirmed the kid's name is Patrick Henry?" Enright said. "So Mr. Sheepskin was just there as muscle?"

"I guess, he had the gun," Abraham said. "How many stitches we doing, Doc?"

"About twenty so far."

"And I almost had a date tonight," he looked at Joe and nodded. "Your lady friend's lady friend."

"From Family Services? Nice. I heard Marlo likes you."

"Still? Maybe she likes damaged people," Abraham said a bit wistfully. "I like the name Marlo."

"Doc will have you looking like Denzel inside of an hour," Enright said. "So tell us about the father."

"Baseball cap, never looked me in the eye, a dirty blue down jacket and black gloves. Six-three, maybe six-four, white, looked a lot more solid than his friend. He hits like Tyson."

"Never saw his face?" Joe asked.

"I was busy bleeding, sorry. The shorter one...I can work with your artist if you guys actually do that kind of thing. Won't get all of it, but I'll know those eyes again anywhere, any time. That one looked at me with such hatred. What'd I ever do to him?"

Joe looked at the two cops who'd been taking notes. "Anything else you can tell us?"

"The little one accused me of touching the boy."

"That's probably where the rage came from," Joe said.

"Could have been a whole lot worse...a shot was fired."

"That shot might have saved my life," Abraham said. "I don't think the big bastard was about to stop on his own."

"He didn't give you a concussion," the doctor added. "Be grateful he was wearing gloves and got stopped."

"I've been seeing my lucky stars ever since the gun hit me, doc," Abraham said as Joe ushered everyone out.

"Not much to go on," Joe said. "How we doing on security cameras?"

"First speed-look through them, just hats, no faces, but we've had copies shipped downtown for analysis," one of the cops said. "Should we finish getting statements from everyone up on the eighth floor?"

"Good idea," Enright said. "And clue in Detective Ed Bittinger to everything we've gotten so far."

13

"I'm never getting my son back," Cory said to Travis as he climbed back into the pickup after putting the post back in place, bringing the chain across the road that led to his house and what was left of his family.

"We're going to get him back, Cor," Travis said. "But you know we gotta get your old lady and the girl out of here first, before they send in a fucking platoon."

"I haven't scouted a new place. It's moving too fast."

"I got room. No matter what your boy tells them about you, nothing leads them to my place. He's never been out there and doesn't know me, so you and them will all be safe staying with me until we get him back. I'll send a coupla guys over to clear out the barn."

Cory stewed, thinking about the marijuana drying in the barn and how he would tell Abby as he pulled up in front of the house. She came flying out, then stopped in her tracks when she saw Travis in the passenger seat.

"Heyya, Abby, long time," Travis said as he stepped out. He knew she didn't like him and couldn't blame her – she saw him as a serious rival for her husband's attention. In truth, he went a whole lot farther back with Cory than his bus-station-bride did.

Cory had an arm around Abby and was trying to lead her back inside as he said, "They might have transferred him out of the hospital and I got no idea where they took him."

Abby gasped and had to stop, as if hit by a body blow. Until now she'd convinced herself Cory would get their son back and then they'd all head to South Dakota or wherever Cory said. Instead, he showed up with Travis, the last person she ever wanted to see.

"What do you mean they transferred him, Dad?" Betsy said from the doorway to the house. She'd been listening.

"The feds got hold of him and now they're questioning him. They took your brother somewhere, Bets...this is more serious than anything we ever faced before," Cory said as he led his wife toward the house.

"All that is real?" Betsy said, surprised. "Feds and interrogation and wanting to put a stop to our kind?"

"As real as a festering toothache," Travis said off-handedly as he eyed Betsy a bit too closely. "Betsy, you have gotten so big and just as pretty as your mama."

Betsy shied away from him and stepped inside to let everyone in. The whole household seemed to be packed up into yard and garden bags piled by the front door.

"We gotta get outta here now, Ab," Cory said as he went to pick up a couple bags, but she stopped him.

"What about Patrick Henry? What's happening with him?"

"We don't know yet, but first let's get you two away from here and somewhere safe," Cory said.

"Where's that?" she snapped.

Cory looked from her to Travis and then saw her racing away, into the rear of the house, so he followed.

"Let's you and me get these bags in the back of the pickup, Betsy," Travis said. "How old you now?"

In the stripped and barren back bedroom, Cory caught up with Abby, who was uncharacteristically shaking her head, defiant. It was rare that she stood up to him.

"Put us in a motel, Cory. Don't make us go to his place with all those...guys and everything around."

"We're not going to a motel, Ab," he said. "There aren't a lot of choices right now."

"We could pay cash and I'll do the check-in."

"No," he said as he grabbed her forcefully, but then let go. "I can't be out searching and worrying about you being spotted in a motel at the same time. Travis has a big house and lots of protection and no one will be looking for us there, no matter what Patrick Henry tells them."

"He won't say a thing!"

"They know his name," Cory said. "These people have ways that no one can resist. That's why we gotta get out of here and do it quick. They could already be on their way."

Seeing the futility of resistance, she sank into herself and followed him to the front of the house. Walking behind him, she noticed splotches of blood on his jacket sleeves and it terrified her. She just pulled another jacket from a hook by the door and insisted he put it on. He noticed the blood and looked at her guiltily, flooded with shame at having lost control again. She'd worked so long and hard on him and they both thought he'd gotten past that kind of violence.

The bed of the truck was filled with everything they could take and Betsy was lugging a tarp to tie it all down and cover it. Cory ran over to the barn and pushed his way through the remaining hanging marijuana plants. At the cabinet, he pulled out his hidden stash of money and took his two rifles. Back at the truck, he slid the guns under the tarp and sent Betsy to fetch the family savings from the hollow in the tree. As she went, she really wanted to go get her own separate funds, but didn't dare. If they found out she'd been stealing, there'd be hell to pay.

Abby looked at the three-person pickup truck seat and the four of them. Travis picked up her concern and slid into the middle while Cory looked wistfully back at the house. They'd lived here longer than any other place in their under-the-radar life. Abby sat in the passenger seat and pulled Betsy onto her lap. It was a tight squeeze, especially when Cory climbed in with his big shoulders.

"Careful where you shift," Travis joked, indicating the gearshift that rose up from the floor by his knee, his leg crammed right up against Cory's from the crowding. He was the only one in a good mood.

MARLO DIDN'T TAKE the news about Abraham easily. Kat was once again ditching out on her clients to go talk to her friend whose office was just down the hall from her in the eight story Family Services Building.

"Is Abraham going to be okay?"

"How do you feel about stitches and swelling?" Kat said. "He got hit really hard and quite a few times."

Marlo thought about it and nodded her okay, but then realized her hands were shaking. So were Kat's.

"Think I should go see him?" Marlo said.

"Helluva first date to tell the grandkids about."

"Let's not get ahead of ourselves! Just that boy is enough to set me off kids forever. He's a terrorist in training, just like his father and the other guy." A shudder ran through her and she said, "What they did to poor Abraham is just sickening."

———

TRAVIS WALKED in the front door carrying two of the large plastic bags holding the Trammell's worldly goods and announced, "Honey, I'm home." He was still in a great mood.

Simon was alone watching a documentary about the Unabomber on the huge television. He looked up, shook his head and said, "Kaczynski, man. Smartest guy there ever was...so why is it he was so dumb about it? Letter bombs? Really? That's the best he could come up with sitting in his cabin for years being pissed off? So much wasted potential, know what I mean?"

"We got visitors," Travis said as he shut off the TV just as Cory arrived with a couple more bags. Behind him, Abby's jaw dropped at the sight of the arsenal just inside the front door. There were more guns everywhere in the house and Betsy stared in open-mouthed awe.

She wasn't the only one who was stunned. Simon gaped at the girl and at Abby whom he'd met before – he'd attended that silly thing they called a wedding. The hug he gave Abby was as awkward as always and it sent a shiver through her. The look he threw at Travis clearly said: 'are you out of your mind?'

"They're going to spend a night or two in Lenny's old room. He sure don't need it," Travis said and led the family back into the bowels of the spacious old house.

Cory and Travis quickly returned and went to the pickup for the rest of the stuff. Cory stayed at the truck to slip his guns and ammo under the bench seat. When Travis arrived back inside with a couple more bags, Simon stopped him. "What the hell is going on?"

"We didn't get the boy and now there's...well, there was a fight at the hospital and it's too hot for them to stay in their place."

"So you bring them here?"

"Only a night or two."

"You don't owe him this. He just dries weed for us."

"There's things you don't know," Travis said. He owed Cory a lot he would never talk about with Simon.

They stopped talking as Cory walked through with more bags, then resumed in whispers as he disappeared in the back of the house.

"So how'd you leave things at his place?"

"I sent some guys over there to clear out the weed, they'll be done before dark," Travis said.

"A fight? He went crazy, right? So cops will be showing up at his place, sooner or later?"

"I suppose."

"There'll be traces of you and me at his property, plus our guys are over there leaving prints that could lead right to us. His place is a huge fucking loose end."

"Maybe you should tie it up for us," Travis said.

"You want that?" Simon said with a long steady look.

"Yeah," Travis said, thought and added, "I want that."

"Want what?" Cory said as he returned from the bedroom to get the bags Abby had left.

"Just business shit. Your girls settling in okay?"

"Abby's not exactly happy but she'll get over it. I can't thank you enough for giving us a place, Trav."

"Mi casa, compadre."

Cory glanced uncertainly at Simon, then pulled out the

pages he'd stolen from Patrick Henry's hospital file on his first visit. "You know how to find addresses from names?"

"Sure, my man," Travis said as he led Cory toward the kitchen, but they were interrupted by the rather frantic arrival of Leo Stacker. He was pretty agitated, far from his usual joint-rolling mellow.

"We got a problem over at Fluff and Fold," Stacker announced, ignoring the presence of Cory who wasn't part of the team. The indiscretion irritated Simon. All the careful separation he had worked so hard to create in their business model was going to shit in one day.

Cory looked to Travis and laughed, "Fluff and Fold?"

"A laundromat I own," Travis said a bit defensively. "What's up over there?" he said to Stacker, unnerved by Cory being there, but that horse was out of the barn.

"I was just doing my Tuesday rounds and Twitch is out of sorts. Accounts is screwy."

"I got everybody out over to..." Travis said, then looked at Cory and stopped before revealing where he'd sent most of his guys. He turned to Simon, "Could you look into it for me? For us, Simon?"

"I don't do on-site account work."

"I know, I know. I wouldn't ask except everyone's out helping tie up those loose ends, you know what I mean?"

Simon knew. At last he nodded and left with Stacker.

Travis gestured after him to Cory. "Simon's computer connection is so secure the NSA couldn't hack us."

"That's his kind of stuff. Still..."

"It's safe, Cor. Who we looking up?"

"The two agents who took Patrick Henry."

JOE STARTED to open up a bottle of Pouilly-Fuissé, but Kat got up from the laptop opened on the dining table and took the bottle from his hand. She put it back in the under-counter wine cooler and started to fill the silver ice bucket. She was making an announcement. Using silver tongs, she put ice into two cut crystal glasses and splashed in surprisingly healthy shots of Booker's bourbon. Joe was still getting adjusted to the notion of silver ice buckets and tongs, but now was not the time to marvel at how far he'd come. She seemed disturbed.

"Which bothers you more, the boy or the father?"

"Does it make me a selfish and uncaring person if I'm not very concerned about Patrick Henry?" Kat said. "The close call with the father is another matter."

"It makes you human."

"Then call me extra human," she said and drank down a good half of the glass.

She tapped on the laptop's space bar and the video they'd been watching started up again. It was a copy of the security tape Enright had sent of the beating of Abraham. It was brutal and Kat had finished her drink before Travis fired the shot into the ceiling.

Joe wanted to usher her to the couch and away from the video, but even to his eye, the living room did not look inviting. His furniture was interspersed with hers and there were stacks of cardboard boxes visible in every direction. The sun porch was equally a mess and neither of them had the energy to try to make his things fit into her perfect world. They stayed at the dining table and that meant staring at the open computer where Joe backed up the video and froze it to look at the guy in the sheepskin. He could almost make out his face.

"That coat is expensive," Kat said indicating Travis' coat on the frozen frame of the video.

"Meaning not many places will carry them?"

"I bet not more than two or three in the Twin Cities."

"I'll ask Byron to look into it. Good catch."

"There's no escaping this case, is there?" Kat said. "What other clues have you got so far?"

"Not much. The boy's name, but no place of birth. And no idea about his father, mother, the friend with the gun, where they are, when they might turn up again, what they might do next or what it's really about," he said. "I wish I'd just come back upstairs Monday morning and joined you in the shower. Then we'd never have heard of this kid."

"Now who's an uncaring person?"

"Ain't we a pair. So how about that shower?"

"My back is feeling a bit dirty."

"I might work my way around there," he said and stood, offering his hand. She finished off his drink, then let him pull her from the chair. She knew they were fleeing the day and it felt like the perfect thing to do.

Despite Abby's protests, Cory knew he had to leave. All their bags of stuff were in the bedroom at the back of the large house where they'd be plenty safe even though Travis' house and the men in it scared her. He told her he'd buy a sturdy door lock to install on his way back from his other errand, but he knew Travis would never let his guys near her. There was no convincing Abby and that battle was way down his list of priorities at the moment. Patrick Henry was at the top and he had only two clues – Brandt and Nolan. He was going out tonight to locate them.

There was no sign of life at Brandt's house and it didn't seem like the kind of neighborhood government agents lived in. The locks on the building and his apartment door posed no problem, but what he found was an utterly empty apartment. He stood in the living room and realized it was a front. This was just one more confirmation for Cory that there were dangerous government people on his tail.

Half an hour later he parked on Mississippi River Boulevard outside a very nice-looking apartment building. Katherine Nolan lived on the top floor, right. There were lights on and it looked like she was home.

14

Simon hated going on rounds – collecting cash, checking on balances and distributing new product to the dregs of the earth Travis had assembled to sell drugs. When he first joined the operation, he'd accompanied every one of their runners to get a full grasp on the network. After that he'd revised their protocols and taught Travis how to enforce discipline and make everyone accountable. These weren't the sorts of people who could easily be made responsible, but after a little weeding of the troops – which had resulted directly in Lenny's timely demise – Simon thought there was too much fear among the guys not to obey the new rules.

Stacker pulled his beat-to-shit old Chevy right up in front of the laundry out in Coon Rapids. The ancient neon sign above the door read: 'Coo apids Fluff an old.'

"Don't park in front, you moron," Simon said.

Stacker started back up and drove on, at last remembering that not parking near the site had been one of the changes. Never leave the car, yourself and the location in the same potential photograph. He'd remembered that for the first few days after Travis laid out the new rules, especially after all that happened with Lenny, but mostly he still parked in front. It was cold and he didn't like walking that much. Besides, with that system, he'd walk a couple blocks with drugs on him going in and cash on him going out. How smart was that? Not that he'd ask Travis to explain; he just didn't usually follow the rule. He brought back all their cash, so what was there to complain about?

Simon pulled his scarf over his face as they trudged into the wind to the laundry. "What's his name again?"

"He's from Nord-East, everyone just calls him Twitch."

Nord-East was Northeast Minneapolis which had a large Polish population. Second, third, even fourth generation Americans still were given old-world names in honor of the grandparents. This neighborhood cultural hegemony left some names of native-born Americans with almost no vowels.

Twitch was the right name for him anyway; the guy couldn't sit still and looked skinny enough to blow away in today's breeze. They had heavy users selling for them. Any police recruit on his second day would pick him out as a user, abuser and seller of drugs. And he'd be right. Once he was back alone with Travis, they'd have to have a talk. They couldn't have idiots like this guy screw up when they had much bigger things coming up soon. 'World changing things,' Simon thought. Better to have fewer locations with better people than dig this low down the human food chain.

The two men trying to solve the cash controversy at Fluff and Fold drove Simon crazy. Stacker was barely able to keep his accounts straight, yet he was a collector. Twitch couldn't actually add up three numbers; two at a time was his limit and even then he was uncertain. He and Stacker were going over the flush-able day log for the third time while Simon watched someone actually using the laundry to clean their clothes. He bet Twitch pilfered the coins put in the machines. Exasperated, Simon took over the day log, corrected the math, took some of the cash from Stacker and gave it to Twitch, who was happy and felt vindicated. They'd both been wrong, but he wasn't going to waste his time and argue. Outsiders were nearby and that always made him uncomfortable.

Simon left before Stacker delivered the resupply to Twitch and peered out from behind his scarf at the closed gas station and garage across the street. It had gone out of business years ago and appeared derelict, but he knew different.

"I didn't know Travis had bought that place," Stacker said as he joined Simon, indicating the gas station.

A deep chill ran through Simon, but he managed to hide it as he said, "What do you mean?"

"I seen you coming out of there last week, so I figure Travis is expanding like he always is."

"Huh," Simon said as his mind raced. Stacker had stumbled onto something no one knew about, not even Travis.

"How's a garage fit into his plans anyway?" Stacker said as they walked toward the car.

"You didn't ask Travis?"

"Nah, man. He don't confide in me, know what I mean?"

"Anybody else tell you what it's about?"

"I didn't mention it to no one. 'No cross-talking' is one a the rules, right? Everything is strictly 'need to know' and all that good stuff...I don't cross-talk."

'Good,' thought Simon as they got into the car. "Let's go over there, I'll show you what it's all about," Simon said. "You'll like it."

Stacker grinned at this unexpected confidence. Maybe his loyalty was going to pay off.

He drove past the old pumps to one of the two garage bay doors Simon directed him toward. Simon hurried to the glass entry door, which was blacked-out inside, unlocked it and then the bay door started to open. Stacker drove his car inside and Simon looked up and down the street as the door closed behind the car.

It was damn cold in the garage but it was far from empty. It was fully stocked with a giant array of tools and, parked in the other bay, there was a plumbing truck. It was a converted Ford F250 that was twenty years old and had a rack above with pipes of all kinds and sizes, plus long tool cribs mounted to each side of the rear bed. Simon shivered as they entered and pulled on his gloves. He started laying out a sheet of plastic near the workbench, then beckoned Stacker. "I could use a hand."

Stacker helped him spread out the plastic as he gawked around, trying to figure it all out. "I don't get it. How's a plumbing truck and a garage full of some very cool tools help Travis? You building us a meth lab or something?"

"You'll be able to see it better from the plans," Simon said, urging Stacker to join him at the workbench. There he had a roll of hand-drawn plans laid out, held down with a hammer on one end and a screwdriver on the other. It was an elaborate and detailed drawing of a big tank and a bunch of little ones with hoses and connectors. None of it made a bit of sense to Stacker.

"I'm still not seeing it."

Simon knew he should just get on with it, but it felt good to have a chance to be admired.

"You know how fuel injection works?"

"In a car? Gas vapor is sprayed into a cylinder, a spark

plug makes the gas explode and the confined explosion drives the piston in the cylinder to turn the crank shaft."

"Excellent," Simon said with genuine surprise.

"I had garage mechanics for my shop class before I got kicked out," Stacker said with a tiny swell of pride.

"This is like a giant version of what you studied. Fuel injection on a huge scale."

"How big?"

"Building size," Simon said with a smirk, then enjoyed the awe and confusion in the first person ever to learn what he'd been working on for many months.

"A building?"

"An elevator shaft up the center of a tall building is really just a squared-off cylinder. A huge one."

Stacker leaned closer to the drawings, then looked across at the truck and a large, squat tubular tank for liquids near it. Simon watched with fascination as the pathetic little man tried to work it out – fuel injection on a building-size scale and the resulting explosion. At last Stacker started to understand and his eyes brightened.

He turned to Simon. "Why?"

"Why stick a garden hose down an anthill?" Simon said, "To make them scramble and take notice before they die."

Before Stacker had fully turned back to the truck and tank for another curious look, the hammer bashed into the side of his head with a vicious finality. He crumpled to the floor, his body perfectly centered on the plastic.

Simon used kerosene to clean the hammer, wiping it extensively on Stacker's jean jacket before putting it back in place atop the plans on his workbench.

He hated to have to kill face-to-face. In person was not his style, but this situation was both unexpected and urgent. He'd been seen and that was just unacceptable. He had been momentarily understood by Stacker – which was quite enjoyable – but full recognition was perilous and had only happened once before. Back then it resulted in a beating that taught him a life lesson. Since that day, he had allowed no one to see or understand the totality of all the plans he had in motion at once. His prudent secrecy had paid off ever since that failure; he'd never been in jail, never been arrested, almost never even remotely suspected.

Two hours after he wrapped the body in the plastic, he drove Stacker's car right through the chain across the dirt road and headed up to what had been Cory's home. The body was in Stacker's own trunk and Simon was glad he'd found a way to could kill two birds with one stone that would also create an impressive, yet untraceable display of power. Earlier he'd dropped off another car from the Cushing Avenue Towing yard and parked it within walking distance of Cory's place. He hadn't been seen going back and forth, so there was no possible connection between him and the two loose ends he was going to clean up spectacularly.

As the headlights played over the house where Cory's family had lived, they illuminated the propane tank. This was shaping up nicely, as was his cover story for Travis.

KAT WOKE UP WITH A START, thinking about that boy in the psych ward. She wondered if he was scared, if his tough-guy persona had evaporated and he was crying into his pillow. She wasn't going to get back to sleep anytime soon and she had now become resigned to this being a case that Joe would not let go. She knew there was a study on medical paranoia she'd been meaning to look up to help her understand the boy and his mother. At the very least, if the article were dull, it would lull her back to sleep.

When she left the bedroom in her robe to grab the laptop, she planned to curl up in the sun porch loveseat under an afghan, but there were boxes everywhere. She turned a light on and cleared enough room to sit. With a spot open, she stopped to look out the windows which gave her an amazing daytime view up and down the wooded park that followed the river dividing St. Paul from Minneapolis. At night, there were pools of visibility under the streetlights that left patches of darkness between. She noticed exhaust coming from a pickup truck parked in the shadows well up the block and wondered who was getting home from work in the middle of the night. Finally she nestled into the loveseat, tucked the afghan around her and started her search on the computer.

In the pickup, Cory shut off the engine after he saw Nolan looking out the windows of her apartment. Had he been spotted? Should he go in and confront her? But then what? There was no good exit once it got to a confrontation. So he watched her sitting haloed in the light from a lamp.

JOE LEFT before dawn to catch up on all of his cases before his meeting with D.A. Mike Westermann. Now that he had several felonies to build a case on, there would be no resistance to his pursuing the mysteries around the boy, aiming at the parents and Dad's friend. Police resources could now be justified to help solve this bizarre case.

As his car warmed up, he scraped the night's frost off his windows. Kat's building had six garages built out back, one for each apartment, which left his car on the street gathering frost. Her car was like her – nice, neat, clean, new and presentable. His car was like him – a pile of junk with enough rust to show how many years it had endured snow, ice and street salting by the city. As he drove away and headed toward downtown, he didn't notice the rusty beige pickup truck parked up the block looking a bit out of place in this neighborhood.

Cory sat back up after Brandt drove past and was intrigued; he wondered if the bosses knew these two agents were having an affair. This might explain why the guy's apartment was empty. While he decided whether to follow Brandt or wait for Nolan, he saw one of the garage doors rise and spotted her racing from the building. She backed out in her Prius – figures, she pretends she's saving the earth while she abducts boys from their families.

He made a U-turn to follow her and she was oblivious to the pickup behind her as she led Cory on a tour of how the wealthy robber barons had once lived while they'd been stealing the people's land and enslaving them.

———

THE SUN HAD JUST RISEN when Simon got back to Travis' house. No one was up that early and none of them had a clue what he'd been doing. He counted on them believing he returned in the middle of the night, so sat in the living room with the TV on and the volume off. The burner cell phone he would use once was in his breast pocket – handy when the time came. He tuned it to a local news station and settled in to feign sleep. They'd think he'd dozed off in front of the TV.

While he'd always been cautious about hiding his actual movements, this day was more important than most. Big things were going to happen soon and it was crucial that only Travis have even a partial understanding of how he'd taken care of some of their unfinished business. Everyone else should know nothing of what he'd been doing.

He could actually use some sleep, but there was no way, he was too keyed up. He loved anticipating the moment the world started to discover what he'd secretly set in motion. His greatest excitement came from knowing they had no idea he was behind it. He could indulge in the joy of his triumph yet feel no personal danger. No fear of being caught and blamed and imprisoned.

Having Cory under the same roof with them brought back a memory of delicious anticipation when he was the only person in the world to know a major event was about to happen. Much like he felt now, awaiting the morning news.

Once he'd installed Travis and Cory as leaders of the boys army of Redwing, he had wanted to experiment with his power. He found a boy who'd burned down a neighbor's garage. He'd instantly look guilty of the crime Simon had in mind, which would leave him unsuspected.

He created a fuse from end-to-end cigarettes, kicked the boy from his class so he'd be near the fire in the dormitory that was about to erupt and then established his own alibi inside a locked classroom filled with boys.

The fire flared up exactly as he'd planned, sprinklers went off, locked door automatically opened and the emergency allowed all inmates about twenty minutes of free rein. Wonderful mayhem followed – chaos throughout the system – and he alone could anticipate the bedlam.

He'd made a perfect experiment in instigating anarchy.

15

Joe had a handful of folders open on the conference table in Mike Westermann's office. They represented all his on-going cases for the Wednesday morning update. Mike felt that the first two days of the week told them what their strengths, weaknesses and opportunities were and the last two were when they had a chance to make adjustments and broker deals. Wednesday was the day to reconsider their approach collectively. So Mike, the imposing District Attorney, would be at one end of the table and Stacy, the Chief of Prosecution, was at the other. In between were all the ADAs who weren't in court; each shepherding folders.

Straight across from Joe was Ronald Sheldon. Technically he was Assistant Chief of Prosecution, but everyone present, including Ronald, knew he was never moving up from there. Early on he'd identified Joe as a threat and always treated him as such. He was a petty man consumed with frustrated ambitions. Joe had harbored suspicions that he'd betrayed the DA's office in a previous murder case, but he couldn't prove it at the time, so he kept mum. Next to Joe on one side was Tony McCullum, the DA's unofficial encyclopedia and historian. He was the oldest hand present and had no ambitions beyond staying on staff forever. So far, his chances looked good. Joe considered him an ally. And on his other side was his usual partner, Liza Upman.

While they waited for Mike, who was now in his third elected term, Stacy questioned each of them about their most urgent cases. Mike was still by the windows with their panoramic view of the Wabasha Bridge and the Mississippi River far below his eighth floor office. He was, as usual, using two cell phones at once and looking far more like a fashion model than the college football star he'd been. As he returned to the long conference table, he silenced everyone and tossed down a phone. He picked up a remote control and turned on three televisions at the end of the room, each tuned to a different local station.

"Looks like we've got a major fire and the department is already calling it arson," Mike said as they looked at the unfolding fire, which was near the edge of the county. Local news helicopters were showing a house, a barn and other outbuildings – plus much of the wooded land around it – all burning ferociously.

"Mike, can you freeze it?" Joe said and Mike clicked a button. Joe leapt out of his seat and went to the screens. Frozen on one TV was a towering pine tree he was sure he recognized. As he inspected the frozen image, he could make out a tree-climber's strap still clinging to the bark near the lowest of the spreading branches at the top. "I stood under this tree on Monday."

"Why?" Stacy said as she looked at the screens.

"That's the tree Patrick Henry fell out of."

"The mystery boy whose father assaulted an orderly at St. Johns?" Stacy said as she handed their boss the boy's case file from Joe's stack.

"Yeah. Boy falls out of tree, he and his mother refuse medical help, his father beats a hospital worker and now the place he was hurt burns to the ground in an arson..." Joe said. "It just keeps getting stranger every day."

"What tiger's tail did you grab, Joe?" Mike asked.

"I thought it was just an abandoned boy at the time."

"Can't you tell when you got a major case?" Ronald said and looked around for support. He didn't get it.

"I calculate zero chance all those events are coincidental," Tony said.

Mike looked at pictures of Patrick Henry with a bone sticking through his arm. "He refused treatment for that? Did Daddy do that to him?"

"No. We have an eyewitness who saw him fall from that tree," Joe said, pointing to the television. "The tall pine that's burning right now."

Mike discovered photos of Abraham's brutalized face.

"Forty-seven stitches....beaten by a gun, then fists," Joe said. "Dad and his friend ganged up on him. Our theory is the gunshot was not meant to hit anyone."

Mike clicked the remote and watched the fire ravage the land where Cory and family had recently lived.

"That fire might be the father covering his tracks after the assault," Joe said.

"Yeah," Mike said as he looked again at the photos of the boy and Abraham. "There's some real violence in these people. So why's he climb a tall tree in the first place?"

Joe shrugged and looked to Stacy who said, "They estimate he's nine, maybe he was just being a boy."

"Forty feet in the air?" Ronald scoffed.

"Theories?" Mike asked and everyone turned to Tony who never failed to have a precedent from the last hundred years, or however long he'd been with the DA.

"There's a card that hasn't been turned over yet," Tony said. "I'll have to get back to you."

"Wow," Liza said. No one had ever seen Tony stumped.

"Find us that missing card, Joe," Tony suggested.

"Where are you at with your other cases?" Stacy said as she inspected Joe's stack of files.

"Liza and I got a conviction yesterday," Joe said.

"I know. Congrats. And you're up to speed on all of these?" Stacy said to Liza holding up Joe's folders.

"Up to speed and raring to go," Liza said.

"Mike?" Stacy said. "An assault, a gunshot, abandoned boy and now an arson, should we..."

"...Liza take the whole stack," Mike said. "Joe, grab Byron and find out what the hell is going on with all this. I'm not seeing a clear through-line yet but I sure as hell don't like the direction of the flow."

———

CORY NOW THOUGHT he should have followed Brandt, but it was too late to change. He'd tailed Nolan right past downtown, where he'd expected her to go, then she'd driven into East St. Paul. He parked down the street as she went into a crappy little house for half an hour, then came back out. He noted the address and might check it out later in case that was where they'd taken his boy for some reason. But his gut told him this was completely unrelated. He followed her again until she pulled into the parking ramp below one of the tall buildings in St. Paul Plaza. He raced off to find a quick spot to leave the truck on the street.

On the northern edge of downtown, St. Paul Plaza was home to a collection of government buildings, including so-called city services and, notably, the FBI. Cory didn't want to go into the public parking area and be photographed while getting the parking stub at the gate. Still, he had a growing certainty she would lead him to his son, so he kept following. Luckily he found a parking spot, skidded up to the curb and anxiously fed quarters into the parking meter, giving himself two hours. A ticket would identify the truck and mean, at the very least, he'd need new plates.

He raced back toward the entrance that Nolan had driven down and sprinted past employees waiting in line to swipe their cards to leave their cars in the two stories of underground parking. He'd passed nearly a dozen security cameras, but he just had to adjust his priorities. He kept his head hidden under the brim of his cap as he raced deeper into perilous territory and there was no sign of her anywhere as he ran around the lower garage level. Finally he snugged his cap even lower and went to find the stairway up. He darted in but discovered that the stairs would only allow him to go up to the lobby level. There was a locked door from the stairs that rose to the other floors to keep pedestrians from going upstairs without key cards.

On the ground floor he fell in behind a group coming off the elevator and followed as they moved like cattle toward the front of the building. The lobby was filled with security personnel, x-ray scanners and a line of people waiting to enter the upper stories. The building hadn't originally been built to have a secure entrance, but had probably been retro-fitted after 9/11. It was still possible to drive into the below-ground parking, but to enter the upper floors, one had to be screened. He quickly acted like he'd forgotten something and headed back to the stairs to go back down. He was shit out of luck.

He raced back the way he came and walked around to approach the lobby from the plaza level. From outside he watched as people entered, put their purses and packages on the conveyer belt into the x-ray machine. Damn government.

Upstairs Kat entered the outer office of the Psychological Therapy Section, said hello to the receptionist and some co-workers, then saw she already had a family awaiting her as she went to her office. She glanced through the print-out on her desk of her day's schedule and it looked full – she was still trying to catch up for time lost to Patrick Henry. There was a note for an urgent call-back to Marlo Kerwin, so she made that first, hoping it was good news about the boy.

"He beat up an older boy and flooded the bathroom at the psych ward," Marlo said by way of good morning.

———

JOE DARTED into Enright's office in the DA's building and found the big man on the phone holding a hand up for him to wait. Joe was very impatient.

"You know and I know it's the brother, Bitt," Enright said into the phone, "but until the Little Canada Police come to the same conclusion, there's not a lot we can do." He rolled his eyes to Joe and said, "Right now?"

Joe vehemently shook his head and waved the folder, then fished out a picture of Abraham's wounds.

"Hold on, Bitt, I got an emergency here," Enright said, covered up the phone and looked to Joe.

"Patrick Henry's case has grown from assault and a gunshot in a hospital to a major arson. We gotta go."

"That fire on the news?"

"That's where the boy fell from the tree. Mike said it's you and me running the case. Let's go see the site."

"Can I meet you there?" Enright said, indicating the phone and Bittinger and his continuing nursemaid role.

Joe wrote down the location from his cell phone history, then stopped Enright before he got back on the phone. "Who's the best arson investigator in St. Paul?"

"I hear great things about Denny Polaro at the FBI."

"Fire crews are still fighting the blaze anyway...see you there in an hour?" Joe said.

Enright nodded and Joe dashed away to his office to get his coat and make a call to the FBI office, then he'd walk the eight blocks to St. Paul Plaza.

CORY NERVOUSLY STOOD in line for the security check into the Children and Family Services building. He'd waited and watched until a mother with three active kids and a baby in a stroller arrived. They'd make the kind of distraction he needed. He'd gone back to his truck to fetch one of his disguises – a scraggly blond wig he wore under his baseball cap – and was sure he looked sleazy enough to blend in. The kinds of people who not only didn't question their abusive government, but stood there with their hands out, asking it to take care of them. Hopeless fools.

The two guards who manned the scanning machines had their hands full with the woman and her brood when two of them toddled off in different directions and a third one wailed. The guards let him walk into the infernal machine with barely a second glance. Cory almost blew it when he dashed through in near panic at being scanned, feeling sure he'd just been tagged by the government. They waved him quickly by and he walked rapidly toward the elevators.

He found Katherine Nolan listed on the guide outside the elevators and was convinced the building was filled with government fronts. Even though he had no idea how many agents were nearby, he headed into their hornet's nest, because his son might be here. He took the stairs two at a time and emerged from the stairwell to find his way to the glassed-in entrance to the Psychological Therapy Section where this Nolan was purported to work. He was amazed how transparent their fronts were: 'Psychological Therapy' was probably where his boy was being interrogated and turned. If he didn't get him out soon, it would be too late.

There were no cameras immediately outside the doors; even they didn't want a record of what went on inside there. While he lingered, a black woman came down the hallway and stopped at the reception desk. In a moment Nolan came out to meet her and he needed to listen in.

His heart racing and his fists clenching, Cory put his head down and slid inside the room.

"The boy just keeps getting more violent," Marlo said.

"May I help you, sir," the receptionist said as he watched Kat and Marlo huddle to the side of the main room.

Cory didn't respond and inched closer to listen.

"They might not be able to control him," Kat said, "I will be so glad when we can finally just wash our hands of him."

"Excuse me, sir? Are you in the right place?" the receptionist said, her voice rising to grab his attention. Now every eye turned to Cory. Without looking up or responding, he slipped back out of the room and raced down the hall. He was two flights down before he slowed to see if he was being followed. Luckily he wasn't.

———————

As HE WALKED through St. Paul Plaza on his way to the FBI headquarters, Joe automatically looked up to the window of Kat's office in the Children and Family Services building and wondered how her morning was going.

16

Simon had the television tuned to a news station but muted and was avidly watching until he heard the first morning activity in the house. He pretended to be asleep as Travis straggled out and turned up the volume when he saw the fire coverage. Simon faked waking up and didn't say a word, but he couldn't take his eyes off the images as they watched together. It was a spectacular scene.

The helicopter coverage was of the blaze at Cory's house, where fire trucks were still arriving and men were already scrambling all about. The fire had reached into the woods around the little house, exactly as he'd planned and it was thrilling because the massive response was even bigger than he'd expected. The sound from the TV brought out a couple guys from other rooms to admire his handiwork.

He suppressed his excitement as one of the guys recognized the place from just having cleared out all the marijuana drying in the barn. Simon was alone in appreciating his real ingenuity, but it was enough to gloat in silence while they watched his work in awe.

"Isn't that where we were yesterday?" one said.

Travis looked at Simon. "What do you think, Simon?"

He couldn't tear his eyes away from helicopter shots showing so many fire engines and a swarm of men. He'd sent a message that had forced the world to respond and they were his puppets. He yanked their strings and they moved.

When he realized the guys were all looking at him, he covered himself enough to say, "He must have gone back to cover his tracks."

"Who?" one of the guys asked.

"Cory. That's where he lived until yesterday," Travis reluctantly admitted, with a sidelong glance at Simon. "That weed you cleared out...he'd been curing it for us."

"Man..." the guy said. "Good thing we got the product out before it started."

"Toast me up a coupla those waffles," Travis said to the guys, sending them away. Then after they headed toward the kitchen, he sat in his usual chair, picked up the mini-blowtorch and lit a flame as he looked at Simon. "So?"

"Loose ends have been tied up."

Travis looked in the direction of the room that Cory and his family were staying in. "Helluva big way to tie up a loose end."

"We had dual problems," Simon said and tore his eyes away from the inferno he'd created. He needed to look his partner squarely in the eye when he lied.

Travis glanced warily toward the kitchen and whispered, "What other problem did we have?"

"Stacker," Simon said. "His difficulty at the laundry made me dig into his accounts last night."

"He'd never dare."

"He dared big time, Travis. Big."

Travis moved out of his chair and sat on the couch next to Simon, now intensely focused. "How big?"

"I can do some forensic accounting, but first glance ...I gotta say in the area of a hundred thousand."

"No way," Travis said in disbelief. "He's not that smart and he'd never be that brave."

"He'd been faking it with us. In the end, he admitted it...so I took care of it for us. No loose ends."

"How'd you leave things with him then?"

Simon looked back at the raging fire and nodded toward it. "The Lenny solution," he said.

Travis stared at him, then at the TV. Lenny had died in a way that sent a clear message to every man who worked for him and yet left no way for them to point fingers at him or Simon. Count on Simon to stay clear of blame. He looked back to his unwavering eyes and finally smiled as he said, "I guess the rat-bastard deserved it."

Simon nodded.

"Thanks," Travis said. "I thought Stacker was a guy I could more than half trust on rounds. Maybe you'll find the hundred grand...he can't have spent it all." Travis got somber a moment as he looked toward the kitchen. "But these losers, ya really can't trust any of them."

"It's down to you and me, Trav. As always."

Travis nodded and patted Simon on the back as he said, "So it's clean then? Nothing is coming back at us?"

"Not a thing," Simon said, then added, "We gotta give some thought to Twitch too. He could O.D. himself."

Travis nodded, then called out, "My waffles ready?"

Simon watched firemen racing about and felt certain everyone in St. Paul – in the whole state – was talking about what he'd done. He'd set in motion an enormous show that everyone would obsessively watch. He had the power to make the world jump to his will. They had no choice, what everyone did was determined by him and him alone.

He could hardly wait for the next part.

WHILE HE WAITED in a small conference room sitting at a mahogany table and looking at nicely upholstered chairs, Joe thought about how much better the federal budget was than the county one. He had a tiny office, a metal desk and a chair he'd bought himself. Here he'd been led past spacious offices with matching desks, chairs and bookcases. The FBI knew how to do office. To hear Enright tell it, they often knew how to investigate and they definitely dressed better. It seemed too orderly for Joe's taste.

The door swung in and an agent said, "What's the DA's office want with the FBI?"

It made Joe look up and then stand, but still he had to look up at the tall female agent in a dark suit that mirrored menswear, except she didn't wear a tie.

"I'm waiting to see Denny Polaro."

The agent stuck out her hand and said, "Special Agent Denise Polaro, call me Denny." As they shook, she added, "Man's world and all that," and pointed out toward the predominantly male population in the offices nearby.

Dark, short-cropped hair, a Mediterranean complexion and deep, brown eyes gave her a brooding look at first glance, but her smile and youthful face more than offset that first impression. But to a suspect, Joe guessed, she would look pretty damn intimidating even though she couldn't be more than about twenty-six. Height and confidence, which she had in abundance, had to help too.

Joe found her studying his face earnestly, especially the

scar on his upper lip, a lasting vestige of his rough child-hood. When he was a kid the wound on his lip hadn't healed evenly. Now it didn't so much diminish his good looks as make him memorable and distinctive.

She looked down at the pink slip with his name on it, then back at his face. "Joe Brandt? I've seen pictures of you with your shirt off," she said and laughed when he gaped at her in surprise. "Helluva scar on your arm."

"Guilty as charged," Joe said. Everyone in St. Paul had seen photos of his injuries in the newspapers, but most of them had forgotten about them – and him – since then.

"Dad and uncle, if memory serves."

"I wish they weren't in <u>my</u> memory."

"There's a lot of bastards in the world," Denny said and pointed at the lip scar. "Had to have hurt a bunch."

They edged about in awkward silence a moment as he now studied her just as closely as she'd analyzed him.

"I played volleyball," Denny said answering his unspoken question. "I saw you play a couple games when I was a freshman at the U. Deadly shot."

"You were on our Big Ten championship team, weren't you?" She nodded. "Captain?" She nodded again.

"So, we have more than collegial bonding on the menu?"

He nodded, they finally sat and Joe explained to her about Patrick Henry, the assault and the gunshot. And he could tell he was sparking zero interest in her.

"The big arson fire that's still burning is where the boy fell from the tree," he said.

That got her attention, but she still shook her head. "Arson is fire department and all the rest is you guys. You don't need us. Sorry."

"You're supposed to be the best arson investigator in

town and I think I've got something major going on. The same players are behind the boy, the assault and the fire."

"Well, my ears are burning from the compliment, but my specialty is explosive devices, bombs. They intersect with arson, but you only got a match-crazy dad, that's not me."

"It's a big fire."

"Size isn't everything..." she said with a smile.

He laughed and found he liked her even knowing she'd made a crack about his height soon after meeting him. Very few people ever mentioned his scar either and she had asked about it within a minute of meeting him. He liked forthright and she had a ready smile.

He pointed at the TV on the wall and she nodded, so he turned it on. It immediately brought up news helicopter coverage of the fire at Cory's house. It was showing the fire in the barn raging.

"It's admirably big. Still..."

As the helicopter flew alongside the property, the billowing smoke obscured nearly everything below. But then there was an explosion and something the size of a small dog house flew aloft, then abruptly fell to earth.

Denny was out of her seat even before another blue canister soared upward in front of the rapidly retreating helicopter. "Propane tank," she said.

The smoke momentarily cleared as they heard more small explosions and saw four more gallon propane tanks launched like missiles around the site, sending the fire crews scurrying back in retreat.

"Okay, Mr. Basketball, you got my attention," she said as she watched with fascination. Once the six tanks had exploded and flown about, the most forward fire crew crept forward aiming a torrent of water in a high arc. She exclaimed out loud as the smoke cleared. "That's a five hundred gallon propane tank. In a fire, that is a bomb."

From the door she beckoned. "You driving or am I?"

FIRE DEPARTMENT CARS blocked the road nearly half a mile from the site and Denny had to pull the FBI car over. As they badged their way onto the scene and signed in, Joe saw that Enright was already there ahead of them and he had Bittinger in tow. Maybe at last he was breaking loose of his hasty conclusion about his friend's brother. It was good to see him on a case where he belonged.

They were allowed to walk closer to the waning fire, toward three pumping trucks lined up on the road. Russell Filmore was the fire captain overseeing the parallel operation of all the fire crews. He wore thick turnout pants and coat, rubber boots and the distinctive helmet. He also had plenty of sweat and ash smeared on his face. He'd been working the fire, not just watching it. He shook hands with Enright like old friends, but when he spotted Denny he split away and headed right toward her and Joe, his hand outstretched and a smile on his face.

"Special Agent Polaro," Filmore said, "welcome to my little bonfire." They shook hands heartily.

"You know ADA Joe Brandt?" she said. "Russell Filmore is way more friendly that your average fire captain."

Filmore shook Joe's hand, then Bittinger's as he joined them while Enright glad-handed with firemen nearby.

"Denny, this is Detective Ed Bittinger, Special Agent Denise Polaro."

Bitt said, "The FBI have all the luck."

She chose to take it as a compliment. Old school, judging by that narrow little mustache.

Filmore ushered them toward the trucks and to the end of the dirt road that led into what had been a thicket; it was now ash-filled mud. He said, "You guys are sure fast. How'd you find out about the body in there?"

"We didn't," Joe admitted, more than a bit shocked.

"The guy's head was bashed in before it started," Filmore said as Enright was introduced to Denny. He hadn't met her before even though he'd recommended her.

Joe watched crews dragging out flattened fire hoses and bringing gear back to the pump trucks. Smoke and steam still billowed from the woods plus the two major hotspots farther from the road which were the remains of the house and barn. "How'd you guys find the body so fast?" Joe said.

"We were concerned about the large propane tank out back of the house," Filmore said with a grin at Denny. "That's why you're here, I gather."

They all looked up along the track of the road and past the remains of the house to see the long, low shape of the propane tank, like an elephant lying down.

"There's a school on the other side of these woods," Filmore added for all of them.

"A propane tank like that can make quite a bomb," Denny said. "Good work keeping it from blowing, Russell."

"Your crews went into the fire?" Joe asked, impressed. "There were also smaller propane tanks exploding, right?"

"Six of them," Filmore said to Denny. "From the barn area and we don't know if they were just left sitting around or what." He pointed into the area ahead of them where a blue tank was visible in the mud. "Six different directions and each one firing off like a rocket."

"Could they have been directed?" Denny said.

"That's up to you to tell us when you inspect."

"I don't like the sound of six of them," Denny said. "Why didn't you foam the big tank?"

"We couldn't get close enough to stream foam on it," Filmore said. "Denny knows this, but for you guys...if you keep the hoses on the tank, cool it enough, it probably won't blow. This access road burnt off pretty quick and I could send one crew inside to hose and another to make sure they could get back out. We were cooling the tank and that's when we spotted the body leaned up against it."

"What if the tank had exploded?" Enright said.

"You'd have found parts of the guy in a couple counties," Denny said. "Very small parts."

"Thanks to my guys, the body is well preserved," Filmore said and received a pat on the back from Denny.

"Can we go in and look around?" Joe asked.

"Hell no," Filmore said with a look to Enright.

"He's enthusiastic, Russ," Enright said.

"We've got an abandoned kid, a savage beating, now an arson plus a murder...all connected to this property."

"When it's cooled down and our team says it's safe to enter, by all means," Filmore said. Then he handed Joe a pair of binoculars. "Best I can do,"

Joe looked through them while Denny stepped up next to him and pulled out binoculars of her own. Filmore leaned close to Enright to whisper, "How'd he talk her into coming? She's the best."

"I can see that," Bittinger added in a loud whisper.

Joe studied what remained of the house, which was now just ashes surrounding an ancient round-topped refrigerator that was still standing. The barn was also nothing but ashes settled around what looked like farm implements and Stacker's Chevy. It had been gutted when the car's gas tank exploded and had torn apart the whole rear end. More than half of the woods nearest the house and barn had been burnt to nothing but pathetic skeletons.

"How'd you guys call it arson while it was still burning?" Enright asked. "We were told it was deliberately set before we even drove out here. How'd you know?"

"Because they're smart, Byron," Denny said.

Filmore grinned and gave the men a school lecture. "Fires spread organically. They start somewhere and then move outward from that center. You see enough of them, you get to know how they follow the fuel, what blocks them or makes them turn and what they can leap over."

"This one didn't spread naturally?" Joe said.

"There were four distinct centers from which fire fanned out almost simultaneously. That ain't natural and it told us from the moment we got here that we were dealing with a fire set by someone. That made us suspicious, so we looked for booby traps, which, in turn, helped us spot the body near the propane tank. Someone had an agenda."

"You think the body was put there so the tank explosion would destroy it and make it impossible for us to ID it?" Joe said.

"Yup," Filmore said. "All the reports have to be done, but it will come back that this guy was already dead and then deliberately placed beside the tank. By all rights that tank should have exploded – and would have if we weren't so good at our jobs. Then you guys would be piecing the body together for months and might never have known if the caved-in skull was pre or post-mortem."

"Thank you for being so good at your job," Joe said as he raised the binoculars again and zeroed in on the body. It was charred but recognizable and the side of the nearly-shaved head against the tank had been smashed in.

Filmore beckoned them past the crews prepping hoses to reload into the trucks. They stood on the little road where the chain was and from there could see all that had once been hidden by trees and brush. "Watch the wingtips, folks. It's mud from here on out."

"So where are these centers of the fire?" Joe asked.

"May I?" Denny asked Filmore.

"Be my guest."

She gestured with her binoculars as she spoke. "The house there, the barn arranged around the car, the propane tank where you see the county M.E. already at work, he's suited-up like Russell's guys. The fourth was a well-placed stack of branches." She stopped and shared an appreciative look with Filmore. "He wanted us to know he did this."

"So he wanted us to know it was arson, yet he also wanted nothing left to sift through?" Joe said, puzzled.

"Mostly he wanted the whole woods burning when we got here," Filmore said, taking over. "That's why the fourth center was that pile of branches. He set it up so the fire would spread quickly through the woods, creating a wall of flames."

"Why?" Enright said.

"He knew if we saw the propane tank and we could get to it, we'd try to keep it from blowing. If the woods were an inferno, it'd make it hard for us to get close enough to cool the tank. He counted on it blowing up for sure."

"Sounds like a pro."

"No doubt about it," Denny said. "He knew exactly how all of this would burn and how the crews would react. Only spoiler was Russell and his ballsy men."

Filmore smiled. "A lot of fire captains, they see a propane tank, calculate the distance to the closest houses, then clear everybody back and let her blow."

"Seems prudent."

"I hated this asshole from the moment we drove up and saw what we were dealing with. I wouldn't give the bastard the satisfaction of watching the tank explode on live television," he said, pointing to the hovering helicopters. "These guys usually like to watch their work. He's probably watching right now."

"Going into the fire sounds dangerous," Joe said.

"Yeah, but my men were as safe as they'd be in any normal fire. I wouldn't put any of my guys at unneeded risk. Two crews, I was with the forward team arcing the water up to hit the tank and the other team had an infrared spotter gauging the heat of the tank, watching our back."

"How are we going to catch this guy?" Joe asked.

"You probably won't, at least not directly," Filmore said grimly. "Good thing you brought in Denny. This guy is so good, I damn near admire him. It's hard to get four centers to flame up at the same time."

"So he wasn't just running around with a book of matches?" Enright said.

Filmore stepped back and gestured to Denny.

"He was probably creating his alibi in a Starbucks filled with early risers by the time all the fires sparked up at the same time," she said. "Flames didn't leap until dawn, but I bet he set it all up several hours earlier."

"How the hell he do it then?"

"I'm dying to get in there and see," Denny admitted. "Like Russell said, he wasn't trying to hide his hand. My suspicion is we're going to find a timer and a battery, plus wires leading to four ignition devices."

"Sounds like a Heath Kit," Enright said. "I made a radio in seventh grade. I was pretty proud of myself."

Joe studied the whole scene and shook his head. "So

now we have to add a professional arsonist and a dead body to the mystery of a boy falling from a tree."

"Just to confuse it more for you," Denny said, "This set-up is a lot more ambitious than it needed to be just to burn down a house. This prick is an artist."

"Swell," Joe said as they all tiptoed back out to the road pavement.

Denny exchanged cards with all of them and promised to investigate the site with Joe when Filmore said it was cool enough, then stuck around to confer with the fire captain.

Joe was going to ride back with Enright and Bitt, but as they headed to the SUV, Enright was awfully quiet.

"What's bothering you, Byron?"

"If one incident doesn't make sense...okay, there are crazy people. Two incidents don't make sense, maybe we'll see the pattern, the underlying reasoning. But a child's accident triggering an assault preceding an arson fire that contains a murder victim that was supposed to explode...we breezed right past pattern. Every new step contradicts everything else."

"Still waiting for the other card to be turned over."

17

I t took every ounce of discipline in him for Simon to hide his rage in front of the guys watching the fire on TV. He had thoroughly enjoyed the six small propane tanks taking off like rockets, but then he'd waited. And waited as they watered down the large propane tank. No explosion. He'd left a bomb he hoped might knock a chopper from the sky or take out some firemen. He'd have made the national and international news. Instead, nothing. It was a five hundred gallon propane tank, he'd brought a bunch of smaller ones and used the adapter he'd built for Cory to add propane to the large one. There was plenty of fuel to make that tank have an impact heard around the world. And he'd left Stacker hugging the bomb so he'd turn into confetti. Instead, nothing.

When they showed an aerial view of the body and the tank, he got a questioning look from Travis. Then it got worse when Cory let himself into the house and they were all surprised he'd been out. Everyone thought he was in the back room with his wife and daughter. Simon was quick with the remote and froze the image on TV of a newscaster talking to the camera, so there was nothing that Cory would recognize. They needn't have worried, he didn't give the TV a thought. Everyone grunted hellos as he passed carrying a door lock and a few tools.

"Give us a minute," Travis said to the guys, who went to the kitchen for more waffles. He turned to Simon. "How we handle this? His place on the news? He'll go insane."

"We pick the right time and prep him," Simon said, feigning calm that he didn't feel. "They did it to him."

"Who?"

"The same people who kidnapped his son."

Travis thought about it and finally nodded, satisfied.

"That's Stacker?" Travis said pointing at the TV.

"He was supposed to explode and take forever to ID."

"That ain't what we got."

"I'll take care of it. Just keep Cory from finding out until we're ready for him," Simon said. "It'll be okay."

Travis let it go largely because Simon was in such a black mood. It was rare that one of his plans didn't go exactly right. Damn Stacker.

Abby and Betsy had pushed the dresser out of the way to let Cory in. He said he was getting closer to finding Patrick Henry, but it was taking time. It freaked Abby out, because she didn't have much faith in Cory's ability to overcome the government. 'Nobody could,' she told herself.

Betsy went back to her book on the bed and Abby joined him at the door as he started to install the sturdy sliding lock with tools from his truck. "Anything wrong?" he asked.

"How soon can we move?"

"Did something happen?"

"You know they have a gun range in the basement?" Betsy said. "They shoot night and day."

Cory relaxed slightly. It was just about noise and those

assholes shooting at any hour. He could talk to them about that. "Want to get out of here for a while?" he said.

Both Abby and Betsy leapt at the chance, but he shook his head to his wife. "She's seen you." He turned to Betsy and handed her a jacket, "but she's never seen you."

"Who?"

"The agent who took Patrick Henry, the woman at the hospital. I know where she works and I think Betsy can get close enough to help us find our boy, but she'd recognize you, Ab."

Abby tested the lock on the door and unhappily said, "Okay." But at the same time, she slipped one of Cory's Phillips head screwdrivers up her sweater sleeve. It was definitely uncomfortable between them right now, but once he got their son back, Cory told himself, everything would get back to normal. It'd be good.

As Cory and Betsy filed into the living room, again the TV was paused and he idly wondered why Simon and Travis were alone watching the news, but didn't dwell on it.

"Say, Trav," Cory said as he and Betsy stopped by the door, right next to the arsenal. "Sound carries from the range. Could you guys watch the firing hours?"

"I'll post a memo, Cory," Travis said. "Really, we'll keep that shit down."

As they left, Cory knew he was better off with Betsy as back-up than Travis again.

On the couch, Simon was deep into his brooding. If it had worked, it would have been huge and that prick Stacker would have just been nothing but tiny bits. Now he was the lead story. Nothing was going to come back on them, but it was a disappointment. It was supposed to be a signature move, not just a simple arson like any moron could light.

After Cory and Betsy left, Travis watched out the

window as they went to the pickup. "Cory's always on the move, ain't he? We could use a self-propelled guy around here," he said, turning to Simon who was a lump on the couch. "Replace Stacker, maybe higher up the chain. We need a good man with half a brain and we know the Boy Scout would never even think of stealing from us."

Simon finally turned his thoughts from the fire to Cory. "He's got a world-class grudge against the government and sure doesn't take it lying down," he admitted.

"Yeah," Travis said. "Cory goes out and takes matters into his own hands. Lot to admire."

"A guy like him could be an asset. McVeigh sure could have used him instead of Terry Nichols, the half-useless fuck," Simon said as he turned back to watch repeated footage of the flames soaring over Cory's former house. Fire engines, men with hoses, helicopters, a big mad scramble. It was all his handiwork, but right now it felt like the 1812 Overture without the cannons.

JOE SCRAPED mud off his shoes into the waste basket and Enright sat in the one guest chair in his tiny office.

"I've been thinking about sheepskin coats."

"Yeah, it's going to be a cold winter," Joe said.

"Maybe, but coats like the one that guy was wearing at the hospital? They cost more than my first car and make you look like that asshole anarchist stealing land out west for his cattle, what's his name?"

"Bundy?"

"Knew it was the name of a serial killer," Enright said. "That coat makes the angry little guy stand out."

"That's all we're getting off security tapes, isn't it, coats and hats? No faces."

"We get more attitude out of the tapes than evidence," Enright said. "I'm thinking the coat might lead us to a guy with a short fuse and a huge need to look cool."

"That's almost a clue," Joe said.

"Maybe I can add to that," Denny said. She sported a 'visitor' badge on her overcoat as she stopped outside the door and found there was barely any room for her to join them. "They don't give you much elbow room, do they?"

"Elbows are federal," Enright said and stood to offer his seat, but she declined. "Bunions are local."

"I missed those regulations," she said with a laugh. She turned earnestly to Joe and leaned down to put her hands on his desk. "Propane tanks."

"Yeah, we saw that. Big bomb that didn't go off."

"Six modest bombs did," she said.

"You have our attention," Joe said.

"I've been thinking about the men who do things like this," she said and leaned back against the door jamb to explain. "McVeigh had one clear, singular objective and gigantic ambitions. Kaczynski, on the other hand, was a serial, small-scale bomber who held grudges and spouted philosophy. This guy is more complex. I think he wanted firemen to die, but he failed at his major objective."

"Thanks only to Russell Filmore," Enright said.

"Laying a trap for first responders?" Joe said, "Damn, that sounds like the Middle East."

"Yeah, but the kid, a house and barn, the guys at the hospital. This screams out home-grown...all-American."

"Lucky us," Enright said. "Where's that leave us?"

"The bombs that did go off were all five gallon propane

tanks like you can pick up anywhere. And all of the household size tanks exploded in the barn. My guess is they were emptied into the big tank."

"If they were empty, how'd they blow up?"

"Fumes explode more efficiently than compressed gas, which is actually liquid under pressure."

"What were the tanks there for? Just leftovers?"

"I think your guy devised a way to upload those thirty gallons into the main tank," she said. "The house was abandoned for years, so the big tank was probably depleted long ago, right? He wanted it to blow the victim and half the Ramsey County fire department to smithereens, so he had to make sure it had enough fuel."

"Thirty gallons of propane would be enough?"

"With a partial tank, there's room for the fuel inside to expand and the result will be a larger initial explosion than a full tank would have given him," she said.

"And we're thinking this guy knew all that?" Joe said.

"That we do," Denny said.

"I can buy those five gallon tanks at gas stations, hardware stores, a ton of places," Enright said.

"I said it would be a clue, not a straight path."

"Many thanks. Any other guidance you can give us."

"Wear brown shoes with blue suits."

"I'll write that down."

"My SAC says I can consult," Denny said, "but follow-up is all on you. See you later to walk through the site?"

"It's a deal," Joe said, standing to shake her hand.

Enright watched her walk off. "Highly combustible."

"The propane? Yeah."

"No, I mean her.

EVERY INTERACTION with the world-at-large became a teaching opportunity for Cory. He and Betsy stood outside the Family Services Building and he was giving her a lesson in how to get past the security men. She shouldn't look anyone in the eye, she should keep her hat down and she should wear a big scarf around her neck on the way in and hide it completely in a pocket on the way out. The notion that those people were the enemy – an idea she'd heard her entire life – finally resonated for her. The government really had kidnapped her brother and her family really were in danger. Her dad was right and it freaked her out almost as much as having him send her alone into the government center. He couldn't go inside with her.

"You're a kid and their front is Family Services, so you won't stand out," he said. "If someone pretends to want to help you, just tell them you're looking for an office number on another floor. They'll point you to the elevators, but don't get in one. Stairs, always the stairs and be aware of security cameras in the halls."

She looked at the building but was afraid to move.

"It doesn't hurt when the x-rays go through you."

"You always said never to let them do that."

"I know and I hate it, but they never held your brother captive before," he said, giving her a hug. "I went through it okay."

"All right," she said as he ushered her to the door.

Cory watched her get through security without half a glance from the guards and then disappear inside.

Up on the third floor, Betsy followed her dad's directions to the Psychological Services. It had a glass door and she saw the receptionist, people waiting and no sign of the pretty woman her dad described in detail.

She was peering through the window into the psych place when she heard two men nearby and started to panic. She plopped onto the floor and pulled out her paperback.

The men stopped at her and she looked up only as far as their knees. Suits, fancy shoes. She imagined they had badges and guns. 'Agents,' her dad called them.

"What'cha doing, little lady?" one of the men said.

"Waiting for my mom," Betsy said, her heart pounding.

"You shouldn't sit in the hall."

She nodded and got up without looking and made a motion to go into the office until the men moved on.

Her hands were trembling, but no one bothered her as she walked off with purpose. She made her way up the hall and turned when no one was nearby, then just headed back. After a few laps she saw two women come out of the psych office. One was black, the other had dark hair, a sharp nose, very pretty like her dad had described. Betsy watched the women step into the ladies room. She darted in after them and slipped into a stall without being noticed.

"That boy has stolen practically my whole day," Marlo said, talking over the stalls as if they were alone. "I been on the phone with the locked ward like seven times and there's always more blood in the water."

"You heard about the charred body, right?" Kat said as she emerged to wash her hands.

"Yeah. Think the boy knows about it? Think we could pry some info out of him?"

"Not even with a crowbar...we only got his name by accident. Who names their kids after Revolutionary War figures anyway?"

Betsy had to stifle a gasp when she heard that last comment and realized her worst fears were true, they were

talking about her brother. Then she heard them pushing the
door open as they left and darted out to follow, her head still
spinning with images of burned and beaten bodies. What
could it all mean? She reached the hallway just as the
women were parting ways. Head down, she inched
past them.

Kat noticed the girl. "You looking for something?"

Betsy barely glanced at her, spun away and hurried
down the hall, turned a corner, found the stairs and raced
down them as fast as she could go.

She was pulling off the scarf and stuffing it in her pocket
on her way down as she passed a guy in a wool coat going
upstairs, two at a time. She kept her head down and he paid
no attention to her.

Joe continued up the stairs. He planned to take Kat for
lunch and he had news to share; he doubted she'd heard
about the body found at the site where the boy fell. He was
hoping she'd help him arrange to talk at length with the kid
himself. There had to be clues there.

Twenty minutes later, Betsy was still running through
the exact words of the conversation she'd heard for her dad.
But just then Cory pointed at Kat crossing the plaza outside
the Family Services Building. "That's her, right?"

"Yeah."

Kat and Joe walked at a brisk pace trying to beat the
lunchtime rush at Mickey's Diner. They wanted one of the
coveted booths and a little escape from the crush while they
updated each other. They never spotted the father and
daughter following them with their hats tugged low.

"Remember both their faces, Bets," Cory said. "She's the
one who took him away from your mom at the hospital."

"I think the woman works for some kind of psych thing
and they're hurting Patrick Henry."

"Every office there is a front for various government agencies and some of them are into mind control," Cory said as he watched Joe and Kat. "So we have to assume they're working on him. We need to rescue him soon."

"I'll do anything it takes, Daddy," Betsy said.

Inside Mickey's Diner, Kat and Joe held hands across the table in the booth as they awaited bowls of chili and grilled cheese sandwiches – winter comfort food. They talked about the body leaned up against the propane tank, as well as Marlo's continued interest in Abraham, despite the forty-seven stitches.

"She likes character," Kat said.

"I'll keep that in mind next time I get beaten up," Joe said as Betsy squeezed through the crush of people waiting inside the warmth of the railroad dining car converted into a diner. She had her back to them and had not put the scarf back on. She just looked as if she were waiting for one of the stools at the counter to open up.

"So when can you let me work on the boy?" Joe asked.

"The physical violence has continued, so I have to do another report. Maybe you should join in this afternoon, see if together we can break down his resistance. We only have him a limited time before he has to move on."

"Good idea."

"He's a tough one, but you might be able to drag something out of him with your devious ways."

"I'll have time before I meet with the FBI agent," Joe said and just then the waitress pushed through the throng. He caught a startled look from a girl staring at him as the waitress reached past her. She looked halfway familiar, but he was more interested in his steaming chili.

Betsy scurried out of Mickey's Diner, flushed from having looked in the eyes of the damned agent. She was stunned by how casually they talked about torture and her brother. When she got to Cory, he thought she had probably been blown, so he decided to drive her back to Travis'. On the way, she updated him.

18

T he Wabasha Hospital children's psychiatric ward was a strange mix of institution and child-inspired decor. The entrance was huge glass doors that were locked and had embedded wire mesh along with an intricate locking mechanism. A key and a buzz from a staffer were both needed to open the door. Fire alarms were required by law but these had been adapted to be difficult for children to trigger and had a delay that allowed staff to reach the doors before they automatically unlocked. The ward had an entire wall at the entry where children were encouraged to draw and kid art was taped up everywhere.

Joe and Kat were let in by Dianna Willets, the head nurse, who used the key on her lanyard. Kat had official standing to talk with the boy, so she decided to meet with him alone. Joe needed to go over the seventy-two hour observation orders with Dianna anyway. Patrick Henry had already proven a disruption and had actually shown no signs of psychological maladjustment, just anger. Joe insisted they needed every hour until Friday morning with the boy, so the orders would have to stay in place.

Kat was led toward the 'time out room' which was Patrick Henry's location after his latest infraction. She peeked into the school room where a handful of kids almost paid attention, then a kitchen where other kids, a nurse and a psychiatric assistant were making cookies that smelled delicious. The children looked normal if more distracted than other kids, but Kat knew better. She'd had clients who'd been here for good reason. Mostly due to abuse or neglect, but a few had committed serious crimes. The youngest in-patient was six and the oldest was twelve. At thirteen, the kids had to move to the teen psych unit.

Within his first hours, Patrick Henry had gotten into a fist fight and, one-handed, had more than stood his ground with a bigger boy who was known to be a bully. More recently he'd flooded a bathroom and this had gotten him locked in the time out room. The psychiatric assistant letting Kat in thought the boy might prefer to be alone and had done just enough acting out to get himself put there.

The room was really a padded cell with thick mats on the floor, quilting on the walls and light fixtures inside protective cages. It allowed an utterly out-of-control child a place to vent without hurting himself or others.

The boy sat in the farthest corner from the door, studying his broken arm.

"How's it going, Patrick Henry?" Kat said as she stepped in, but stayed near the entrance. "Want to come out?"

"Leave me alone or let me go."

"I'm afraid I can't do either," Kat said, cautiously stepping closer. "The law requires that I work with you."

"Your law, not mine."

"Let's go to the play area and you can tell me why it's not your law," Kat said, then inhaled deeply. "They're making cookies. I bet we could get a couple. Let's go see." She stepped out of the room, left the door ajar behind her and looked into the kitchen. The boy didn't move, even when she returned with two steaming hot chocolate chip cookies. The aroma wafted into the room, but he didn't look up or even seem to inhale the smell. So she stayed back.

When a ruckus started up somewhere nearby, she was tempted to close the door, with herself inside with Patrick Henry and the cookies.

"I'm afraid we need the room," Dianna said as she approached carrying an eight year girl who was wildly out of control – a real patient. Dianna had her completely wrapped in her arms, as firmly yet gently as possible, to keep the ferocious girl from hurting any of them.

The big psych assistant stepped past Kat, went to the boy and offered a hand down to him. "You walking or riding?" When Patrick Henry didn't budge, the man picked him up and carried the unresisting boy out of the room as Dianna moved in.

"Play room," the psych assistant said to Kat, who was enthralled as she watched Dianna let go of the girl with surprising gentleness for someone who looked almost feral.

Dianna stepped out, locking the door as she looked at Kat. "She belongs here, your boy doesn't."

"Good to hear," Kat said. "He's got enough problems."

Joe was already in the play room and was directing the psych assistant to set the boy atop the climber there. The large room was filled with games and toys all along one side and another had a wonderful climber that was half child's fort and half sea-going or outer-space-probing ship. It looked like a fun place and was meant to give the kids a sense of power in their imaginations. Patrick Henry sat where he'd been placed, but still looked quiet, inert.

Dianna pulled Kat back to watch from just outside the

boy's view and accepted one of the cookies. "This is a fattening place to work," she said.

"Looks like you get a helluva workout, actually."

"I think he's traumatized, but not in the way most of the kids we see," Dianna said. "They've been abused by family in one way or another, their trust shattered by the people who are supposed to love and protect them."

"And Patrick Henry?"

"From what I've seen so far," Dianna said as they watched Joe approaching the climber and the boy. "He doesn't have trust issues with family, but he has major distrust of the world. Society, people outside the family. Us. All he talks about is going home."

"He must have been taught that distrust, right?"

"That's probably true," Dianna said as she headed off for her other duties "but he's still moving out on Friday."

Joe stood near the climber, looking up at the boy. "My name's Joe Brandt, Patrick Henry."

"Some day you'll be sorry for doing this to me."

"Why is that?"

"A day of reckoning comes to everyone," the boy said.

"Your mom tell you that?"

No response.

"I bet it was your dad. He seems like someone who thinks a lot about reckonings."

Patrick Henry glowered at him.

"Your dad tell you what 'reckoning' means?"

"Paying for what you did that you shouldn't have."

"Like climbing a tree and breaking your arm?" Joe said. "Is he going to beat you for stealing his climbing gear? Is that going to be your reckoning?"

Silence.

"How come they named you for a minor revolutionary?"

Joe said. "Why not name you George Washington or Benjamin Franklin or Paul Revere? That I could understand. Who even remembers Patrick Henry?"

"He was the greatest American Revolutionary!"

"No, definitely not one of the best," Joe said, sensing he was getting under the boy's skin. Irritation might get him talking.

"Your kind don't know a thing."

"What's my kind? People who don't steal and get themselves locked up?"

"People who trust government and become its slaves."

"I don't think you know what you're talking about," Joe said to rile the boy. "You're just saying things you heard your dad say without knowing what they mean."

Patrick Henry leapt to his feet and stood atop the climber. Joe braced himself, but the kid wasn't attacking, he was ready to orate, looking down on Joe: "It is natural to man to indulge in the illusions of hope..." he began and Joe listened to the whole memorized speech.

"I'm impressed. You got every word exactly right. You learn it in school?"

"I don't go to school with your kind."

"But you're obviously well-educated."

Joe sensed him swell with pride. "We have the best education of anyone. Betsy reads a whole book every day."

"So Betsy Ross is your sister?"

Patrick Henry glowered, realizing he'd let out a detail he shouldn't have.

"Not Ross, fool. The flag's the rallying point for oppression, not liberty!" He was red-faced-angry. Then sullen, realizing he'd blurted out too much. He sat back down and definitely emitted an aura of entrenchment. It was going to be nothing but silence from here on out.

CORY BUZZED the intercom from the front gate and was let in immediately, they were regulars now. Betsy was sorry to be back already, but she had a new respect for her father and how he had safeguarded them over the years. So much he'd told them was different from the books she read and that had made her think he was just crazy and afraid. But listening to those women, watching that couple in the diner, she felt their contempt for 'our kind.' She now appreciated her dad's protection.

Abby was stir-crazy after being locked alone in the room with the dresser across the door. This house, these people, Travis, they all scared her even more than the outside world. She'd thought about leaving but didn't know how she'd ever find Cory and Betsy again.

She was a bit wild by the time Cory and Betsy returned. It was a desperate hug she gave him and he knew he had to come up with a better situation for them. Abby again suggested a motel, but that remained out of the question. That would leave them way too vulnerable.

Telling her he'd fix it, he went in search of Travis, passing the empty living room where, for once, the TV was turned off. Travis heard him coming and pulled a couple beers out and popped the tops as Cory joined him.

"I gotta be in two places at one time," Cory said.

"Science stuff is Simon's department," Travis joked.

"I'm serious, Trav. I have a line on the agent who took my son and I have to go back and follow her."

"Okay. So what's the problem?"

"It's Abby. Look, we appreciate it, both of us, that you took us in."

"Mi casa."

"Thing of it is, she's kinda squirrelly around all the guns and, well, truth is, your guys coming and going."

"They can make me feel squirrelly too. So you gotta scout a new home and follow this agent at the same time?"

"That's the shape of it."

"Want me to follow the agent?"

Cory instinctively knew that wasn't a good idea.

"I was hoping you might know another place we could stay a short while...until we get Patrick Henry back," Cory said. "Then we'll be out of your hair."

"I like having you around," Travis said and meant it, then suddenly exclaimed, "...fuck me, why didn't I think of it? The farm in Anoka."

"Where you have the weed grown?" Cory said.

"Yeah. We got a caretaker who sits on the place all summer, but we close up the house for the winter. I'm not the owner-of-record, as Simon would say, but it's ours."

"We'll take it."

"Hell, maybe it could be permanent. We'll need someone there next summer."

"Let's get there and then see how it goes. Abby will calm down after Patrick Henry is back."

Travis knew this idea would please Simon immensely; he'd become nervous having them around since the fire. Plus Stacker's body would be identified soon enough and Cory was bound to see it eventually on TV somewhere. Putting them at the farm kept them at arm's length and uninformed which was safer for all of them.

"Colder than shit in there and we put antifreeze in the plumbing," he said, "but...look, you guys pack up, I'll get Simon and we'll all drive out there. It won't take long to get the place back to livable, toasty warm by sundown."

Cory surprised the hell out of Travis with a man-hug,

then took off to tell Abby the good news. She hadn't
unpacked much and was so excited to get away from the
guys, it was all of fifteen minutes later when they carried
bags back to the pickup.

Travis drove one of the old, non-descript cars and Simon
rode shotgun. Cory followed in the pickup with his family
and their possessions, including the two guns under the
seat. He was actually sorry to be leaving Travis' place and
the protection it provided, but what he needed most was
Abby feeling comfortable. She was used to tending a home
in the woods, so the farm wouldn't freak her out like Travis'
house had. She'd be okay and that meant he could get back
out there following Nolan.

DENNY WAS EXPOUNDING on the ideal ratio of flammable
fumes and oxygen as she drove them back out toward the
fire site. Joe understood almost everything she explained
and remembered having liked chemistry in school, but
unlike his new FBI friend, he'd never tried to blow up the
school lab. She'd channeled those instincts and joined the
good guys, but clearly still got very excited by explosives.

She parked at the end of the dirt road and popped the
trunk. She grabbed two pair of rubber boots and pulled hers
on over her shoes and tucked in her slacks. Joe followed suit
and joined her slogging through the mud onto the property.
She was carrying a tool kit from which she'd already
extracted a telescoping probe, a flashlight and a camera. She
led the way to the barn and Stacker's Chevy.

As she strode ahead of him, Joe called Enright and told
him where they were. "Denny's going to explain how our
bomber did it. I figured you'd like to know."

"I like the idea of understanding the arsonist."

———

HEADING toward the Anoka farm Simon asked, "How'd you get them to leave so soon?"

"Cory listens to me. Always has," Travis lied. "I convinced him it was a good idea."

"Having them around would have put a real crimp in our operations faster than you think."

"He'd be a real asset to have join us, though, don't ya think?" Travis said. "Smart, reliable..."

"If he were still like he used to be, sure, but just look at him with his family around," Simon said. "They're a huge distraction. He's just traded one form of oppression for another."

Travis nodded and said, "Yeah, he's not free like us. Not like the guys in The Movement you tell me about."

He always met Simon half way when it came to the revolutionary stuff; toying with anarchy helped keep Simon around and part of the business. Travis had felt lost after Cory knocked up Abby and got hitched. He had always worked better with a partner and Simon was the smartest guy there ever was, so it was natural. He came with baggage, but Travis found it pretty easy to shout 'fuck you' at the government when Simon needed to hear it. A little mayhem kept Simon's devious mind working overtime to create new and profitable enterprises for them both.

"He chose not to be free," Simon said. "I wish we could bring him in, but I'm not seeing it happen." Simon always met Travis halfway when it came to his weakness for Cory who had been a good convert early on, but then he'd gotten too many ideas of his own. Travis was a good partner because he didn't bother with ideas, but was truly adept at keeping a group of idiots around to do the scut work. The Stackers of the world gravitated toward him and they could be useful if they didn't start noticing too much.

The farm in Anoka was a step down from where Cory and his family had been living. Beyond a thicket of woods between the property and the road, there were a few acres of open field which surrounded a tiny dilapidated house. The garage was truly caved-in and the house had plastic sheeting covering the roof. It looked to Cory like the walls might not be too sound and nothing but cardboard covered a couple windows. Even so, Abby was happy and relieved as they drove along the little road that crossed the field where all that weed had been grown last summer. Betsy was distraught at the look of the place, but knew enough not to say anything.

Simon went inside to undo the winterizing and to get the wall space heater going. Travis drove off to buy them food, which even Abby admitted was generous and kind-hearted of him. The Trammells carried their bags into their third home in three days. Abby was pretty horrified by the sheets on the sole bed, but they had their own linens. Cory flipped the mattress over and left the rest for Abby and Betsy. He wanted to help Simon get the heat, water and electricity going, because he was really anxious to head back to the city. He didn't want to miss Nolan when she left for the day, she was still his best target.

The lights all came on and soon the water was flowing. It was freezing cold, but Abby could start cleaning. She was determined to make this work for them; there wasn't an ounce of complaint in her. None from Betsy either when she saw that there was a TV in the rear room and knew there wouldn't be guns firing all day and night right below them.

At last the wall-mounted space heater clicked on and Simon cranked it up to heat both the front and back rooms. It was the stove that was frustrating Cory, he was having no luck. Travis returned with four bags of food, but one was devoted to beer, as if it were a food group. There were actually a couple halfway nutritious things in the bags and a lot of the kind of crap he and his guys usually ate.

Simon took over getting the stove working and Cory got ready to drive back to St. Paul. Now that traffic was getting into rush hour, it was going to take a long time for him to get to downtown in order to follow Nolan.

Abby didn't want him leaving so soon, but she'd won the more important battle – they had moved out of Travis' house – so this one wasn't worth a fight. She kissed him a passionate good-bye and pleaded with him to bring back Patrick Henry. She watched him drive off then turned her attention to the house. She inspected the refrigerator with horror, then focused on cleaning up with the frigid water. Once the stove was working, they'd have hot water.

Half an hour after Cory left, Abby had the sink and counter scoured and was turning to the refrigerator when Betsy called from the back room, "Mom, can I talk to you?"

Abby left Simon tinkering with the stove and Travis opening beers as she went into the back of the house. Betsy closed the rickety door and just pointed at the TV.

They watched without sound as helicopter images showed their home burning, then the barn explosions and the roof of the house crumpling in the flames. Betsy began to weep quietly and the two hugged desperately. That's when a title came up about a murder victim being found on the property. Abby turned to stone reading 'Murder Victim' and 'Arson' on the screen over the devastation of their former life.

She turned to her daughter, put her finger to her lips and wiped away Betsy's tears. It was time to take action.

It had remained so cold in the house, they still had their coats on and Abby whispered, "I'm going to get the keys and I want you to go start his car. I'll follow you and I want you to drive away from here. Fast."

"What?"

"Don't think. Don't question. When I give you the keys, walk out. Say you left a bag outside if they ask."

"But..."

She held Betsy at arm's length and stared right into her eyes. Hard, as forceful as she had ever been in her life. "You got it? Start the car and be ready to drive the second I run out and jump in."

Betsy felt the urgency and had begun to realize her parents knew things she didn't get yet, that they protected her. So she nodded, then followed her mother out to the front room. The one guy was on his knees at the foot of the stove, the other was hoisting a beer, grinning toward them.

Abby saw the keys on the counter by the groceries and went to rummage in one of the bags, giving Travis a smile.

"Want a beer, Ab?" Travis said.

He was teasing her. She didn't drink and he knew it, so she shook her head and poked through another bag. She found a quart of orange juice and went to twist the top off, pretending not to be able to do it. Travis took it and, as he turned the top off the bottle, she stealthily palmed the car keys. She held them behind her back and Betsy slipped up behind her to take them secretly. Then she casually went out the front door, without a word or a look behind. Neither man gave her exit a second thought.

Simon got to his feet and headed over to the space heater to fetch the matches he'd used to light it's pilot.

All three of them heard the car engine start at the same time as Simon saw the TV in the rear room was black, but had been plugged in. He could see that Abby was backing toward the front door and unable to mask her fear.

Slower on the uptake, Travis went to the window to look outside in surprise at the sound of the car.

That's when he heard the gunshot and jumped in shock.

A single bullet hit Abby in the head and she slumped to the floor at Travis' feet. A Phillips head screwdriver fell from her lifeless fingers.

Travis spun and saw Simon with a pistol in hand.

"They were watching TV and figured out about the body and the house," Simon said as he headed for the door.

Betsy already had the car in gear and the passenger door opened for her mother when she'd heard that gunshot. When she saw the two men running out of the little house toward her, she stomped on the gas and sped away down that little road, her eyes filling with tears.

19

J oe and Denny stood at the end of the muddy road near what was left of Cory's house and watched Enright slog toward them ankle deep in the mud and ash. He was wearing a large pair of galoshes and nothing about it was graceful.

"Outright laughter will be held against you," Enright shouted ahead to them.

"We're just laughing inside," Joe said.

"You're just in time," Denny said gesturing about with muddy latex gloves. "Lots of interesting things to see."

"Did he engrave his name anywhere?" Enright said.

"Well, there is a signature," Denny said. "I'll track down similar cases when I get back to the office."

She led them into the barn area and right to the car where the hood was up. The front end was fairly intact, but the car looked as if it had been cut in half by the explosion of its gasoline tank. She pointed out various remnants of the trunk and some shredded pieces of the car.

"There were six depleted propane tanks in the trunk of the car. Each went up after the car's gas tank exploded."

"And they were part of the plan?" Joe asked.

"Yeah. I'll show you in a minute over at the five hundred gallon tank," she said as she pointed to parts of exploded five gallon tanks around the barn. "They went off like rockets and I think he had them aimed."

"Why?"

"Experimenting. It could be they wouldn't all fit standing up and he had to wedge them in, but this guy...I think he was wanted to see how they'd go up. He thinks of himself as an artist."

"Did he sign this painting?" Enright asked.

"Sort of," she said and led them to the front of the car. The motor compartment of the Chevy was intact and there were bare copper wires stretching out from its twelve volt battery in four directions. Denny had pulled their trails out of the mud in every route, following the leads.

"So I was right about this guy, he's clever. Ingenious design really," Denny said. "He had four parallel explosive devices set to go off at once, triggered by a cellphone."

"Forensics have the phone already," Enright said. "I checked with them on the drive out here."

"Duplex wires," Denny said, using her telescoping probe to point out the four sets of parallel wire strands heading different directions. "It's high quality lamp cord, the plastic casing melted off in the fire, but it wasn't hot enough to melt the wire so it's easy to follow."

She pointed out the wires leading under the rear of the car, toward the wooden house, to the base of the large propane tank and to what had been a pile of shrubs at the base of a tree, all now reduced to ash. At the last location, she showed how the parallel wires went inside the end of a shotgun shell. The brass casing had also survived without melting and had been held in place by a rock.

"The beauty is in the simplicity," she said. "All made with easily accessed materials."

"So common they won't lead us anywhere, I expect," Enright said. "How's it work?"

"He emptied the birdshot out but left the full gunpowder load. Twelve gauge shells," she said. "He set it up so the wires just barely touched inside the shell. One wire was positive, one negative. When the battery charge hit them, the wires touching created a short and that spark set off the gunpowder inside the shell. The flash of exploding powder was even aimed by careful placement of the casing. All four explosions went off at once when he called from wherever he was establishing his alibi."

"I hate the smart ones," Enright said as they followed Denny to the five hundred gallon propane tank.

There was another shotgun shell aimed at ashes that had once been a sizable pile of brush. At the side of the tank it was clear where Stacker's body had been sitting because there was a ghostly silhouette untouched by fire.

"He knew the center was the thinnest part of the metal skin and was clearly trying to get the tank to blow," she said. "And it would have, if not for Russell."

"What's this?" Joe said pointing to a neat rig – metal fittings and a thick hose attached to the top of the tank.

"His invention," Denny said with evident admiration. "Up here is where a hose from a propane truck would attach to refill the tank."

"He used this to load fuel from the small tanks?"

"Exactly. It's illegal to upload from a small tank to a big one or to fill propane tanks without proper equipment and a license."

"Is that why I have to buy a full tank for my grill and leave an empty at the hardware store?" Enright asked.

"Yeah, they're loaded up at a proper facility."

"We think it's Dad?" Joe said. "Pretty sophisticated for the guy with the fists we saw in the hospital video."

"That question is up to you guys," Denny said with a shrug. "One other point of interest..."

She led them to another set of parallel copper wires. These were much thicker than the others and went from the house and off the property.

"The other end leads to the garage of the house next door which is over two hundred yards away. They were stealing power from their neighbors who never knew about it. He strung heavy duty extension cords end to end to reach the neighbor and tap in, probably hidden under leaves and dirt to cover his tracks."

"Squatters?" Joe said. "They just moved in, stole power and set up house?"

Denny and Enright nodded, thinking about that as they looked around the ashy remnants of the property.

"I thought squatting went out a hundred years ago," Joe said, trying to imagine living in danger of discovery every day. In truth, it wasn't so hard to picture, he and his mother had lived with similar, unrelenting anxieties.

"I made calls on the drive out. Owners are the three kids of the last known resident who died years ago," Enright said. "They all live out of state, haven't visited the land since Dad died and have been waiting for developers to make an offer on the property to make them rich. A shopping mall or housing development, they hope."

"So the boy's parents picked a good spot to squat," Joe said. "I found out the kid has a sister, so now we think it's Mom, Dad, Patrick Henry and a girl named Betsy. This was home. So why'd they burn it down?"

"Did you find the makings for his explosive devices in

the barn? Tools, wires, shotgun shells?" Enright asked as they walked back toward the remains of the barn.

"Not a bit," Denny said. "If Dad did it, he's got a unique skillset and took every last thing with him."

"Then why'd he leave behind chainsaws, a snow plow and all this?" Enright said looking at the surviving parts.

"The boy was wearing spikes and using a tree climbing belt when he fell," Joe said looking at the assortment of charred but recognizable chainsaws. "Maybe Dad was a tree trimmer," he suggested, "but why a snowplow?"

"Tree trimming is seasonal work," Enright said. "He probably works cash and carry, trims trees in the fall, plows for cash in the winter. From the looks of their life, they were living way off the grid."

"He named his son Patrick Henry. 'Give me liberty or give me death.' I'm guessing he really hated tyranny," Joe said, looking at them for support.

"Don't look at me," Denny said. "B.S. in chemistry and M.S. in CrimSci. History isn't me."

"Where's the tyranny in having his boy's broken arm treated?" Enright asked doubtfully.

"The tyranny that keeps track of citizens," Joe said. "You stay off the grid if you don't want the government to know who you are and what you're doing. The boy can quote Patrick Henry verbatim and his famous speech is a lot less about founding a new country than it is about fighting the overlords. These days there are a lot of groups who think the tyrants are the government. We're the authority they hate and fear. We are the enemy."

"Sometimes I like that you're an intellectual nerd," Enright said with a smile. "So what's this tell us?"

"The boy says the American flag is a symbol of oppression," he went on. "They hate any aspect of the government, including hospitals."

"How is this is helping us find him?" Enright said.

"We found no record of the boy's birth and I don't think we're going to find anything at all on the family," Joe said. "In all modern ways, they don't exist."

"No credit cards, no gas bill, no driver's license?" Enright said. He was becoming convinced.

"We can quit looking for current records to lead us to them," Joe said. "We should look for stolen license plates and stolen vehicles with snowplow mechanisms, but there won't be any official paperwork on this family."

"We could look for people who disappeared off the grid before the boy was born," Enright said.

"Earlier...I'm guessing Betsy is older. The boy said she reads a book a day."

"We've had units out canvassing the area with pictures of the kid and he's unknown at the school on the other side of the woods," Enright said. "No neighbors know him."

"Dad also brought another guy to the hospital," Joe said. "How's he fit in with these squatters? Where's this Marlboro Man lead us?"

"I'd rather think of him as Cliven Bundy, who's also seriously anti-government," Enright said. "I grew up loving the Marlboro Man."

"Didn't he die of lung cancer?" Denny said.

"I loved his image, not his real life. Anyway, I doubt our Bundy fellow is nearly as off-the-grid as our squatter. He's more like Cliven and his moron breed, they don't feel the need to hide."

"If either of them is the pyro, he's pretty clever," Denny said. "The profile of arsonists doesn't describe a guy who beats people up. Firebugs are sneaky instead."

Each of them thought about the two known assailants as they made the slow trek back out through the mud.

DENNY DROVE off and Joe joined Enright to drive back. Neither of them saw the girl hiding in a remaining thicket of trees. Betsy was shocked at the staggering reality of the fire site and sank even lower when she recognized the agent she'd seen inside that diner. Her dad had been right all along; they really were all conspiring against their kind. Her family was in their crosshairs and those bastards had even burnt down their house. All she really wanted was to find her dad and get him to go back for Mom. She was just as afraid of Travis and his guys as she was of these agents and she knew enough to know she couldn't do anything without Dad. If she could just find him.

It had taken a lot of driving to find an area she recognized, but once she spotted the library, she knew her way and had parked at a distance, just like Dad would.

She gave the agents time to go away, then hurried through the burn area to the tree where she hid her own stash of money. The tree's branches were charred and the trunk was black as tar, but it still stood. She shinnied up and found her hiding place was filled with water. And under the water was her triple-wrapped plastic bag of money.

TRAVIS HADN'T HELPED A BIT. He'd just sat with his head in his hands, muttering and occasionally raging. Simon had called guys and had them drop off a shitty old car a mile away and leave the key in it. While he waited for them, he pulled the plastic from the roof and wrapped the body in it. Then he walked to get the car and drove it back to the farm house. That way, no one knew – or could testify – he and Travis had ever been to the house. Travis was still in shock, so Simon struggled by himself to get the body into the car's trunk. With it packed, he was ready to roll, but still had his toughest chore – enlisting Travis. He would be key to making this new and evolving plan work.

The whole time he'd been dealing with this mess, he'd been thinking and it was now becoming clear. His long-term plumbing truck plan was starting to gel with the problem of Abby and, ultimately, Cory. Once he worked it all out, combining this problem with his project at the garage would more than make up for the failure of the propane tank.

His instinct was to burn down the house, but he had two problems. He needed Cory to return and find the blood on the floor. That sight would shock him and help make him buy the story Simon was concocting. At the same time, Simon didn't want a meaningless fire at a shitty little house to alert the police. It would have to stay standing for now and he'd come back to take care of it when there was time.

But what he needed, more than anything, was to get Travis on board. "We have to get going," he said.

Travis looked blankly at him, then over at the blood on the floor where Abby's body had been. He'd almost not noticed all that Simon had been doing until now.

"Why in fuck you kill her, man?"

"It's all Cory's fault, you must realize that."

"What do you mean? Jesus, you shot her."

"What has Cory brought us? Nothing but trouble, HIS troubles, not ours. We have to get back to what's important for us, Travis, and Abby was going to fuck that up. She was going to bring down everything we've been building."

Travis stared at him blankly, unable to follow him.

"We have to focus on our business and all that we do for The Movement. We can't lose track of that."

"All you do for The Movement."

"With this next project, you're about to be dealt in."

Travis shook off his stupor for a second and stared into Simon's eyes. "Really?"

"They're excited by the new plan and have been asking to meet you, but what happens? Cory comes back into our lives and dumps his shitstorm in our lap. That's the last thing The Movement wants. We don't want them to back away from us now, do we?"

"I've been wanting to join them for a long time."

"I know and I've been going to bat for you. Now they're listening and they like the looks of you. Abby stood in the way of all of that. She stood in your way."

"How?"

"She saw the fire on the TV in back and was trying to get away from here, from us, so she could tell Cory."

"Yeah, and Cory's going to go absolutely apeshit."

"That's why we have to direct his rage."

"How'n'fuck we gonna do that?"

"Tell him the government has been satellite tracking his truck," Simon said with absolute assurance.

Travis was shocked. "What? How'd they do that?"

"They didn't do it, but he'll believe it, won't he?"

Travis thought a moment, then nodded. "Probably already does. He took the radio out of his truck and refuses to carry a cell phone...so they can't track him."

"Great. So you and I have got to make him believe they really tracked his truck here and sent in a team of agents after we left," Simon said. Travis sat up straight and listened as he worked it around in his head.

"We lie to him?"

"You want to tell him we killed his wife because she stood between us and The Movement?"

Travis shook his head, cringing at the thought.

"He already believes they took his son, he'll buy they shot his wife," Simon said. He studied Travis mulling it over and felt he was making incremental progress. "Once we get Cory cleanly off our backs, we can get back to The Movement and your first project for them. It's a big one."

"How do we get him off our backs?"

"We make him believe the government stormed in <u>after</u> we took off. Abby and the girl were fine when we left."

Travis nodded. Some of it was getting through.

"The same agents who snatched his son, the ones he's stalking right now," Simon said, coaching Travis, "they must have come in here and grabbed Abby and the girl and someone got badly hurt. We know nothing about it, because we weren't here at the time."

Travis thought about it, slowly nodding. "What about the girl? She knows it didn't happen that way."

"We send everyone out looking for her. We find her and she disappears. Any chance she'd go to the police?"

"No way. Cory indoctrinated her since the day she was born that they're the enemy."

"Good. She won't get far and our guys will find her."

"But what about him? The way the Boy Scout's acting... you know he went crazy when he beat up that guy at the hospital?" Travis said. "He's gonna fly even farther out of control and get himself caught pretty soon."

"Not with us redirecting his energies, he won't. That's the key to getting him and his problems out of our lives. Once he's gone, we can get back to our business."

"And The Movement."

"Exactly," Simon said. "Think you can sell him on those agents coming here? Coming to take his family, shooting one of them?"

"When we were working together I couldn't keep him from believing shit like that," Travis said, nodding. He was coming around to accepting the lie they had to sell.

"Good. We keep him believing, it'll all work."

"How's this help us?"

"He will become our anti-government agent and distract them from the new action we're taking for The Movement."

Simon would never say it out loud, but in his mind, he shouted, 'He's going to become my Timothy McVeigh.'

20

"We were able to get clear fingerprints. His name's Leo Samuel Stacker," the M.E. said to Joe and Enright as they stood over the partially charred body on the slab. "He did not die in the fire, no smoke in his lungs. The cause of death was blunt force trauma, maybe a hammer, but he was killed somewhere else and moved. The blood pooling in the body doesn't match the sitting position he was found in beside the propane tank."

Bittinger joined them carrying a thick police file. He looked at Stacker and said, "Right-handed hitter?"

"Yes, definitely. Standing behind him."

"If his head had been against an exploding propane tank, what would you know about him today?" Joe asked.

"That he died," the M.E. said.

"So now we actually know something they don't want us to know?" Joe said. "Almost feels like progress. Bitt?"

Bittinger was paging through the man's file. "Theft, assault, abetting, dealing, drug crimes – mostly petty. A few stints in county, one for two years in Stillwater. And miraculously, he's been arrest-free for the last year."

Enright looked over the body. "No tattoos. What kind of self-respecting drug dealer doesn't like needles?"

"One who has mostly been too small-time for us to care about. Biggest events in his life were getting himself killed and almost blown up. In that order," Bitt said.

"I don't have lab results back yet, but from the look of his teeth, meth was his preference," the M.E. said.

"Whoever killed him and put his body in an arson site is somehow involved with Patrick Henry. It just can't be a coincidence," Joe said. "But how and why?"

"Let's go through known associates," Enright said tapping the file in Bitt's hand.

As they headed off, Joe asked Bittinger, "So you're with us on this now?"

"Yeah, plus I'm not allowed to set foot in Little Canada until Jordan's case is settled," Bitt admitted.

"Ouch. Captain Volante?"

"He said I was jumping to false conclusions. They think it's about the gun, not about the victim."

"Huh," Joe said. He felt relieved to have actual police involvement in their revolutionary crime wave. The DA's office had been shouldering too much of the load.

"We need a more thorough canvass of the area around the fire and accident, plus now we got this guy Stacker to figure out," Enright said. "Glad to have you aboard."

———————

WITH BOTH ENRIGHT and Bittinger joining Joe in his inadequate office it was hard for them to spread out Leo Stacker's file. They were combing through it looking for known-associates and, more importantly, parole officers and cops who knew Stacker and his friends. Their corpse had been a low-level dealer, 'M&M's' according to his most frequent parole officer who was on the phone with Joe. He sold marijuana and meth, his own personal drug of choice. He had no ambitions, just selling enough to keep himself in drugs. At one point he'd been caught-up in a larger exchange that took down a mid-level distributor and that arrest had sent him to Stillwater for a two-year stint.

"His one and only virtue, if you could call it that, was that he could be trusted to do anything to stay in supply," his parole officer said to Joe. "He was always faithful to his own needs, but he wasn't creative in how he met them. He made a decent go-fer, I guess."

Enright finished talking with an officer who had arrested Stacker at the same time as Bittinger ended a call with one of his many friends in drug enforcement. Finally, they started comparing notes.

"A couple months after Stacker got out of Stillwater, the narc who arrested him was pistol-whipped," Bitt said. "Never saw the guy, cold-cocked by a right handed man who apparently flew out of control."

"Would that be Dad or his friend?" Enright said.

"Maybe the friend with the pistol at the hospital also bashed Stacker with a hammer...but it was Dad who went crazy on Abraham. A switch in M.O. or are they tag-team?"

"Playing for the same team anyway," Enright said. "If Dad trimmed trees and plowed snow, could it be the guy in the sheepskin who was the dealer Stacker worked for?"

"Guys who sell M&Ms don't usually get themselves killed, no matter how much they screw up," Bittinger said. "Hospital, sure, unless they O.D. But hammer to the head, no, that's not usually a low level guy."

"Let's run it by Stacy and see what she thinks."

THE THREE OF them took the file and notes from their various calls to Stacy's conference room where there was room to spread out and run it down for her.

"The body was leaning on the propane tank so he'd be blown to smithereens," Joe said.

"Vaporized, I think is the term," Enright said.

"He was killed somewhere else and brought to the property to be vaporized," Joe amended. "Maybe they needed to get rid of the body and cover up something else too."

"So they had two problems?" Stacy said. "They had an extra body and they had to ditch the ranch. Why do we think that is?"

"It starts with the boy falling out of the tree. That brought Joe to the property they were squatting, so maybe they feared we'd find something big time. The place could have been a part of their operation," Enright said. "Denny found traces of marijuana in the barn."

"Wouldn't it have all gone up in the fire?" Joe said.

"You ever tried to keep a joint lit?" Enright said. "They're always going out on you."

Joe stared at Enright with an inquisitive smirk.

"So I'm told," Enright added.

"Whiskey never goes out on you," Bitt said.

"So we got a dead dealer at a marijuana site, a boy, a beaten up orderly," Stacy said. "Where's it lead us?"

"If I'm the dad and want to break my kid out of the hospital, why do I bring a guy with a gun?" Bitt said.

"Maybe you don't know he carries," Enright said.

"In the view of this dad, what's he see?" Joe said. "Say I'm him...I see the tyranny of the government and I need backup. So I bring someone I trust, but I don't realize he's the kind of guy who might go apeshit."

"Sounds naïve of you," Enright said.

"I named my son after a revolutionary, I live off the grid, I have very particular ideas about the world and see only what confirms what I already believe," Joe said, running with it. "I really hate the government. Anything that doesn't fit my world view...I ignore."

"Okay, so if I'm you, I only trust people like me," Enright said, "people who also hate the government, right? Who hates the government the most?"

"People locked up by it...cons, ex-cons," Bitt said.

"So these two might have met in prison?"

They sat on that for a moment, each feeling it was somewhere between half-plausible and a stretch. Then Stacy finally said, "More than we had an hour ago. What's next?"

"I'll get uniforms out to the neighborhood and dig more into Stacker, ask my narc buddies," Bitt said.

"I got an avenue to follow that's too dumb to mention," Enright said, "which makes it right up my alley."

"I'll talk to Kat about figuring out the dad, see if I can understand him more."

BETSY KNEW Salvation Army stores had no security cameras. She stood inside the large store absorbing the warmth looking at the pay phone on the wall, but there was no one to call. She had no way to tell Dad what was going on, except to find him. She'd ditched the car ten blocks from the store, just like she'd been taught, and was now planning to transform herself. She had to get rid of the coat and she needed a couple of different hats, a few scarves that she could crumple into the pockets of the bulky jacket she'd buy. Thinking like Dad, she also bought a second jacket in another color and grabbed a well-worn school backpack to hold it all.

The lady at the counter was so accustomed to seeing the homeless, she seemed genuinely pleased to find a courteous young lady like her. She was too chatty and Betsy didn't like the attention, so she got the hell out of there right after paying. She redistributed her money to a variety of places in her used clothes, just as she'd heard Dad talk about, then ditched her old coat in a dumpster.

The girl in the hat and scarf who emerged from the alley was a new person in the neighborhood, so she felt slightly less inclined to be looking over her shoulder. She wondered about Mom, but couldn't let herself dwell on that or she'd fall apart and never find Dad.

Rather than wallow in her fear about her mother, she wanted to take action of some kind. That diner was close to where Dad thought Patrick Henry was held and she had been able to see the dome of the state capitol building from the diner. She could see the Capitol Dome from the Salvation Army store too, but she'd been told cabs, buses and public transport were all wired to keep track of the population, so she'd walk.

JOE WALKED from his office in the cold November wind. His nose was freezing and he had to pull his scarf up to brave the gusts as he hurried up Wabasha toward the Family Services Building. He could have taken a cab, but that always seemed so wasteful for just eight blocks.

Having gone off the clock for the day, he naturally spent

the entire walk thinking about the boy and his father. He had watched the security footage a couple dozen times trying to get a bead on the man's face, but then he became captivated by the other guy's transformed behavior. He seemed furtive as they first approached the boy's room, then at the sight of Abraham loaded up with bed linens, he went berserk. Abraham had done nothing provocative, but the moment he fought back, the smaller guy appeared to retreat, as if expecting the big guy to take over. It felt to Joe like these two must have acted this way before.

Joe wanted to ask Kat about all of this over dinner. Their plan was to drive to a restaurant together, then after dinner she'd drop him at his car and they'd head home separately. He loved that he didn't have to check where he'd be sleeping tonight and still found it almost unbelievable. 'What did I do to deserve to be so lucky?'

The wind was nasty but was stopped by his thick wool coat and complementing scarf, clothes he'd never have bought on his own. They were entirely Kat's influence. He was just snugging the scarf back down around his neck when his brisk walk came to an abrupt halt.

He was looking at the man from the hospital video.

He wore a different jacket, but the same baseball hat. He had the same posture and walk, and those shoulders. Not fifty yards from Family Services, Patrick Henry's father was watching the entrance. He hadn't seen Joe, not that he'd know who he was anyhow. What a stroke of luck.

Joe inched closer as he pulled out his phone to call Enright. He needed police to swarm in and pick this guy up.

He had to take a glove off to use the phone and was just about to tap the speed dial for Enright when he looked up, right into the man's eyes. He knew instantly that this guy recognized him somehow and was lunging at him.

The phone and glove went flying and his scarf was pulled taut around his neck.

"Where the fuck is my boy?" Cory shouted into Joe's face as he yanked him off balance with the tight scarf.

Joe instinctively punched and caught a good one to the man's jaw, but he couldn't breathe. The few people hurrying along in the wind started to notice the fight and gathered around, pulling out cellphones. Joe tried to get another punch in, but this guy was really strong and already had a strangle hold on him. Even as he was fading from consciousness, Joe managed to hit the guy again while the man screamed, "where's my son?" over and over.

A siren sounded in the distance as Joe landed his last punch before nearly passing out. He crumpled to the ground and frantically loosened the scarf as the man ran off at a surprising speed. Bystanders gathered around Joe to help him to his feet as the blood started flowing to his head again. Nearby a homeless man picked up Joe's cell phone and pocketed it.

CORY WAS near the pickup and the sirens already sounded pretty damned close. He shook with rage and his jaw hurt like hell. That little prick packed a wallop.

He'd just started to open the driver's side door when Joe slammed him into the side of his truck. They both went down as he was tackled and they crashed into the road pavement with heavy grunts.

Cory flung Joe off and it sent him flying into the side of a car that was swerving and trying to avoid them.

Cory caught him with a bare fist and pain shot through his hand from the power. He had to get out of here, but the guy was already staggering up and heading back at him. Joe smashed him in the face one more time before Cory grabbed that loosened scarf again, pulled him forward and jerked him downward as he brought up his knee with all his might.

Joe managed to turn his head at the last second and took the knee in the side of the head instead of the nose. It sent him down and this time he was not getting up.

The sirens were close and deafening as Cory leapt into the truck and pulled away before Joe could roll over. The pickup turned the corner and soon blended into traffic, just as a police car skidded to a stop beside Joe. He struggled to pull his DA badge from his pocket as the officers approached and started to help him get up.

Betsy slowly blended back into the crowd of onlookers. Moments earlier she'd pushed through the pack, trying to see what was going on. She'd seen Dad at the same moment she'd heard the sirens, but he'd sped away by the time she got close and she had no way to signal him.

She also had no place left to go.

21

Why St. Paul, Minnesota had a cowboy shop was a question that Enright longed to ask. This wasn't cowboy country, but as he looked around at the fancy boots, the long-rider coats, the insanely huge hats and intricately sequined shirts, he realized it was an ethos. Cowboy was a style, it had nothing to do with riding a horse, herding cattle or rolling cigarettes one-handed. People bought this stuff because of how it made them feel and how it gave them an image whether or not they had ever stepped in horseshit even once in their life. It fit their suspect perfectly.

After he had badged the clerk who had already measured him in his mind, Enright said, "If I wanted to look like Cliven Bundy, what would you recommend."

"Gain weight."

"Thanks, I gotta tell my wife about that one."

"Why would you want to look like the Bundy clan?" the clerk said as a shudder ran through him.

It appeared to Enright that Bundy and those morons had given the cowboy sensibility a bad name.

"I'd like to see what you carry in sheepskin coats,"

Enright said, looking around. "You figure some guys think a sheepskin coat makes them look bigger and tougher?"

"Only works if you got a horse under you," the clerk said as he led Enright to the outerwear section where there were many leather jackets and some sheepskin coats. One of those was exactly the same as the one their suspect had worn the day he assaulted Abraham Lashway.

"This is the one. Any way you can pull up records on who recently bought this particular coat?"

The clerk unlocked the chain through the arm of the coat, took it to the register and scanned the bar code.

"Sell a lot of them?"

"At three thousand a pop, not really," the clerk said. "Sorry to say."

"That's more than every coat I ever owned...combined."

The clerk spun the monitor around to show Enright. "The last one sold was the middle of last winter. Cash. Says here there was an alteration charge as well."

"Could be my guy. What was the alteration?"

"Sleeve shortening, but like I said, cash."

"No security tape I imagine."

"Not ten months later."

Enright pulled out a photo printed from the hospital security tape. It was grainy, but the man was fairly clear. The coat was even clearer. "Any chance it's this guy?"

The clerk studied the photo and shrugged. "That's our coat for sure, but I didn't sell it."

Just then Enright's cellphone rang and it was Bitt. "Joe met the kid's father and now he's in the E.R. at St. Joseph's. He'll live. I'll see you there."

The clerk had already printed out what information he had on the sale and was writing a phone number on it when

Enright hung up. "That's the salesman's number. We don't sell a lot, so he might remember something."

"Thanks," Enright said as raced out the door.

TRAVIS CARRIED four opened beers from the kitchen, handed two to Simon and kept two for himself. They were alone in the living room because everyone who worked for them was out looking for Betsy and the car she'd stolen.

"I can't get over seeing her fall...dead."

"You did not see that," Simon firmly insisted. "When we left the farm house, Abby was cleaning the refrigerator and the girl was making up the bed. Picture it, believe it, because...when Cory gets here, we don't know a thing after that moment. Whatever he tells us...it's all news to us."

"Right," Travis said, letting the script sink in.

Simon watched Travis closely, analyzing him as he drank his beer. "You never saw a dead body before?"

"Yeah I have, just...I was more psyched beforehand, ready for it to happen," Travis said taking another good long pull on the first beer. "Plus, then with Lenny...well that didn't happen in front of me, thanks to you."

"Best for everyone to know about it, but not see it."

Travis finished his first beer. "I never did like Abby much. She pulled him away."

"He seemed off course from the beginning. Back when you two were partners in juvie," Simon said, "you were always the rational one. He just got completely carried away with his ideas, his idiotic code."

"He can be a righteous Boy Scout, but he's always been my righteous Boy Scout," Travis said with a stunted laugh.

"He's the kind of guy The Movement have to drive away, too unstable," Simon said. "You're perfect for them."

"Good to hear."

"Think about what you were doing when you and he were still partners...compared to everything you've built now," Simon said, gesturing around the house with appreciation. "He held you back then and he'll drag you under with him right now if we don't break free."

"All true, it's just he goes back to..."

"First, you got nothing to feel bad about. You opened your home, you gave him refuge. You were good to him, you've been a great friend. He brought everything down on himself. Remember...it's those assholes from the government who traced his truck with a drone or something."

"He's hard wired to believe conspiracies like that."

"Then make sure it stays that way. We have to loosen ties with him but we can't let him be aware of it."

"How we make sure?"

"If he brings his truck here, we have to be really concerned and offer to ditch it for him because there must be a government tracker in it. To keep him safe, okay?"

"Got it," Travis said. "The poor, dumb bastard."

Simon studied him, a bit worried. He had a lot riding on this and it depended not only on getting Cory in proper position to become his McVeigh, but he absolutely needed Travis to get him there and keep him there.

"You cool with all this? I know it's a change..."

"Since he showed up the other day, I've kept trying to picture Cory joining us. You know, us three as a mighty trio" Travis said. "But I could never get it to fit. Him and me...that now feels so past. Not like you and me have been building, what we're now planning..."

"We are all about the future and we've got new allies

who are major players. Major," Simon said. "You're really wise to let you past with him be long gone."

He started his second beer as Simon took a sip of his first. Travis' battle with feelings about Cory reminded Simon of when they all first met. At the time, he'd thought Travis was in love with Cory. He probably didn't realize it on any conscious level, but there was an attachment for him that was real. It seemed clear that Travis was now subconsciously severing that bond, just like people do with past lovers. Simon never understood affection or love, but he had witnessed people actively working to dissolve their affections when the glow had passed. He felt confident Travis would soon start to find all sorts of resentments about Cory. Simon intended be there to help encourage them.

———————

THE TWO UNIFORMED cops who picked Joe up off the street after his fight with Cory had driven him to the St. Joseph Hospital emergency room. It was the downtown St. Paul E.R. and therefore a fairly busy place.

Bittinger thanked them and got brought up to speed on what they'd seen when they arrived. He also learned Joe had given them the license plate on the pickup. He had them chase down that information and was about to head in to see Joe when Enright arrived. With a heavy look at each other, they went in together.

The bruising was already settling in on Joe's face on the side that had taken the knee and his ear was quite swollen. He was holding an ice pack to his face and didn't like the looks he got.

"You gotta stop assaulting perps with your head, Joe," Enright said by way of hello.

"You saw him? Can you ID him?" Bitt said. But he was the one to pat Joe's leg. Sympathy, but in a masculine way.

"Get me an artist and we'll have a picture. I saw him clear as can be. Maybe it will do us some good."

"Why didn't you call in backup?" Enright said.

"I was calling you when he spotted me and attacked. Knocked the phone right out of my hand."

"Why'd he attack you?"

"Good question. I have no idea. I was trying to call because I'm not stupid enough to approach him on my own. Then all of a sudden he was looking at me. He knew me, I could see it in his face, he knew who I am – but how?"

"He actually recognized you?" Bitt said. "How would he know you?"

"Beats me."

"Might want to rephrase that...for future reference," Enright said. "So he knows you're after him somehow, which means he's probably already ditched the pickup."

One of the cops beckoned Bittinger who left to confer. Enright said, "How in hell he know you from Adam?"

"I've been trying to figure that out. He was standing outside where Kat works, he knew my face in an instant..."

"Even I don't recognize you at the moment."

"Very funny. What if he's been watching us while we've been investigating him?"

"Don't see how, but it can't be a coincidence. He was right outside her work? I don't like that."

"Don't like what?" was called from beyond the curtain.

Bitt was trying to slow Kat down, saying, "He don't look good but they said no concussion."

The curtain flew open and there was Kat. Enright sidled away to give her the full view.

"Jesus, Joe," she said as she grabbed his outstretched

hand and leaned close. But she didn't kiss him, his face was a mess and looked painful. Her eyes started to well with tears as she muttered, "I don't like it either."

"You should see his knee."

She managed a weak smile as she squeezed his hand. He yelped and extricated it from her, holding up his bruised and taped-up knuckles. "I got in three or four good ones. His face has got to look at least half as bad as mine."

"I suppose you're proud of that?" Kat said as she lifted the icepack from his face, winced at the sight, and put it gently back down. "What happened to your neck?"

"Scarf burns. I might need a replacement...but, hey, Christmas is coming up," Joe said, indicating his clothes that were strewn across a chair near the bed. Kat looked askance at them, back at him and could only shake her head.

"The license plates were stolen over a year ago from another pickup truck, unrelated to the one Joe saw," Bitt said. "We're looking into stolen pickups with snowplow attachments that fit the color, make and model." Bitt then grinned at Joe, then to Enright and Kat. "I just watched a video from a bystander's cellphone. You clocked him good, Joe. Real good." He looked from somber face to somber face and dropped the smile, but aside to Enright he whispered, "Really fought hard...until he got knocked out."

"You two mind?" Kat said impatiently.

Enright and Bittinger sheepishly stepped out, but gave Joe a thumb's up as Kat turned back to Joe. As they disappeared from sight, Bittinger dropped the whispering and could be heard: "You gotta see the video, Byron. The second fight's damn impressive. He's flung against a moving car and still throws a right hook to the guy's jaw."

"Sorry about that," Joe said as they both listened.

"Wish you were," she said. She was holding his wool

coat, touching the dried blood on the shoulder and lapel. "Maybe we should quit buying you decent clothes."

"I've been saying that all along," he said, doing his best to grin, but it was decidedly lopsided.

She inched the chair closer and sat, growing very serious. "You picked a fight with a killer, Joe."

"No. No. I defended myself from a killer."

CORY TOOK a look in the rearview mirror and his face was pretty battered. Abby was going to have a shitfit. His jaw felt hot to his touch and hurt more than he wanted to admit. Nobody had ever gotten in four shots to his face before. Ever. If that car had been half a second later, it would have run over the agent, which he sure as hell deserved. But he'd probably have died and there would have been no escaping, if that had happened. This was an agent and it had occurred in daylight in front of witnesses. He had to get himself and his family out of town.

The hatchback he'd stolen would do. They might have to take less stuff and there was no hiding the two rifles which now sat in the back seat, but the car would take the whole family on their next migration. He'd left the pickup truck in employee parking at a big box store that was open 24 hours. It had freshly stolen plates and he'd swiped another set for the hatchback, so he'd covered his tracks as effectively as ever by the time he drove off the road onto the little dirt path that led to the farmhouse.

The place was utterly dark even though the electricity had been working before he left. Maybe they'd gone to bed already, it'd been a big day. The headlights played across the forlorn-looking house and he told himself they wouldn't stay here long.

When he opened the front door, he could barely remember the layout, so he felt for the light switch. Something bothered him already. It didn't feel right and the place had an odd smell.

At last he found the switch, flipped it on and reeled back at the sight of a pool of blood on the floor. "Abby!" he shouted in panic. "Abby! Betsy!"

He leapt over the blood, darted into the back room but it was as empty as the front. All their bags were strewn about, but there was no sign of either of them. He was breathing really hard and feeling lightheaded.

He forced himself to inspect the scene as he leaned down, his hands on his knees so he could catch his breath and his brain could wrestle with his fears. There'd been four people here when he left, one of them had lost a lot of blood and now all of them were gone.

He tried to convince himself it wasn't either Abby or Betsy whose blood smeared the floor.

The car kicked up a cloud of dust as he raced away from the farmhouse and nearly spun-out as he turned onto the little county road. He told himself the moment they were all back together, they would be so fucking gone.

———

HE'D COOLED down and had mulled a lot by the time he pulled up to Travis' property. His friend had really come through for him, he had gone above and beyond the call of friendship, but now Cory realized anything Travis had to say about the farm was guaranteed to be bad news.

He was buzzed in at the gate without any comment. As

he raced toward the house in the dark, Travis opened the door. "Didn't expect to see you tonight. Are Abby and Betsy still at the farm?" Simon's coaching was flowing well. The story should prove they knew nothing.

Travis was surprised by Cory's beaten face as he rushed inside, right past him and found Simon alone on the couch, a documentary on Ruby Ridge playing. "Hey, Cory. They all settled in?" he said before he turned around. Then even his cool was momentarily disturbed when he looked at Cory, his face now all swollen and red.

"You're both okay?" Cory said with disappointment that knocked the breath out of him. It had to be Abby or Betsy.

"Where are they? What happened to them?" Cory said.

"What are you talking about?" Travis said as he looked to Simon for help. "What the hell happened to your face?"

"I fought that agent. So where are Abby and Betsy?"

"Last we saw them was at the farm," Simon said, taking over for Travis. "Half hour after you drove off everything was working, so we left. Aren't they there now?"

"There was nothing there but a pool of blood."

Simon faked shock and Travis did his best to catch up. Cory having a fight hadn't been part of their script.

"Abby was scrubbing out the fridge when we left," he said, then ran off and returned with a bag of frozen peas.

Simon was drawing out what Cory had discovered at the farm and was quite believably surprised by every detail.

"No lights were on, all our bags of stuff were still there, but the blood..." Cory said.

Travis handed the peas to Cory and said, "Whose blood? What blood?"

"I don't know, I don't know," Cory screamed. "They were fine when you left and now they're missing and there's blood all over the floor."

"Holy shit," Simon said. "Maybe one of them got hurt and they walked someplace to find help," Simon suggested.

"After Patrick Henry was taken away and held captive in a hospital? Abby wouldn't do that," Cory said. "They would-n'ta left. They woulda stayed. They wouldn'ta left," he said. "Not Abby."

Simon said. "Damn."

Cory looked at Simon, then at Travis. He was blind and couldn't think, as he stared at the frozen peas as if they'd just appeared out of thin air. He couldn't really comprehend and Simon realized he needed to help him along.

"It's not like this would be the government's first assault on your family, would it?" Simon said.

"The government?" Cory said, shocked and disturbed.

"Maybe not, you're right," Simon said. "If Abby wouldn't leave, what else could have happened?"

That left all three of them silent for a long moment.

"Didn't you say an agent walked up to your house, then the very next day they took your boy..." Travis said, but stopped as he saw Simon's signal to slow down.

"Now today..." Simon added gently. "The rest of your family is missing..."

Cory's swollen face got redder as the rage overwhelmed him. He leapt to his feet, seething as he shouted, "The fucking government!"

22

B etsy ordered a hamburger, fries and Coke; all the things she couldn't get at home. She sat at the counter close to the cooking area of Mickey's Diner where she'd listened to those agents. It already seemed so long ago. She was warming up and figured she'd keep ordering food so they'd let her stay, but that only solved the hunger and warmth problems. She was terrified about Mom, wondered if Dad would ever come back here and her little brother was still in custody. What could she do? What was she able to do?

She glanced around warily from under the brim of her hat as she devoured the hamburger. There was a guy down the counter sawing up a bloody slab of beef with a steak knife. In the polished stainless steel of the wall across from her, she could watch him and he was paying way too much attention to her. It made her uncomfortable in several ways, but when she glanced his way again, she ignored his grin and focused on his sharp knife.

She ordered a steak for her second meal and decided they would never get their knife back. She needed a whole lot more than that, but it was the first time she'd thought about protecting herself since her Dad drove off.

———————

"YOUR FIGHT with the agent could have set them off," Simon said helpfully. "Maybe it triggered those agents to go from just tracking you to abducting your whole family."

"They were already taking action against us," Cory said. "They'd already kidnapped my boy."

"You're right. Sorry, didn't think of it like that," Simon said, backing away and letting it all stew.

Cory was staring at his bruised knuckles, feeling the throbbing in his face and doing everything he could to keep from imagining either Abby or Betsy being so badly hurt she'd lost all that blood. Nevertheless, the fury was simmering inside, burning at his muscles to take action.

"They mighta come looking for you and only went after Ab and Bets because you weren't there," Travis said.

"How could they know any of us were there?" Cory said. "We'd only just driven to the farm."

Simon suddenly leapt up from the couch in well-feigned panic and said, "Is your truck here? They might have placed a tracker in it. They could be tracking you right now."

"I ditched the pickup. What are you talking about?"

"Good thinking," Simon said as he sat down, pretending to be relieved, looking thoughtful. "Still, we should find out if there was a tracker in your truck. Then we'd know."

"There's no way they put a tracker in my truck. When would they have done that?"

"They kidnapped your boy, right?" Simon said. "And some man walked right up to your house?"

"Yeah. But..."

"So you're on their radar," Travis said convincingly. "We got no idea how long they've been after you."

"Wish I'd thought of it earlier," Simon said. "I could have swept your pickup for a tracker."

"You can do that?"

"Sure, do it to all our cars all the time," Simon said and caught a look from Travis. He was already starting to see Cory as a dupe. "The car we drove out to the farm was clean. Wish I'd thought to sweep yours. Sorry, man."

"My pickup?" Cory said, trying to keep up.

"You said yourself that agent tracked you to downtown. He was on top of you before you knew it, right?" Simon said. "How'd he do that? How'd he know where to find you? It was your truck, I'd lay odds on it."

Cory stared from one earnest face to the other.

"Travis and I had left the farm long before you got into the city, right?" Simon said and waited for Cory to nod, then went on, "Maybe they picked up your girls soon after we took off and you were the last one they were ready to grab." He was gaining confidence as Cory took in each lie, nodded solemnly, offered few rebuttals and started to believe in their conspiracy theory.

"Could they really have done all that?" Cory said, confronted with two men he respected who had now begun accepting all that he had believed in for so many years.

"I sweep the truck, we'll know for sure," Simon said.

"What if they're watching it?" Cory said.

Part of Simon sighed with relief. Cory had now bought the tracker story, he believed his truck was being watched. A major hurdle had been overcome.

"Once I'm close enough I can detect a search signal. If they're monitoring it I can find their system first," Simon said as confidently. "Where's it at?" In truth, he knew there was no tracker but he really needed that truck.

While Cory explained where he'd left it, Travis picked up the TV remote control. It was time for the second shoe to drop, just as Simon planned. The news would drive Cory fully into their grasp and Travis was getting into the game, feeling superior and closer to Simon than ever.

"Maybe this finally explains the fire, then," Travis said and turned on the TV to start the cued-up recording.

"What fire?"

"We been trying to figure it out," Travis said as the TV news clip showed an aerial view of Cory's home on fire.

Already beaten and distraught, Cory watched in horror as he saw his house and barn burning ferociously. Simon secretly swelled with a feeling of power. He had made all those bastard cops and firemen scramble around and now an independent 'master of his own destiny' – as Cory liked to think of himself – was coming fully under his influence.

"They burned your house down, man," Travis said.

"You've been right all these years about those mother-fuckers. They really are after you," Simon said.

The news clip showed all the highlights of the fire, announced the discovery of the body and the fact that it was being investigated as a murder. Cory was stupefied.

"A body?" Cory said in disbelief. "Who?"

"No idea, but you just know they'll blame you," Simon said softly. "The fix is in...this is how they frame you."

Cory had been leaning toward the TV, terrified. But as the flames leapt and the house fell, he finally collapsed into the couch, leaned his head backward and stared at the ceiling. He was overwhelmed an. "Man, what is going on? What'd I do? Why now?"

"Shut that thing off," Simon said to Travis. He was

certain Cory was in the bag and it was time to wrap him up with sympathy.

Travis couldn't stand the silence and went off to grab some beers. Simon just studied Cory's inertia, fascinated. People's emotions were strange fictions they convinced themselves were true. He knew he didn't have emotions, but he'd always found them an efficient way to manipulate the suckers. All he felt, as he again watched the barn explode and all those men scramble about, was power.

"I just can't believe it," Cory finally said.

"I'll sweep your pickup and then we'll know for sure."

"And if there is no tracker?" Cory said, accepting a beer from Travis, who put the rest on the coffee table.

"Then they're even cleverer than we think. Fuck, I don't know...a drone or something."

"They're not clever," Cory said bitterly. "They're insidious." He looked Simon deeply in the eyes. "You willing to risk it? Check the truck out for me? I know it's a lot to ask."

"Anything for you, man. We have to stick together, don't we Travis?" Simon said, getting up.

Simon's plan called for Travis to stay and help Cory come to grips with the belief that his family was gone for good. He was to support all paranoid fantasies about drones or implants or Cory's many other conspiracy theories. Simon headed off to grab a few things from his room, among them a voltage meter that he'd modified which he could pass it off as a bug-sweeper if Cory asked, but he never did.

"YOU CALL THAT A BOURBON?" Joe said from the couch Kat had just set down a glass with a lot more ice than booze. He was stretched out, propped up against an arm, an afghan across his legs and the coffee table pulled close. He felt like a school boy who had stayed at home, sick.

"You're on opioids, you shouldn't even be having a sip," Kat said as she sat in the matching armchair. She'd had to rearrange a lot of Joe's stuff to make room, but now she sat with her back to the mess. She looked across at Joe – his face and ear red, his lip and cheek swollen. "You have Oxy and a muscle relaxant in you. I, on the other hand, need a double just to look at your face."

"Imagine how it feels from the inside."

"I'd rather not," she said, swirling around what really was a double. "You worry me, Joe. You are aware of that, aren't you? Your fights are supposed to be verbal and in court, not with..." A shudder ran through her.

"Byron and Bitt are working on how the guy knew me, and how he found me. But what this guy has been doing mystifies me. Help me figure him out," Joe said.

"Maybe a few things his son said will help. He's got a lot of very strong and quite odd beliefs."

"Yeah."

"Dianna told me he's terrified the surgeons put an implant in him when they operated on his arm."

"What kind of implant?"

"He seems to believe in every crazy idea," she said. "Mind control, trackers, anything to keep tabs on him and his family. Security cameras freak the boy out." Kat then had to laugh to herself. "He believes the air system on an airplane can vaccinate you against your will."

"That's gotta be his dad," Joe said. "Serious paranoia and anti-government rage. What's the psychological term for being like that...lunatic fringe?"

"Wish we could write it off that easily," Kat said. "It's disturbing that people actually embrace this stuff."

"So Dad's some kind of self-styled revolutionary who hates the government and names his kid after our most celebrated near-anarchist," Joe said. "He indoctrinates his son to believe we're the ones who are indoctrinated, to believe that only he has found the wisdom of independence."

"Yes, Dad's paranoid, but it seems he cares about his boy, he's connected. He's not your classic loner."

"Yet he lives off the grid, entirely outside society."

"Sure, he has an inability to live amongst the rest of us, but he's got a family."

"Which tells us what?"

"That he's not a Unabomber. Not a Ted Kaczynski, he's not a hermit writing treatises alone in a mountain cabin."

"Even though he kills a guy and positions him to blow up when he burns down his own property?"

"Only after moving his family somewhere else. I expect in his view of the world, the family is his tribe."

"And we are holding a member of his tribe."

"Which makes us the enemy, his oppressors," Kat said as she finished her drink and got up for more. "You know what happens if a paranoid person's worst fears start to come true? His anger builds until it boils over...then he lashes out."

He touched his face and said, "Which hurts like hell."

As she poured herself another drink, the front door buzzer went off and it was Enright; he said he was bringing them something. She had the door open for him by the time he made it up the two flights of stairs.

"Built-in exercise program," Enright said as he entered, a bit breathless. It was his first time in the apartment and he gestured at the stacks of boxes and the mismatched furniture. "I guess you two needed to have a little bit of Calcutta..." he said, then gestured at Kat's furnishings, "...in what is otherwise Paris."

"Good to see you too, Byron." Joe said from the couch.

As Kat took his coat, Enright looked over Joe propped up under a cashmere throw cover, then said to her, "You cut the crusts off his grilled cheese sandwiches too?"

"He deserves a little pampering tonight," Kat said.

Enright sat in the armchair. When Kat held out a glass with bourbon and ice to him, he grinned and said, "Careful, I might never leave." He took the glass and a sip, then added, "Personally I hate those crusts."

"What is it, Byron?" Joe said.

"All business? Okay." Enright pulled a copy of a police drawing of Cory out of his pocket. It was a damn good likeness, a sketch that used images from the videos along with Joe's extensive input. It looked real and Kat didn't like the look in the man's eyes. He was a killer.

Enright hemmed and hawwed, looking uncertainly at Kat. "Maybe you don't want to listen to this," he said. "Joe and I have to have a heart-to-heart."

"Then I'm in," she said and sat by Joe on the couch.

Finally Enright took a small pistol from his jacket pocket and pointed at the police sketch. "He knows who you are and he's made his intentions clear. Sorry, Kat. You gotta take this, Joe. I'll square it away with Bitt and the police. I'll register it to you, all on the up-and-up."

"I don't want it, Byron," Joe said.

"A murder, arson, now direct assault...sorry, Kat. I'd be a lot more comfortable if you'd give us a minute."

"I wouldn't be. I'm as uncomfortable as hell and having a gun in Joe's hand with drugs in his system isn't a combination that makes me feel more secure."

Enright nodded. "You're right. What am I thinking?" he said and changed tactics, offering the gun to Kat. "Here's the safety, on the side here, flip it this way only when – and I mean <u>only</u> when – you want to shoot."

"I don't want to shoot."

"Neither do I. Ever," Enright said. "But I want to be able to. Whatever these guys are about, it's serious and so far we've been lucky." When neither of them would take the gun, Enright at last put it back in his pocket. "I like having you around, Stretch. You got a baseball bat?"

'I'd rather have a gun,' went through Joe's mind, but of course he didn't say it out loud. A baseball bat had changed the course of his life. So...never again.

Kat fished in her purse and showed a little black plastic spray bottle. "I've got pepper spray."

Enright inspected it. "Yeah, that's a good one."

"We'll be safely locked in our home, way up here on the third floor," Kat said as she saw Enright out.

Then she gave Joe more of his pills so he could rest.

23

After a quick detour out to the farm house to rig it so it wouldn't come back to haunt them, Simon drove to the Cushing Avenue Towing yard. Under many layers of shell companies, Travis owned the place, which had no tow trucks and no employees. Its very true purpose was to obscure one rusted-to-shit Ford Falcon that was important only to him and Travis. That old car was buried behind a rotating group of functioning junkers their men used for deliveries and errands. 'Never drive anything flashy' was one of Simon's mottos for business operations. Behind the functioning cars were many completely derelict junkers and, unremarkable even in their midst, was the nondescript Falcon.

He drove Cory's beige pickup into the lot and parked far away from the light from the street and beyond the intentionally broken main overhead lamp in the lot.

Of course he hadn't swept the truck for trackers, even if he could. In his bag of supplies he'd brought from the house, in addition to the voltage meter, was a government-issue magnetic tracker device he'd purchased long ago at an espionage store. He'd tell Cory he'd found it hidden in the truck to prove the government had traced him to the farm. Cory would blame himself for leading the feds to his family and his guilt would allow him to buy into the government conspiracy story more deeply. It was working perfectly.

Getting Abby's body from the trunk – which it had been in for hours – into the space behind the pickup's seat was like a three-dimensional jigsaw puzzle. But soon enough she was behind the seat that was rammed all the way forward. He covered her up with a tarp, stacked the tools back on top and then looked about for anything he might have missed. Under the seat he found the license plates that Cory had taken off the truck and put them back on. He wanted it to be easily identified as Cory's pickup. Finally he wiped down the gun he'd shot Abby with and slipped it in with the body.

Cory felt lucky to have Travis to help him get through all these compounding tragedies, but after Simon left, he'd become restless. He couldn't just sit and wait, he wasn't ready to give up yet, so he borrowed one of the pistols from the gun rack – a handy little Ruger .380. He left despite Travis' objections and drove the hatchback on side roads into St. Paul, then parked a block from Kat and Joe's apartment.

There were lights on in what he believed was Nolan's apartment. There was no one outside when he approached from the rear and inspected the building's back door lock. Juvie had taught him many things and picking a lock was one of them. He was a bit rusty because he hadn't done this much after his partnership with Travis ended, but it wasn't a sophisticated lock and he was quickly in. The wooden back stairs looked creaky, so he tested each step as he went up. Sure enough, it was damn noisy and he heard people nearby in the kitchen in one of the apartments as he crept up.

He let himself back out silently and one peek through the glass in the front door showed the main wooden stairs. He figured they would be just as bad and he'd be even more exposed. From across Mississippi River Boulevard, he assessed the brick building and decided he could climb up right above the front door. Each unit had sun porches that protruded to the front, leaving a sizable nook between them above the front entry. The lower floors all had their shades drawn and there was no traffic going by at all. With the street quiet and a park on the other side, he'd be unseen as he climbed. Wedged in the inside corner and using the framing around the windows of the sun porches, he made his way up, barehanded but secure.

Inside, Joe was very drowsy from the second Oxy and the muscle relaxant Kat had insisted he take. He hadn't had anything since the E.R. and the pain had been creeping up. Kat had to help him to their room and into the bed, so she decided to forego getting him fully undressed. The meds would keep him sound asleep for hours anyway. She gently kissed his swollen face, tucked the covers up tight and slipped out of the bedroom. She still had her second glass of bourbon waiting and sat down to study the drawing of the man who had fought with Joe.

Just as he reached the darkened sun porch, Cory saw movement inside Nolan's living room. From his perch, he had a view of a portion of the living room and the whole sun porch, but he could see no one, just shadows. Then the movement inside stopped. He put his gloves on and tested the nearest window in the sun porch. It was unlocked, so he lifted it an inch, but the shadows in the living room abruptly moved again. He had just enough time to slide the window back down.

Kat left the drawing of Cory on the coffee table, wound her way through Joe's stuff cluttering her place and entered her office, the second bedroom. She flipped the light on and sat at her computer to do a little research, hoping to find something to help her profile this strange, paranoid attacker. She vaguely worried about what the state would do with the boy, since he couldn't stay in a psych ward indefinitely, but the first priority was to get his father safely locked up.

Skimming an article on paranoia left her feeling rather paranoid herself. The connection between obsessive, undifferentiated distrust and acts of violence was undeniable. Joe was sleeping off the results of an assault that was proof of that correlation. As she read on, she felt her anxiety rising. It was disturbing enough to her that she walked back out into the living room to look around. She told herself that so much had happened, plus her previously comfortable world had been thrown out of whack with all the strange stuff about. It was disturbing.

She couldn't completely calm the vague, but rising fears so she opened her lower desk drawer and fished out a blue plastic case. She hadn't felt the need before, but now she just hoped she remembered the combination. The top of the shoebox-sized case was embossed, 'Glock.'

Cory had a secure perch outside the window as he waited for all activity inside the apartment to stop. The lights were still on in the living room, which was piled with boxes, and he wondered if this just another front. But there had been movement inside and the night before Nolan had looked out these windows.

Finally satisfied that all motion inside was over for the night, he ever-so-slowly and quietly slid the window open. He stepped through, silently pushed the window back down and stretched his cramped legs. He tiptoed into the living room and his eyes fell on the drawing of himself. He froze as he realized his anonymity had entirely vanished.

Having felt a draft of cold air, Kat stepped out of the second bedroom with the opened blue case in her hands. She stopped and looked right into the face of the man she feared most. He was standing in her home staring at her.

Kat fumbled with the case, trying to extract the Glock and one of the two loaded ammo clips. She was screaming like a Banshee as Cory maneuvered rapidly through the mess of boxes and swatted at the gun case. It went flying and in a flash he had his hands around her throat. The screaming stopped and they were nose to nose as he saw terror in Nolan's eyes. She'd tell him what he needed to know.

Her thrashing about slowed while he listened for sounds from the other apartments, but heard nothing.

She collapsed in his hands and he put her on the couch, knowing she wouldn't be out long.

The old floor lamp came down on him like a hammer.

Barefoot, profoundly disoriented and unfocused, Joe watched the big man fall completely off his feet between the couch and coffee table. Cory skittered out of range under the table before Joe could get another shot at him, then grabbed Joe's foot and yanked him down. He pounced on top of Joe and this time he wasn't going to stop.

Somehow through his daze and deep in survival mode, Joe pushed off the floor with all his might. His smaller, compact size gave him leverage and the jolt he threw out made Cory's first punch go wide and hit the floor. Hard.

Cory yelped but didn't fully let go of Joe.

The bullet changed that.

Kat had found the gun and, with surprising expertise, she'd slammed a clip in place as she flipped off the safety. Kneeling, with a two-handed grip, she fired right at Cory and hit her target.

Joe managed one more gigantic shove that sent Cory tumbling backward, but he rolled onto his feet. He looked at Kat with the gun aimed at him knowing his own gun was still in his jacket pocket.

Cory dashed for the door, flung it open and was sailing down the entry stairs two at a time before Kat could even think about taking another shot.

———————

"THAT WINDOW THERE?" Enright said for the second time in disbelief. Cops were all around them, taking photos and samples of Cory's blood, dusting for fingerprints and digging the bullet Kat had fired from the wall. Enright stood with Kat in the sun porch looking at the window Cory had opened. He peered down toward the brick wall above the front door, then across at the other sun porches and saw shades open and people in every apartment looking out. Police lights flashed atop the cruisers on the street as Bittinger parked out front. Enright signaled to him, then said, "So our guy climbed up the front of the building?"

"Who thought you had to lock third floor windows?"

Enright realized Kat was trembling and put an arm around her shoulders to comfort her.

"I just couldn't shoot the second time," she said.

"You shot the first time, that's the one that counts," Enright said as he led her to the couch where Joe was propped up under the afghan. He was very drowsy.

He looked at them and seemed surprised to see Enright, as he said with a smile at Kat, "We make quite a team." She gently kissed him and whispered, "Go back to sleep." He complied, despite the hubbub of all the police around them.

Kat sat beside Joe as Enright sat on the coffee table across from her, next to the Glock case and the gun which no longer had a clip in it. "Shall we talk about this?"

"I'd never told Joe I own it. My dad insisted I have one and Joe's so dead-set against them, so, well..."

They both glanced at Joe sleeping.

Bitt arrived, gave Kat a ferocious hug, patted Joe on the head and took charge of the police presence. He looked like the most stressed person in the room, especially when he noticed the gun case and pistol. He gave Enright a worried look about it and received a hand signal to wait. Enright picked up the little Glock subcompact and that was when Kat noticed he was wearing latex gloves.

"I hadn't even looked at it in two years," she said.

"Light, powerful, easy to carry in your purse," he said, then handed the gun to one of the policemen, who put it in an evidence bag along with the ammo clips. "I'm glad you had it. Might have saved both your lives."

"I'd like to keep it," Kat admitted as she thought about the whole battle. For the first time ever, she was glad her dad had insisted she have that gun and the training to use it.

"No can do," Enright said. "Evidence." He then reached into his coat pocket and pulled out the little pistol he'd offered earlier. "Not half as nice as yours, but I want you to carry it until we have this prick in custody."

"Yeah," she said, taking it. "What about Joe?"

Enright spotted the lamp, which was now being bagged as evidence, and said, "He's got a couple ugly lamps left."

24

Betsy spotted the neon sign for a motel and decided to investigate even though she didn't know how she'd check in: they'd question her age, they'd have security cameras and they'd want a credit card. But she was freezing and she felt really exposed on the deserted streets near downtown. The motel had a few cars in the lot and stucco flaking off the wall outside the dimly-lit office. Even in low light, it looked ratty, but at least it didn't have security cameras. She waited in a shadow and watched a young woman in glittery high heels go into the office and breeze back out in about twenty seconds. She couldn't be much older than she was and Betsy started to get her hopes up.

"Hey there, girly-girl," a man said from behind her, startling the hell out of her.

She spun about and saw a drunken older man studying her just the way the guy in the diner had looked her over. A shiver ran up her spine and she hurried away as he called after, "Come back and party, honey-bunch."

As she reached the corner, she realized she had pulled the steak knife out of her coat sleeve. She looked back and no one was following, but she kept right on going. She thought about going back to the car, but finally decided that those men from the farm might be looking for it. She remembered in a book she'd read that a guy snuck into a boarded-up building to spend the night in safety and warmth. None of the buildings nearby was boarded-up, but she tried every door she came to, hoping one was unlocked.

It must have taken close to an hour before she tried a door that actually opened. She peered inside and the only thing illuminating the entryway was an ancient "Exit" sign that bathed it in an eerie green. A plywood sheet blocked off the stairs and the space was filled with trash and had a nasty smell, but she was alone and there was a working deadbolt on the door. She secured the outside door, pulled on every piece of clothing and scarf she had in her backpack and huddled up to try to sleep. It was damn cold, but she felt fairly certain she wouldn't be bothered.

ONLY TRAVIS and Simon knew what was really in the depths of the towing yard even though the guys who worked for them would often fetch the crappy old cars kept there. Simon made sure they all had up-to-date license plate tags, so they moved on the streets as if invisible. Deeper in the lot, there were a lot of totally junk cars that had come with the derelict business when they bought it; that was part of why they wanted it. One long-term resident of the yard was that precious old Ford Falcon that hadn't run in decades and attracted no attention from anyone at all.

Banks left a paper trail and posed all manner of difficulties for a cash business like theirs, so they kept a large stash of money buried deep inside the Falcon. Even a police search of the yard would be unlikely to locate their cash box, because Simon had custom-made it out of parts of the car itself. Their safe was indistinguishable from all the other junk in the yard. Only he and Travis knew it was there and he was the primary depositor of their cash. He'd secretly helped himself to the hidden money to fund his garage operation, but Travis rarely visited the stash and would never be able to figure out how much had been redirected into Simon's new project anyway. Now with Stacker dead and known to be an embezzler, any shortfall would be laid at that bastard's door, not Simon's.

Simon had taken one of the old cars from Travis' house when he went to find the pickup, which he then drove back to the yard. But all their other working cars were out with the men searching for that damned girl, so he walked a mile before calling one of the guys to come get him. With Abby's body in the pickup, he wanted to make sure that no one stopped at Cushing or knew he'd been there. As he waited in a dark entryway for his ride, he felt confident the girl would be found. There was an all-night 7-11 across the street, but he didn't want to be seen even this close to Cushing until long after Abby's body was gone. It would be leaving very soon in the truck, of that he was certain.

He was anxious to get back to ensure that Travis wasn't losing his grip on Cory. For his upcoming plan to work and leave him free to enjoy the aftermath in all its glory, he needed his fall guy. And there was no better patsy than a man with a grudge and a history of violence.

When the guy he'd called came to pick Simon up, he proudly announced they'd just found the car the girl had stolen, in an industrial area east of downtown. There was no sign of her and that bugged Simon, but not as much as the idiots preparing to bring the car back to the house. He stopped them cold and had them stake it out in case Betsy returned. The girl was a dangerous loose end that needed to be cleared up. The car might still lead to her.

———————

To Kat it felt like she'd just finally drifted off to sleep. After all the other cops had finally left, Enright and Bitt had helped her get the drowsy Joe back into bed and then taken off. Bitt had left a patrol car outside, so she felt safe enough to sleep. She was hoping for a few hours of rest before the sun rose, but just as she relaxed into her slumber, Joe sat bolt upright and turned on the light. He was clearly in pain, his medication had worn off.

As he fumbled on the nightstand for a pill, he saw she was awake. "All of that happened, didn't it?" he said.

Resigned, she propped up pillows and sat up. Joe was horrified to see the bruising all the way around her neck.

"He did that to you?"

"Right before you knocked his block off with a lamp."

He looked her over, softly touched her bruises and then gave her a most tender – and much appreciated – kiss.

"Why do I remember a gunshot then?"

"That's when I saved your life."

He sat in deep thought for a long moment, trying to organize his drug-addled memories of the fight. At last he said, "Thanks."

She pulled his arm around her shoulders, then snuggled tight until he said, "How'd you get his gun away from him?"

"I have something to tell you," Kat said.

Her explanations ended up taking what little remained of the night. They'd made coffee and cooked breakfast while Kat tried to reconstruct the shooting for him.

The sun was peeking through the kitchen curtains by the time she'd told him everything, including about the Glock, which the police had now taken, plus all her extensive gun training, the pistol Enright had succeeded in giving her and what it was like actually shooting someone.

In turn, he'd told her about the two guns he'd ever touched in his life. He'd taken them both from his mother when she still lived in the house where he'd grown up. She was intending to use them when he'd confiscated them from her. At the time, he had promised himself it would be the end of his relationship with guns. Still, he couldn't fault her for shooting the guy trying to kill them.

———————

THE GUY in the yard let Cory in. The pain in his back had settled into a very deep and steady throb that reminded him with every heartbeat that he was still alive. He wanted Abby to patch him up as he felt the back of his jacket with his hand to find that it was matted with blood. Of course, Abby was nowhere to be found and all their things were still at the farm. He was never going back there, so he'd have to find bandages in Travis' house.

When he heard the muffled sounds of shooting from the gun range in the basement, and no one was at the couch or in the kitchen, he headed down to see if it was Travis. He needed advice. Travis had steered him right for years, until he opposed Abby and said, "Guys like us don't need permanent connections." It had seemed like an echo of Simon's world view, but Travis had remained free of entanglements all these years, so he clearly believed it.

Ever since he'd taken up with Abby and left the partnership with Travis, Cory had believed his friend had been truly wrong about relationships. Now, he was starting to wonder if Travis hadn't been right. Those family connections he'd formed were now tearing him up inside and left him susceptible to the government. Maybe that's what Travis had tried to protect him from.

"I don't think they're coming back," Travis said as if reading his mind. He was reloading a thirty-round magazine and they were alone in the gun range, where Travis had been shooting since Cory left. Nothing felt better to him in times of stress than firing hundreds of rounds.

Ashamed of his failure, Cory was hesitant to reveal the wound in his back, so he sat on a stool at the loading bench and watched as cartridges were threaded into one of a stack of magazines for the automatic weapon.

Travis noticed blood all over the cuff of Cory's jacket and then discovered the bloody back. "Jesus, man. Was it the cops? They follow you?"

"One of the agents who took my boy. I got away clean."

"You sure about that?" Travis asked as he led him up the stairs.

"Yeah."

Together they wrestled Cory's jacket, shirt and finally undershirt off. The bullet had grazed right across those big muscles of Cory's back and dug a trench. Travis wadded up the t-shirt and pressed it to the wound and had his friend lie face down on the couch. He was glad the guys weren't around, a bullet wound would get talked about.

Travis went to fetch the medical kit Simon had stocked for them. It had come in handy a few times. He put towels under Cory to keep the blood off the couch, then went to work on his friend's back. It was a great back, rippling with muscles like most guys only dreamed of having.

"What do you think I should do?" Cory asked.

"I'm not saying anyone is dead, but you've done everything possible to find them, right? Travis said. Cory nodded. "It can't be good, if they're even still..." He let that soak in. "It's anybody's guess what those bastards would do to them. They just shot you, for fuck's sake."

He cleaned the wound with alcohol and knew it had to hurt a lot, but Cory was silent, just as Travis expected.

He knew what Simon wanted him to say, but he also sensed how crazy his friend would become when he heard it.

"Just say it, man," Cory said. "Don't hold back."

"The government have them," Travis said. "Can you see them coming back as the people you lost? That's if...if any of them are even...still alive."

A shudder tore through Cory like an earthquake before he turned on his side to look at Travis. Twisting hurt like hell, but his mind was too filled with his family to allow the pain to consume him. "Am I crazy to hope they're okay?"

"You're the one who told me about implants. Mind control..." Travis said, going back to Simon's script. "What'd they do in the hospital to your boy, you suppose?"

Cory rolled back. Travis laid out a series of four by four gauze pads on the wound and started to tape them in place. "I mean, if they really did get implants..."

'It's already too late,' Cory thought. 'They're gone.'

"What's your gut say?" Travis said as he pressed the tape in place and his hands lingered to firm it down.

"I don't know," Cory said. He looked back at Travis imploringly. "I trust your gut more than mine. I barely even got half a vibe off that guy in juvie..." He stopped himself, ashamed he'd brought up the forbidden subject.

Travis was silent as he added tape and took his time applying it while they both remembered beating Garmon.

From the front steps, Simon could see inside through the glass in the door as he got out his key to let himself in. He saw Travis sitting on the couch with his hands on Cory's bare back as he lay there face down. To Simon it was a confirmation, even before Travis leapt up and looked a bit guilty after he'd entered. When he was inside, Simon finally saw the bandages.

"What the hell happened?"

While Cory pulled himself off the couch and to his full height, Simon caught a shrug from Travis. With his shirt off, there was something feral about Cory, Simon thought. He was bigger and stronger than normal people, he had a rage inside that seemed to radiate and fill the room. As long as he was in their control, he was perfect for his plans. Out of their control, he would be the toughest tiger in the jungle.

"One of the agents shot him. Grazed him," Travis said.

"I got away. No one's following," Cory said and went to pull on his bloody shirt, but Travis stopped him.

"I'll find you something," Travis said and ran off.

Cory looked guiltily at Simon. He'd left the house, he'd approached those agents, he'd gotten himself shot. All of it against Simon's wise advice.

Travis came back with a t-shirt, his largest sweater and a pain pill. "You better take this. That's gonna hurt like a bitch pretty soon."

Cory threw back the pill and pulled on the t-shirt.

Simon turned to business and reminded them why he'd gone out. He extracted the bogus magnetic tracker device from his pocket. "There it is, man," he said, offering it to Cory. "It was on top of the gas tank. Even if you'd been looking, without my electronic scanner, you'd never have found that sucker."

"This was in my truck?" Cory said, staring at the device in amazement.

Travis angrily shook his head. "Those bastards."

"This led them right to the farm house," Simon said. "Obviously I cut off the signal before bringing it here."

Cory stared blindly at the tracker, too numb to think. He paced about, clutching the sweater, blood already seeping through the bandages into the t-shirt, but he didn't notice. He was torn between tears and frenzy.

Travis remembered one of the lines Simon had fed him. "You can't get them back, Cory, but you can get even."

"Revenge is sweet," Simon added. "And that's something we could help you with."

Cory looked at Travis and finally to Simon.

"What I gotta do?" he said.

25

E nright watched Joe approach down the hallway of the City Hall and Courthouse. Unlike the last time he'd see him following the break-in, Joe was awake and dressed like a regular ADA, but his face was still anything but normal. The ear was especially red, but the crooked smile was back. He was coming from court, where he'd just been denied an extension of the seventy-two hour psychiatric evaluation. The boy would be secure only for one more day.

"You haven't gotten your cell phone back?" Enright asked. "I had to come find you the old fashioned way. Mike's mounting a tribunal in a few hours."

"The police found my cell with a homeless guy. Now forensics is processing it in case our guy touched it."

They headed to the elevator as Enright said, "Your intruder didn't leave any clues for us. No prints from the brick or the window or anywhere inside your place."

"It's still all a bit fuzzy for me."

"Seen the paper yet?" he said, holding up the St. Paul Pioneer Press with the drawing of Cory on the front page.

"At least there's no picture of me being beaten up."

"Or the way you look right now."

"Thanks."

As they reached the front entrance, they found Bittinger heading in. "Who's the woman answering your cell phone, Joe? Police tech?" he said, then looked at his face closely. "Looks like a pomegranate, know what I mean?"

"Yeah, we're all glad it's not in the paper," Enright said, showing the front page to Bitt.

"That's why I'm here, we're getting calls up the wazoo," Bitt said. "We got witness interviews...want to tag along for the semi-rational ones?"

Enright's SUV was illegally parked outside the door and being guarded by a policeman, who nodded to them and strolled off as they climbed in.

Bittinger worked out of the Grove Street offices of the St. Paul Police. The plan was he and and Enright were going to divide up the interviewees who had made it through the first round on the telephone with other officers.

"What about Elephant Man?" Bitt said, speaking of Joe.

"He watches from the observation room?"

"Okay. I'll set it up and send over an icepack."

A 'wanted' drawing in the news always brought out the crazies, the needy and the guilt-stricken. Many could be ruled out on the phone, but it still left a sizable group of questionable witnesses for in-person interviews.

Joyce Pond wasn't questionable. She was old, but she was a reliable witness who had actually chatted with the man at a library less than a mile from the arson site. Joe sat in the observation room with a borrowed cellphone so he could call Enright with any questions he wanted to add. When Joyce talked about the real estate listings she'd seen the man printing out, Joe called Enright.

"Was he looking for a new place for the family before burning the other one down?" he said to Enright.

"Was it traditional real estate listings, Ma'am?"

"It was almost like tax records, but with addresses that he was writing down," she said. "He was quite polite," she added. "He didn't look like a killer."

After Joyce there were a dozen dead ends and Enright's tolerance was flagging. The public as a group was a strange and disquieting experience: confessions, impossible sightings and a couple alien abductions. Fortunately they kept going until a very excited Kurt Messner was shown in.

"His name's Cory. He's been trimming trees and plowing my drive for a couple years," Kurt said enthusiastically.

"Last name? Address?" Enright asked, his interest definitely piqued.

"Sorry. He always insisted on cash payments. I just knew him as Cory. He's got a boy name of Patrick Henry, like the patriot. Wish I knew more."

"You know more than we do so far," Enright said with renewed energy as he answered Joe's call.

"I'm coming in."

"Cory beat up one of our men yesterday..." Enright said, trying to soften the blow before Joe stepped in.

Kurt was aghast when he saw Joe's swollen face and ear. "Cory did that?"

"Yeah. He attacked me and unfortunately got away."

"He's got muscles like you won't believe," Kurt said. "I sure as hell wouldn't want to tangle with him."

"Neither did I," Joe said. "So how well you know him?"

"He's a bit stand-offish, but nice enough. Hard to believe I've had him at my house a dozen times. Jesus."

"Inside? Maybe he left fingerprints?" Enright said.

"No...never came in. Just came to the door to be paid

after he'd plow and shovel. Trimmed trees for me a couple
years ago and another one just last Sunday," Kurt said. "He
climbs with a belt, carrying chainsaws and scrambles right
up like a monkey. He had his boy cutting up the branches.
Scared me to death seeing the boy with a small chainsaw,
but they were a great team. Boy's a math genius."

"How'd you contact Cory?"

"Almost forgot!" Kurt said excitedly. He pulled out his
cell phone and scrolled through his recent calls, then
showed them a number that Enright wrote down. "He never
answered when I called. I'd leave a message and he'd show
up. With snowstorms he'd stop by on his own, check with
me and then do it. With the tree, I had to call."

Enright left the room with the number and Kurt studied
Joe's face. "Am I going to need police protection?"

"We'll have him in custody very soon and then he's
going away for a very long time," Joe said. "You ever chat
with him? What's he like?"

"He's the kind of guy who names his son Patrick Henry
and home schools him and has him memorize the famous
Revolutionary War speech. Very patriotic, I guess."

"Patriotic? Did he talk about love for our country? Did
he serve in the military? Anything you remember might
help us narrow in on him."

"His 'cash only' insistence...I always assumed it was sort
of a tax dodge," Kurt said. "That won't get me in trouble, will
it? Paying him cash?"

"It's his duty to declare it, not yours. So no."

"He did rail on about taxes and the government once,
then he abruptly stopped. I got the impression he saw the
government kind of like they were the enemy. Don't know
how that jibes with the patriotism, to tell you the truth."

CORY HAD BEEN asleep in the room he'd shared with Abby and Betsy until he was roused by Travis. In the living room the TV was frozen on the drawing of him. Together with Simon they watched the report that tied this 'person of interest' with a murder and arson, to which now aggravated assault and home invasion had just been added by the police. Cory watched in stunned silence.

"Everyone in Minnesota is looking for you, Cor," Travis said, putting an arm around him to console him.

"How'm I gonna get revenge on these bastards?"

"Start by not getting yourself caught before we can put a plan together," Simon said.

"They talk about Abby, Betsy and Patrick Henry?"

"They don't say shit about them...that's how they do it," Simon said. "They broadcast everything they're trying to pin on you and hide all the shit they did themselves."

Simon figured Cory would soon learn it was Stacker at the scene of the fire so he needed to get ahead of that.

"This thing is biting us in the ass, too," Simon said and found Travis looking at him quizzically as he ventured into unscripted territory. "They killed one of our guys."

"Who did?" Cory asked, quite surprised.

"This is the way they work," Simon said, "first they pinned that arson on you and then the government put that body on your property. They're looking to cook you."

Cory shook his head in disgust but he believed it.

"The body they left at your house when they burned it down...he was one of our guys. One of us, Cory," Simon said. "That shows you how far they'll go to frame you."

Travis stayed silent, doing his best to catch up with this new direction Simon hadn't warned him was coming.

"These agents have such a hard-on for you," Simon said as he clicked the remote to freeze the picture of Cory with 'Wanted: armed and dangerous' below it.

"If we hadn't seen it before – everywhere from Waco to Ruby Ridge – it would be hard to believe they'd actually kill a guy and plant his body just to fuck you, but that's the way they work," Simon said. He was getting excited.

"You guys remember those two brothers who bombed the Boston Marathon, right?" Simon went on and they both nodded. He was an expert on the crimes of the government.

"Something most people don't remember is what the FBI did about a month after the marathon. They scoured the world for every friend of those brothers they could find. They located a guy in Florida and were in the middle of an interview with him when they shot him in cold blood. Killed him and said he attacked them. Ten fucking agents and he attacked them...with a kitchen knife, they said. Fuckers."

"And they killed one of your guys?"

Cory had just made another important transition. He agreed to the conclusion first, before having all the facts. Simon had been waiting for this moment.

"Yeah, Leo Stacker."

"I've met him," Cory said, jumping out of his seat.

"They pin a murder on you on top of the arson they set," Travis said having finally caught up. "They're saying three assaults, so they just pile it on."

"I am so completely fucked," Cory said.

"You've been right about the government all along," Travis said with enthusiasm. But as he watched Cory seem to implode, it confirmed what Simon had been saying – Cory really wasn't right for The Movement. Not like he was.

"Gives you an idea of how long they've been watching

you," Simon said. "We're keeping all the guys away now, plus Travis and I have put everything on hold ourselves."

"That's right. It's getting dicey here," Travis said.

Cory was swirling and Simon figured he was ready to commit. "The murder adds more weight to their case against you," Simon said. "They target you, zero in on a guy you know, then blame his death on you."

Cory's paranoia spiked as he tried to encompass the government making so many assaults on him. It confirmed that they were out to destroy him, once and for all.

"This screws us all, Cory, not just you," Simon said. "That tracker on your truck might already have led them here. They might even be going after all of us right now. We're all being pulled into this clusterfuck."

Travis added, "We been doing emergency clean-up all morning, having lost one of our guys like that, worrying they might follow from you to him...to us."

Cory slumped onto the couch, head in his hands as tremors wracked his body. "They really aren't coming back." He turned to Travis with tears in his eyes. "I kept thinking it would get fixed somehow."

"It's not going to get fixed," Simon said. "Your family's gone. What we have to do, all of us, is protect ourselves and figure out how to avenge them. We need to show them there are consequences."

Travis sat down, arm around Cory's shoulders as the big man sobbed. Simon watched, fascinated how the right words and a bit of effective misinformation could mold a susceptible man into someone willing to do the unspeakable.

Cory was primed and ready.

Betsy almost walked right past the newspaper rack in the small shop, but the picture on the front page stopped her in her tracks. And it took her breath away. Stunned, she bought a paper and her heart sank as she read below her dad's face, all the lies about things they said he'd done. No matter what they said, she knew for a fact he didn't burn their home down. 'And who was dead?' she wondered. Just half-asking the question brought her back to Mom and she started to fall apart.

"You all right?" the clerk in the shop said to her.

She ran out, down the block and around the corner before she looked back. And she found the knife in her hand as she realized she was crying. Every terrible thing Dad had ever told them about the world was true.

She wiped her eyes, threw out the paper and realized there was no going back to that farm house. She wanted nothing to do with that guy's place filled with guns. She just had to hope Dad would return to the plaza soon, because she couldn't see any other options.

Not much could quiet a roomful of assistant district attorneys, but as Joe entered Mike Westermann's office for what was called a 'tribunal,' the place went silent. This wasn't even the first time he'd shocked his colleagues so dramatically. Once he'd taken his shirt off to show them his childhood scars and stunned everyone spectacularly. This time his new wounds were even more visible.

"Jesus, Joe," Stacy said. "I went into law because it's a non-contact sport."

"I guess I missed that on the job description," Joe said as he tolerated everyone's cringing at his face.

"I once came out of a Northwestern game looking a bit like that," Mike Westermann said. He'd played linebacker for the University of Minnesota and had never shied away from contact sports. "I saw the video, Joe..."

"Along with fourteen million of your friends," said Ronald Sheldon with a slight sneer. Joe was a constant focus of his disdain.

"You landed four solid punches," Mike said with a glare at Ronald. "I doubt any of us could have done better against that guy."

"I'd'a called backup first," Ronald said.

Enright looked up from his phone and said, "Just about two hundred thousand hits on YouTube." He held out the phone to show the starting image of the viral video with Joe's fist to Cory's face. "He was calling for backup when the guy attacked him, Ronald. He fought back."

Everyone had the drawing of Cory, because the tribunal had all been convened to discuss the case against him. Mike said, "What we got on this guy now?"

"His name is Cory, he's a tree trimmer and plows snow in the winter," Joe said. "No last name yet, but his son is named Patrick Henry and the boy's birth was not registered in the county or state. We think there's a wife and maybe a daughter named Betsy. All of them live off the grid."

"His buddy who pistol-whipped an orderly before Cory finished the job...we think they know each other from jail maybe," Enright added. "We're also tracking his sheepskin coat. He paid three thousand in cash for it."

"The murder victim found at the fire was a drug dealer named Leo Stacker," Joe said. "We're slogging through Stacker's known associates for Cory or his friend."

"What about the boy?" Mike asked.

"We have him on a seventy-two hour observation at a children's psych ward, but it expires tomorrow," Joe said.

"We learn anything from that?" Stacy asked.

"He calls us 'your kind' and says our laws don't apply to him or his family," Joe said. "Seems pretty clear Dad is a self-styled insurrectionist who hates the government."

"The feeling's mutual at this point," Mike said.

"We got a phone number Cory gives to tree trimming clients," Enright said. "Of course, it's a burner phone and set to no-ring voice mail. Detective Ed Bittinger is on this with us and tracking it down. Seems Cory accesses that voice mail from pay phones – who knew they still existed? – mostly in the vicinity of the library we know he frequents. We're having those phones fingerprinted, might get lucky."

"Bittinger pinged the phone and found it tucked behind an ice cream freezer in a bodega. They didn't even know it was there because the ringer and vibrate were both off," Joe said. "The phone was wiped clean and nowhere near where he lived. This guy is super careful and ultra-paranoid. We left the phone in case it's accessed again."

"You gotta mop this up fast," Ronald said. "Big fires on TV, street fights and a junky murder victim..."

"Meth head, actually," Enright said.

"Either way, you left this guy running around town doing a lot of high profile damage," Ronald said.

"Nobody left him, Ronald," Enright said.

"The big question is what's he going to do next," Joe said. "We have his son and he attacked me because he wants him back. What if the placement of our fight isn't accidental? What if he was at the plaza for another reason than me?"

Mike silenced both his cell phones and the room was filled with disturbing thoughts.

"He names his boy for a near-anarchist and lives off the

grid. He hated the government <u>before</u> his son fell from a tree," Joe said. "Imagine what he feels about us now."

"Just because he's focused on you doesn't mean he wants to take on the whole government," Ronald said.

"He knew who I was. How'd he know that?" Joe said. "He kept shouting, 'Where the fuck you got him?'"

"He was looking for you specifically?" Mike said. "And hours later he broke into your home?"

"He knows more about us than we know about him."

"About the arson..." Enright said and every eye turned to him. "FBI's explosives expert says it was sophisticated and designed to showcase his artistry."

Stacy picked up the drawing of Cory. "This guy is some kind of artist with a firebomb?"

"Might be," Enright said. "Denny, the expert, says that the arson fire was perfectly planned and executed."

"And a drug dealer was left there to be blown to smithereens," Joe added.

"For purposes we can't yet fathom?" Mike asked.

Enright and Joe both nodded.

"I don't like this guy," Mike said. "You two, meet with the explosives expert. I want to know if they think we're in for anything bigger from this guy. Pull together some worst case scenarios. I want to know if this is going to escalate."

———

CORY WAS DRY-EYED AND ANGRY. Simon was glad the time of emotional shit was over and they could now work on directing that rage. The build-up to fantasies of revenge was underway and it was clear that Cory couldn't focus on an actual, tangible goal of retribution. Travis hated the government too, though he didn't buy all the conspiracies that drove Cory. His greatest fear was the power of the authorities to destroy him and his business. He wanted Cory to get back at them for him, so he could move on to bigger and better things with Simon.

"We know where the two agents are. We break bones and leave them in a coma," Travis said.

"Is that enough of a statement for Cory?" Simon asked.

Cory had so much flak in his mind, he couldn't really nail down the specifics of Travis' suggestion. All he felt was the need to do something big, something meaningful.

Travis had been looking for an opportunity to remind Cory of the true depth of their past, the fact that they had been here – almost here – before. Finally he said, "Some people deserve to die for what they've done."

Cory looked Travis right in the eye; he'd heard his friend say those exact words once before, shortly after he and Travis had escaped from juvie. Revenge had been called for then and they had exacted it together. "Yeah," he said.

Simon saw the exchange between them and knew nothing of the frame of reference, but it didn't matter. Travis had handed him what he needed. Now he had to get a serious commitment from them both to take it to that level.

Back then, right after juvie, Travis had been desperate to get revenge and death had been the obvious and only acceptable end. As he looked from his stricken friend to Simon's cold eyes, he saw death was probably just as necessary this time – for Cory's sake. He nodded to Simon.

"If people die," Simon said to Cory, "you know who they'll come looking for, right?"

"I'm already a killer in their eyes and that bitch already shot me once. I got nothing to lose."

"So you're willing to take the heat?" Simon said.

"Yeah."

"You'd have to go on the run after we take action."

Travis and Cory locked eyes thinking about Garmon and how that night had forever changed their lives. It was their greatest bond and Cory felt it in his bones all over again, as they nodded to each other and looked to Simon.

"So we all agree where this needs to go?" Simon said with apparent calm. "Both agents die."

26

E nright insisted on driving the eight blocks from the DA's offices to St. Paul Plaza and Joe rode along for the meeting with Denny at the FBI offices.

"Forensics wants to keep your phone a bit longer," Enright said as he parked illegally and put a DA Office placard up in the window. "They're not done with it yet."

"They expect me to go an entire day without my phone?"

"Primitive, eh?" Enright said as they walked through the wind tunnel formed by the tall buildings and onto the open plaza, surrounded on three sides by government buildings. Kat's was on the middle side. "So why was Cory here if he wasn't tailing you? You saw him first, right?"

"Yeah, he attacked the instant he spotted me."

"You bring that out in some guys." Enright said.

"Like Ronald? Yeah," Joe said.

They headed to see Denny in the FBI Building.

After she winced at the sight of him, she held up her cellphone, "Seen it. You should have picked a smaller guy."

"Wish I'd thought of that."

"Judging by the video, I'd say his face is feeling the pain

too," she said, leading them through the spacious FBI offices and back to the same meeting room.

"My girlfriend shot and wounded him last night when he broke into our place," Joe said.

"Your girlfriend packs?" Denny said. "I like her."

"Me too."

"Then you better be good to her," Denny said.

"From the looks of it, the wound won't stop him, but it probably saved their lives," Enright said.

Denny opened the folder. "I've been researching similar cases...anything reminiscent of shotgun shells or the propane tank. Trying to see what our boy has been up to before this."

"Tell me he isn't prolific," Enright said.

"The shotgun shell explosive device has been used before," Denny said. "Regionally."

"Like what?"

"A grain elevator that led to a spreading rural fire. A couple warehouses which were probably arson-for-hire. A storefront mom-and-pop," Denny said. "No one caught in any of them. Just like our guy in this latest arson, the setter is long gone before the fire goes up."

"So it's the same guy?" Joe asked.

"Could be or he could be learning from others."

"Arson-for-hire...doesn't sound personal. That's just making a living out of what he's good at," Joe said. "I really hope this is business and not some obsession."

"No insurance payout on the mom-and-pop or the grain elevator, but no grudges we could find either," Denny said. "It could be a mix of business and pleasure for him."

"What about propane tanks being used as bombs?"

"It's harder to sort the accidents from intentional, but quite a few tanks have exploded in other places with rather spectacular results," she said and pulled from the folder several photos showing the remains of tanks that had blown up. Half the tank itself remained after the pressure was let out in one section or from the whole top peeling back, but everything around the tank was decimated by the blast. In one photo that included a house that was now just sticks and tufts of couch stuffing. "A lot of power, huh?"

"Damn, and he knows all this..." Enright said.

"Where's this leave us with him?" Joe said.

"Let me ask you. What do you make of this patriotism thing of his?" Denny said.

"Either of you read the Declaration of Independence lately?" Joe said and found their heads shaking no. "It's a call to insurrection, to the overthrow of the existing – albeit nasty – government."

"Yeah, but we were right. Right?" Enright said.

"History is written by those who win," Joe said. "If we'd lost the Revolutionary War, all our Founding Fathers would have been called traitors and they'd be vilified."

"So Patrick Henry wasn't actually a good guy?"

"Judgment call. He stirred up the populace, they rose up and drove out the oppressors. Whether he was good or bad depends mostly on whether you're one of those oppressors or the people freed from oppression."

"So he was a bad guy to King George?" Enright said.

"Yeah and who's King George in Cory's world view?"

"That would be us," Denny said.

They thought about that for an uncomfortable moment.

"When I ran into him, it was right down there," Joe said, pointing out the window. "This plaza is surrounded by government buildings."

They looked out at the work places of much of the government and thousands of employees.

"If insurrection against an oppressive government is what makes this guy tick," Denny said, "then we got a whole lot of 'worst cases' to figure out. The state capitol is six blocks away and right here are the FBI, the IRS, Public Safety, plus state and federal administrative offices."

"It's a long ways from shotgun shells in a barn to government buildings," Enright said. "What level of anger we looking at? Kill the city, kill a crowd or just you?"

"He seemed to be in the plaza for his own reasons. I'm positive he didn't know I'd be there. Attacking me was sort of an afterthought. He seized an opportunity."

"He was probably searching for the boy, right? That's what he was shouting about," Enright said.

"Think that's what was on his mind before he saw you?" Denny said. "What else did the original Patrick Henry say besides 'Give me liberty or give me death'?"

"'If this be treason...make the most of it'."

Enright whistled under his breath.

Denny sorted through the most destructive propane explosions and said, "He might have some grandiose ideas."

They all thought about self-styled revolutionaries. Joe shook his head and said, "He's just a guy in a pickup truck with a vicious knee. How big can his dreams be?"

"He's an arsonist, Joe," Denny said. "Almost by definition an arsonist is a dreamer. He aspires, he's waiting to see the power he can unleash."

"Frightening thought." Joe asked.

"You feel powerless against someone you can't fight or overcome face to face..."

"Plus he has political obsessions," Enright said.

"If he hates the government and has ambitions of destroying us," Denny said, "he's got a dangerous skill set. His plans could expand to just about any scale."

"I really don't like this guy," Enright said.

———————

THERE WAS a pain in Cory's chest that eclipsed anything he'd ever felt in his life. It was an endless stabbing spasm that radiated out through his body and made it nearly impossible to think, to plan, even to react to Travis, who was blathering on.

"We could do both Nolan and Brandt in the middle of the night, assassination-like..." Travis said.

"Alone in their homes doesn't make much of a public statement," Simon said. "It just pisses off every agent in town and invites them to chase Cory down like a dog."

"It needs to be a statement," Cory said. "But how?"

"Leave that to me," Simon said as he rose to his feet. "I gotta run this past The Movement. We're talking about taking out a couple agents, so they'll want to weigh in."

"They're not gonna stop us, are they?" Travis asked.

"Not a chance, but I have to give them a heads up."

"What's The Movement?" Cory asked.

Simon lit up. "When we went our separate ways after Redwing, I found them. Really they found me."

"I never heard of them," Cory said.

"Ain't it perfect? That's their genius," Travis said.

"It grew out of The Grange Movement after the Civil War," Simon said. "It's the most powerful anti-government group in the country. Formed by people who want to be left alone and have the guts to fight back. Free men."

"David Koresh and those guys?" Cory asked.

"More secret, more effective and much more powerful."

"Right up your alley, ain't it, Cor?" Travis said.

"Travis and I already help them out with resources, guns

and finance," Simon said. "Plus I still go stay with them several times a year, take part in covert actions."

Cory thought about it and finally shook his head. "I'm not a group joiner," Cory said.

"The Movement is going to help us make you disappear after this," Simon said. "Take as much or as little as you want from them, but there is no one on earth is better at living an untraceable life of insurrection than they are."

Travis was excited, but Cory seemed overwhelmed as he finally said, "As long as we get revenge."

"Count on it, my friend," Simon said.

———————

JOE TOOK a taxi from the FBI offices to the Grove Street police station for a meeting Bittinger had set up for him. Despite the cold, Enright walked around the plaza, gazing at the buildings. There were too many to guard and they had nothing but suppositions to go on. It might not even be what Cory had been here to do. Denny had given them details about Oklahoma City and the World Trade Center, both the initial truck bombing and the 9/11 plane attack, which had created an overpowering unease in him.

Betsy was heading through the square when she passed Enright. They didn't know each other and had no reason to notice the passing. The only thing they shared was the desire to get out of the cold wind. She had spent hours inside the DMV building, moving from one waiting area to another, so she didn't stand out. Every hour she'd gone out to look for her father and on the last trip she'd spotted the main library.

Unseen by either of them inside the Family Services building, Kat was waiting in line to go through security so she could go up to her office. She was late and for the first time ever, she was carrying a gun in her purse. She fished out the concealed-carry permit her dad had insisted she get. Even so, the look she got from the guard was odd. But one glimpse at the guards' newspaper open to the picture of Cory reminded her of the battle last night. She'd carry the gun until this was over.

"At least it's not a terribly common name," said Anne Jensen, the computer tech Bittinger had set Joe up to meet.

"If Cory is even his real name."

"Let's find out," Anne said. She searched the state and county as well as the entire past and present prison system. Though Joe assured her Cory wouldn't have a current driver's license, they scanned through them, as well as prisoner photos, but came up with no one Joe recognized. Once they'd exhausted the adult records, Joe, as an ADA, authorized her to delve into the sealed juvenile records.

There had only been three boys named Cory in the Minnesota juvenile corrections system who were anywhere in the target age range. When the photo of the third one came up, Joe gasped. In the photo, he was younger and thinner, but Joe knew those eyes, they still held the same rage. Cory Trammell was the man he'd fought twice.

"Huh, look at that," Anne said. "Trammell's last day in Red Wing was 9/11 in 2001. The 9/11."

"Just coincidence?"

"Let's find out," Anne said, doing her tricks with the database. "Nope, it wasn't his release date, he walked away. He wasn't set to get out for several more months."

"How do you walk away from juvie? It's like prison."

Digging deeper, Anne found out more. "Every day but that day. Seems there was a riot among the kids after they saw the planes crash and the towers come down. Quite a few boys walked away in the chaos that followed. It says a door was carelessly left open and the boys just streamed out."

"Who else took off that day."

"Nineteen boys."

"They round them up?"

"Well...no. Basically they got released a few months early. Everyone was pretty distracted following 9/11."

"Jesus."

"BOLOs were put out for all the boys who took off, but they didn't mount a dragnet-style search. It's juvie, after all," Anne said. "Not like it's killers and rapists."

"The youngest rapists go there," Joe said.

"Those who ran and then got themselves arrested again, they added months to their sentences, but otherwise..."

"Can we print out names and photos?" Joe asked.

Anne printed out pictures of the nineteen boys, but none of them quite jumped out like Trammell had. All Joe had was murky security camera frame-captures, the guy in the sheepskin coat wasn't someone he'd met face to face.

There were no clear hits, so Anne tracked them into adulthood, which proved depressing. Juvenile detention often seemed to lead to continued criminal activity. Even so, most of the escapees had since gotten driver's licenses and Anne pulled up pictures. Again, no one looked familiar.

She discovered Cory Trammell never showed up in any record, anywhere ever again. He disappeared completely from all official records on 9/11/2001. That walk-away was his last recorded event. One other boy seemed to disappear for nearly five years. Travis Devins had been just as off-the-grid as Trammell until about a dozen years ago. Then he'd been arrested for an assault near a gay bar. It hadn't been labeled a hate crime, just a fist-fight that escalated to using a brick against the other guy's head. He'd done a few months and there'd been a record of his existence since.

"Both of them were listed as foster kids and neither went back to the homes they'd had before juvie," Anne said as she dug deeper. "When they turned eighteen, even those BOLOs were removed and their records sealed."

Anne managed to find photos of Devins and they agreed he might be the man in the sheepskin coat.

"Can we cross reference them with Stacker?" Joe asked.

A few keystrokes later, Anne had Leo Stacker listed as a known associate of Travis Devins. Bingo.

27

As he drove out to Coon Rapids, Simon found himself smiling. After his failure to blow up Stacker, he'd been seriously disappointed. That explosion was meant to be a signature event, an outrageous mystery the media and authorities could talk about for ages. They might never have solved it, but if they had, they would have blamed Cory. Either outcome would have left him in the clear. It had been a setback, but everything was looking up again.

For him it had long been clear that the key to a successful operation was having someone the authorities would blame. While his new plan had gestated for a long time, the last key to the puzzle had plagued him until Cory walked back into his life with his abundance of trouble. At every juncture, he'd made his own problems worse, turning himself into a major target of the government. What a gift.

Having a thoroughly believable fall guy made any great crime potentially perfect. Someone who was alive at the beginning and dead at the end, someone law enforcement could close their investigation around – a lone gunman, a mad bomber, a crazed killer for the police, media and public to believe in. Afterwards they would wring their hands and call for more psychologists in schools or diligence in police work. And most importantly, the perfect patsy as sole perpetrator would provide all the answers.

There would be no search for the author of the crime, the real creator of death and destruction. They would have their ready-made answers all wrapped up in one dead man.

With Cory to blame everything on, Simon would enjoy his grand statement without a single recrimination or fear.

He'd told Cory and Travis that he had to get approval from The Movement, but what he really needed was time to get ready, to finish his months of preparations in secrecy so he could capitalize on having the ideal man to blame.

When he neared his garage, he parked well away and walked until he had a view of the Fluff and Fold. He'd been careless when Stacker spotted him and lucky the idiot never told anyone. Twitch might also need to be erased, but every loose end would be cleared only when the time was right.

Inside the garage with its blacked-out windows, Simon turned on the lights and the heat before facing his prized possession – courtesy of Travis' Ford Falcon money – the plumbing truck. He dug into his work with fervor while his mind raced and, as always happened when he worked alone, Simon lost track of time. He was his own best company.

Even using an engine lift, it had taken over an hour to wrestle the three hundred and thirty gallon tank into the back of the plumbing truck.

The body of the truck was a Ford 250 pickup, heavy duty for carrying a professional plumber's rig. It had long metal tool cribs along both sides, pipe racks above and a portion of the truck bed that was originally left open to carry anything from a water heater to a bathtub. It was now filled with the large tank. The truck was old and well-worn and had seen a couple hundred thousand miles. It was the real deal, which made it look completely unremarkable.

When he bought it at a blind auction, he didn't yet have a concrete plan, just a dream that had grown feverishly in the back of his mind since the day he'd seen the twin towers collapse. Now that had been a show! Everyone on earth had paid attention, millions of people had mobilized and everyone said life changed that day. Talk about one individual mastermind seizing genuine power.

As Ralph Waldo Emerson had said, 'There's no limit to what can be accomplished if it doesn't matter who gets the credit.' The same was true of blame. Simon believed that the genuine creators of unnatural disasters were rarely those who were held accountable. He felt certain the men actually responsible for major man-made catastrophes had all anonymously reveled in the power of their destruction from the safety of concealment.

With funds from the Falcon, he'd leased this garage before he hunted down the truck. All along, he'd been steadily accumulating the tools and parts he needed, while also devising several genuinely ingenious mechanisms.

First he had the mundane chore of welding the large tank in place, then securing the scuba tanks. He'd already built a fitted top to enclose the open back of the truck to conceal the various tanks, plus some of his inventions. He'd fashioned many connectors and mechanisms to make the device work that he could access behind the tailgate. Closed up, the truck would never look like it was carrying three hundred and thirty gallons of pure explosive power.

While he worked, he ran the calculations for the hundredth time. One cup of gasoline had the same power as sixteen sticks of dynamite, so three hundred and thirty gallons of gas, assuming perfectly efficient energy release, was the explosive equivalent of one megaton.

He'd never achieve total efficiency and the speed of combustion for gasoline was a lot slower than a nuclear bomb, but even so, the raw power was there. The key was that he would vaporize the gasoline so it would explode just like fuel injected into a car engine. Atomized gas would be injected into a gigantic cylinder and detonated, so all that power would blast directly outward. It would wreak an amazing amount of damage to everything around it.

In 2001, jet fuel fell from the planes and pooled in the bottom of the Twin Towers elevator shafts, which left vapor permeating the shafts. The fuel that burned at the bottom weakened the building foundations, then explosions inside the elevator shafts themselves brought down the buildings. His plan was an explosion, followed by fire and then collapse, a variation on what happened on 9/11.

The genius was the scuba tanks. Each scuba tank was compressed at four thousands pounds per square inch and together they would feed into the large gasoline tank, creating more than enough pressure in the output hose. That propulsion went through a rig to distribute atomized gasoline from top to bottom of a multiple-carriage elevator shaft, which would become one gigantic engine cylinder.

Simon congratulated himself – since no one else would ever see the genius of his brilliant inventions.

BECAUSE HE AND Anne had discovered Trammell's friend lived in Anoka County, not in Ramsey County, Joe left Grove Street early. It was already getting toward rush hour and he had to fetch his car near the office, then fight traffic all the way out to Anoka to plead with a judge to authorize surveillance on Travis Devins in hopes he would lead them to Cory Trammell. As it turned out, the drive wasn't much better on the way back, so he missed his chance to get his phone back from forensics. He stewed as he crawled through rush hour.

The judge had agreed to allow surveillance on Devins and the Coon Rapids Police had been enlisted to carry it out. Unfortunately, with budget shortfalls and staffing cuts, it would take until well into the evening before teams could be put in place. There would be a car at Devins' sprawling property in Anoka county, and another at his other known asset, the Coon Rapids Fluff and Fold.

Some desperado.

———

THE DOOR CAME FLYING in and there was Travis standing in the doorway looking at Cory, who was lying in the dark. "We gotta get going," he said.

Alarmed, Cory bolted upright in bed.

"We gotta move you, it's not safe here anymore."

Cory got up and grabbed the pistol from the dresser beside the bed. It heartened Travis to see a gun had become a permanent part of his routine.

"Where to?" Cory said, following Travis to the living room.

"We need to change that bandage before we go?"

"Nah, Trav, I'm good," Cory said.

Travis already had his HK VP9 on his hip, the holster strapped to his leg. They stopped near the door and picked through the pile of coats, neither taking one they'd worn before. Then they stopped at the gun rack.

"You want a holster? Hip or shoulder?"

Cory just slipped the little Ruger .380 into his jacket pocket and was ready to go as Travis buttoned his coat and pulled on gloves. He handed Cory an extra clip for the Ruger and led him out, pulling out his phone to call ahead.

As they sat in Travis' old Plymouth, he said, "I gotta get the place we're going cleared out before I take you. Don't want any of our guys seeing you." He pointed at the newspaper on the seat with Cory's photo on the front page.

"They offering a reward or something?"

"Yeah. Plus who knows what kind of shit my guys and their friends got themselves into?" Travis said. "Easy way out of a jam is finger a guy like you. Famous and wanted."

"How did my life ever get this bad?" Cory said as they drove out of the compound. It was still early evening.

"Life sucks and then you die," Travis said, "but you can fuck 'em back before you go, that's my motto. Simon and me will get you through this, compadre."

Cory nodded his thanks.

"So I'm gonna have to leave you there alone, 'cuz me and Simon have a lot to do to get ready," Travis said. "But you'll be safe and out of sight."

Travis eventually drove down a desolate alley, parked at the end and got out, looking about cautiously. He led Cory to a metal door with a sturdy mesh security grate outside it. He unlocked both and they stepped inside. Cory found himself in the back room of a locksmith shop.

"You own this shop?" Cory said.

"Not owner-of-record...but yeah," Travis said expansively. "Lot a places like this, places that have a certain amount of walk-in business, foot traffic."

"Your guys actually make keys here?"

"That don't come up a lot, but yeah, some of them can.

On paper, this place makes a profit and pays its taxes, gets its permits, pays the electric bill. Looks legit."

"You really learned how to play their game."

"That's Simon for you. Sets things up and thinks of everything. This place got audited a few years ago and we actually ended up with a refund."

Cory didn't share in the joy Travis felt about cheating the government at its own game; it still represented engaging with them. "You sweep the place?"

Travis' first thought was, 'probably hasn't been cleaned in ten years.' Then he remembered their ruse about sweeping Cory's truck for bugs. "I had the guys do it before they vacated and put the sign in the window."

There was a hand-written sign on the front door that Cory read in reverse, 'Closed til further notiss.'

"So there's a fridge back here, a bed behind that curtain," Travis said, showing the small grimy back room. "You want to stay away from the front windows."

"How long I gotta wait here?"

"Not sure exactly, but if it ain't me or Simon at the door, don't open it and don't let anyone know you're in here," Travis said. "Be ready first thing in the morning."

When Cory went to give him a hug, Travis let him and avoided thinking about how the next day would end.

After he heard the deadbolt lock him in, Cory unplugged the phone and all of the key-making machines, then pulled a beer out of the fridge. He propped up on the bed with the curtain pulled aside and looked around at the row of machines, the racks of blank keys, the bicycle locks and door locks. There was a spot against the wall where the dust showed a TV had sat, but the space was empty. Man, was he alone. Way too alone. Way too much time to think.

It felt like a cell. Just like juvie.

His friends didn't say it directly to his face, but he knew either Abby or Betsy was already dead. The government had shot one or the other. He'd led those bastards right there with that bug in his truck. Her death was on him. It could be they were all dead and he'd begun to think death might be better than the alternative. The one certain thing, there was no getting them back. There was only getting even.

He pulled out the compact Ruger and extra clip, then unloaded the bullets onto his belly. He had more than enough to fulfill his number one priority – to take out the two agents, Nolan and Brandt.

28

J oe got back from Anoka in time to meet Kat, then join Marlo and Dianna, the head nurse of the children's psychiatric unit, which housed Patrick Henry for one more night. Kat paged through the boy's chart, reading the notes aloud. "'Extremely bright, well-versed in some subjects, ignorant in others'" she said. "Home schooling, right?"

"Yeah, but not with the religious bent you often see," Dianna said. "He think's 'Christ' is a swear word."

"Can I see him again?" Joe said. "His dad's in serious trouble and any light he can shed..."

The women all looked questioningly at each other, then nodded. "I'll be at the door," Kat said. "Chaperone. Adult male. After hours. Alone in a bedroom."

Patrick Henry was now the only child on the ward who had a room to himself. They didn't dare put him with any of the other boys, though most of them were older than he was. Joe realized it wasn't just adults he antagonized and attacked, he hated everyone. The huge door to the room, which he had earlier somehow detached from its industrial-strength hinges, had now been permanently removed. The light from the hallway spilled in across the bed, showing the boy awake in the dark.

Joe stopped in the doorway and knocked, got no response and entered. Kat stayed in the hall, listening.

"Patrick Henry, I'd like to talk to you again," he said as he tried to pull the chair near the bed and found it bolted in place. Joe sat with the hallway light cutting across him. "I met your father yesterday."

That got the boy's attention and he took a good long look at Joe's bruised face, then grinned. "I can see that."

"His name is Cory Trammell."

The smile instantly disappeared.

'Good,' thought Joe. 'Two responses in a hurry.' The boy had laid out the baseline: as opponents they could communicate. Trying to befriend him wouldn't bring out any information. Joe desperately needed to fill in what he'd learned, so he'd be this kid's opponent. That way, the boy might reveal something he wouldn't give up voluntarily.

"I know you and your sister and your mom hid out with your dad. He had a cash-only business in snow plowing and tree trimming and you helped him. You lived illegally on the property where you broke your arm," Joe said, sensing he was shocking the boy with all that he knew. "You were 'squatters.' Your family stole the use of that property and I've even seen what's left of your bedroom there."

"Fat lot you know," the boy said. "I didn't have a bedroom of my own until I got here and got rid of that nutsack, Brandon."

"What you don't know is your father burned down the house and barn and forest after you came to the hospital."

The boy bolted upright. "Your kind always lie."

"My kind also try to help boys with broken arms. If it had been left to your parents, you would have died."

"Liar."

"Keep telling yourself that, Pat," Joe said, hoping that needled the boy; anger seemed to loosen his tongue. "Your mom abandoned you, Pat. If we hadn't stepped in, you would have died. They left you to die."

At the door, Kat listened in, disturbed by Joe's aggression. She took a step to enter, but he held up a hand to her. He didn't like it either, but this was progress.

"Your dad has a friend named Travis Devins and they are in a great deal of trouble. We're soon going to put both of them in jail," Joe said. "They're criminals."

"You can't do that."

"We have an obligation to do exactly that."

"...'the battle, sir, is not to the strong alone, it is to the vigilant, the active, the brave.'"

"You know your Patrick Henry quotes, I'll grant you that," Joe said. "But your father and his friend have broken a lot of laws and we will be locking them up."

"No! It's a free country. It was founded out of a crucible of revolt against your kind."

"Big word."

Patrick Henry stayed silent, glowering at Joe.

"Your dad went to jail for vandalizing his school."

"Liar."

"It wasn't some revolutionary movement against King George and tax tyranny. He was a stupid boy doing a stupid prank and he got himself arrested. There wasn't one glorious thing about it."

"Liar."

"Sort of like Patrick Henry himself," Joe said. "He talked big, but he wasn't much of a real revolutionary."

The boy practically leapt out of the bed at Joe, who held his ground. "Take that back," he screamed.

Joe noticed Dianna and Marlo joining Kat at the door, but held out a hand again. The boy hadn't touched him and just sat back onto the bed.

"Patrick Henry talked tough about treasonous things, but other than one little incident before the Revolutionary War even started, he didn't come close to actual fighting. He was cowardly when you get right down to it."

"I'm not listening to you anymore."

"'If this be treason, make the most of it,'" Joe said. "Some hero."

"It's only treason to the oppressors. To free men, it's heroism."

"I'm not an oppressor."

"Locked me in here, didn't you?"

Joe had to agree with that and wanted to leave the kid on a high note in case he had more questions. When he left, he found three women scowling at him. He followed them away. "Looks like he gets his delusions from his father, who sees himself in grandiose terms. He's fighting for his family's freedom," Joe said. "Trammell is not going to stop his war against us. I think it's our very worst fear...he is going to fight against us with everything he's got."

Kat looked him over uncertainly, but finally winked secretly. "Reverse interrogation? You didn't ask him a single question, did you, Joe?"

He was pleased she'd noticed the tactic, but he was distracted by really troubling thoughts.

"Did provoking that boy help?" Dianna asked.

"I'm understanding the father better, but that just upsets me more, because it's clear this isn't over for Trammell. One thing the original Patrick Henry said was, 'Nothing will preserve liberty but downright force.'"

WHEN SIMON HAD INITIALLY STARTED DEVISING his plan, he'd identified the best building construction style, scouted a variety of potential sites and zeroed in on a common building type which was ideal for his needs. He had looked for an elevator shaft that had cement pillars which bore the real weight and cinderblocks enclosing the walls of the shaft itself. The walls would be strong enough to resist the outward pressure of a fuel-injected explosion, but weak enough to give way. When they would eventually succumb to the escalating pressure, the blocks would fragment and blast out into the hallways – all at once, on every floor, at the same time, dead center in the building.

He'd invented his mechanism for such massive fuel injection and tooled the unique parts himself, all since he'd acquired the garage for his workspace. What he had left to perfect was the means of mounting it through a block wall into an elevator shaft. Until Cory presented an opportunity he couldn't pass up, Simon had thought he'd have another couple of months to invent, create and practice so that he could perform every step of the crucial process blindfolded. Then he'd be ready to do it under the pressure of live conditions in a hostile environment. Because of this new timeline, he was playing catch-up.

He'd built a practice wall of cinderblocks near the tool bench in the garage. One block at waist height had holes through both side walls of the hollow block, just like he would create on-site. The real issue was threading his delicate injector mechanism through those walls without damage. Once he mastered getting the bundle through the hole in the practice wall, he knew he'd be able to seat the heart of his mechanism inside an actual elevator. It was fairly easy to envision, but quite difficult to achieve.

The injectors were four parallel titanium tubes of varying lengths and curvatures, each with a custom-built nozzle on its end, each had been calibrated to send mist to different elevations for ideal vapor density. The four shafts were bundled together and securely attached to a plywood mounting plate. But the hole on the inside of the cinderblock wall could not be seen as he worked and was essentially the neck of the hourglass. He'd wrapped the nozzles for protection as he tried, again and again, to thread the whole rig through gently, yet efficiently.

When he'd gotten it through five times in a row without a hitch, he felt he was as ready as he'd ever be. So he set up his workspace at the wall for maximum access. He fetched his Hilti, which looked like an Uzi and was a gun of sorts. It used .27 caliber blank bullets to drive anchors directly into cement. He positioned it where he'd need it once he had the mounting plate in place.

He felt great, because he was now preparing to take action, not just dreaming about it. At the same time, he was excited knowing he was the only person in the world who knew a major, life-altering event was about to take place.

———

THE PUBLIC LIBRARY faced St. Paul Plaza and the only people inside were the cleaning staff, a few night guards and one girl who had done an excellent job of remaining unseen. Betsy was hiding in the library stacks when a uniformed guard had come through and walked up and down each aisle. She'd managed to hide all trace of herself until it had been deadly quiet for quite some time and she dared to come out. She'd be warm tonight, though still no closer to finding her family.

Earlier she'd eaten three dinners at the same diner and whiled hours hoping her father might stop by. She'd lingered until creeps noticed her and that had driven her into a small store with security cameras. In her last few hours of desperation, she'd abandoned any serious avoidance of those. Creeps seemed to be everywhere, so she bought a bunch of crap food and took it with her to the library just before closing time. She was now locked in for the night.

The stacks were a blessing. Lots of empty aisles, thousands of books and she'd found a great little spot to nestle into on the bottom of a very wide shelf. It promised to be yet another long night, but she was warm and safe.

SIMON FELT nervous on the trip from the towing yard to downtown St. Paul. He had to drive with the pickup truck windows down despite the cold because of the odor. He wore a Cory-style baseball cap, wrapped himself in a blanket and took the long way, staying off the freeways. If the police ever got so far as tracing how the truck had gotten to the plaza, he wanted it to look like Cory had driven it. A block from the parking entrance, he snugged the cap down, wrapped a huge scarf around his neck and onto half his face. He was wearing a jacket similar to Cory's.

He drove up to the ticket machine where there was a security camera. He didn't look at it as he took the ticket with a gloved hand and drove in shortly before the parking ramp closed for the night. Overnight workers parked there, so it wasn't empty, but there wouldn't be any new vehicles entering after ten. And that meant very few people walking through until the night workers left around dawn.

He parked near a group of cars belonging to the overnight cleaning crew and rolled up the truck windows. After breaking into one of the older cars with no alarm, he stole the employee parking pass and an air freshener, then placed them both in the pickup. After Cory had been hustled off to the locksmith shop, Simon had pulled Cory's rifles from the hatchback and stuffed them in the back of the pickup with the body. He double checked the tarp and tools sitting atop Abby, locked up and left the truck, confident it wouldn't be noticed for the half day he needed.

He was now alone in the parking ramp under the Family Services Building. He turned the reversible jacket inside out, changed to a different hat and wrapped a different scarf about his face as he assessed the security cameras. On the lower of two parking levels below the building there were only a few cameras and those were aimed at the entrance to the elevators and at each turn down the lanes. So he stayed behind the cameras directed at the elevators.

The construction was exactly what he remembered from scouting it a few months ago and precisely what he needed. It had poured concrete pillars and cinderblock walls, the elevator shaft was eleven stories high – two levels of underground parking, eight stories of building and one story of machinery at the roof level - and it was four elevator cars wide. Perfect construction and ideal volume.

FACED with a choice of half a pain pill or a bourbon, Joe

sipped his decision as he sat at home and pondered the mysterious boy and his crazy father. It was not reassuring. Cory Trammell had somehow known what Joe looked like and where he lived, but his son hadn't known anything about him. Developing threat assessments with an explosives expert had been disturbing all on its own, but it was the Revolutionary War rhetoric thrown about as modern-day rebellion and anarchy that was downright terrifying.

After checking that all the windows were locked, Kat sat beside Joe on the couch and snuggled into an afghan with her propped-up laptop. While he pondered the plans of the father, she was trying to figure out a new place to keep the boy once he was released from the psych ward. He needed a new home in the morning and the chore fell to her.

The drawing of Cory was still on the coffee table which had somehow survived the battle. After shooting him and hearing his son speak with confidence about revolution, just a glance at the drawing sent a shudder up her spine. Enright's gun was still in her purse and with any luck it would never be needed. And in any event, Bitt had a police cruiser on an hourly drive-by routine.

The house phone rang and Joe answered. Enright.

"You didn't go get your cell," Enright said. "I had a nice chat with the forensics tech. She found nothing, but she thinks you should take more pictures."

"Swell," Joe said as he got up and took the cordless phone with him as he went to sit in the dining room where he poured a bit more bourbon into his glass.

"I talked with Patrick Henry about patriotism today."

"He educate you?" Enright said.

"These people seem to be re-fighting the American Revolution. What you find out about Travis Devins?"

"He ain't no revolutionary. Suspected of operating a drug

network, but he's pretty slippery. Nothing really sticks. He's never holding, never directly implicated."

"Either of these guys got a history with explosives?"

"Only their volatile tempers," Enright said.

"Let's check known associates for arson."

"We'd have to be luckier than I feel or you look."

"I don't look lucky?"

"You been near a mirror today?"

Joe looked to the living room to discover Kat had abandoned her computer, the afghan and some of her clothes. She leaned on the jamb and beckoned with her head toward their room. He must not look that bad, he guessed as he watched her sashay away. 'Who's not lucky?' he thought.

"Surveillance hasn't been active very long," Enright said. "The laundry is a place where drugs are sold and the house seems to have someone who stands around in the yard, presumably armed, but we got no actionable crimes unless we want to burn the surveillance for an ounce of grass. And no sighting of Travis Devins to compare with the hospital security video."

"Let's leave it to surveillance and call it a night," Joe said as he went to the archway to peer after Kat. She'd disappeared into their bedroom, but he could see the throw pillows being thrown off the bed. 'Hurry up, Byron.'

"You all right, Joe? You sound distracted."

"It's just the pain in my face and ear."

They said goodnight and Enright signed off.

"Your face is hurting too much?" Kat called out.

He stepped to the bedroom door and found both the bed and Kat stripped, waiting for him. "What face?"

29

Alone in the locksmith shop, Cory didn't sleep a wink. It wasn't nerves, it was memories. He'd been progressively working backward – from Abby, Betsy and Patrick Henry all disappearing, to the homes they'd abandoned over the years, to the bus station and Abby. From there he went back to a completely different life when he and Travis were partners. Those were wild days of freedom, when Travis did all the thinking and planning for the two of them. Cory usually didn't reflect on their time in juvie or the night when everything changed, but now, locked in a squalid little shop behind security grates, it all overtook his thoughts.

In 2001, he only had a few months left in juvie and had been rejected by his latest foster family, so he knew he'd be moving to yet another house filled with distrust.

In Redwing, Travis had been his salvation and they'd bonded into a team the other boys didn't dare mess with. The staff, however, had their ways. Many of the guards, cooks, teachers and others lorded their power over the boys and disguised it as official oversight. They demanded obedience, favors or sheer fright. All of them except Simon, no other staff were like him. He stoked rebellion and revolution with every lesson he taught and did it right under the authorities' noses. He got off on attaching the boys' dreams of freedom to his ideas of corrupting the system. Cory had fervently embraced that anti-government message, because authorities had been running and ruining his life since the day he was born. Simon's hatred of established order and his influence on some boys became crystal clear the day the towers fell.

Like it did everywhere else in the world, news of 9/11 spread rapidly throughout Redwing. The guards and other staff were distraught at the acts of terror in New York and Washington DC and then were doubly horrified when the boys reveled in the attacks. Jubilant cheering was especially widespread among boys led by Travis and Cory, since they were the same group who had been influenced by Simon.

The guards attempted a crackdown to drive the rioting boys back into the dorms, but one teacher with keys had a different idea. Simon chose that morning to quit his job and open the door to anyone who wanted to escape. Travis and Cory, along with a number of others, followed Simon out of Redwing and fled to freedom.

The pair stole a car and it was Cory's hope to put fifty miles between them and Redwing before noon, but Travis had revenge in mind. They stuck around to fulfill his goal and that day would set the pattern for the rest of their partnership. There was only one person in the world that Cory trusted and he wasn't about to break that bond, so if Travis needed to do it, he was in all the way. Travis said they needed to beat the shit out of a guy before they could take off, though it was hard for him to explain why.

Cory hadn't noticed much about Garmon, except that he wore green short sleeve hospital scrubs over his pasty white arms and the guy sort of gave him the creeps. He was the night medic in the infirmary. Usually after a fight, Cory was not the one laid up, so he'd only had his knuckles taped a few times and Garmon tended him once when he had the flu. Travis seemed to be sick a lot more and was taken by guards to the overnight infirmary quite a bit. It always made him sullen, but Cory just wrote it off as life in juvie. It pissed everyone off to be there, to be watched and restricted, so being moody was nearly universal.

Travis' revenge plan required that they stake out the employee parking lot at juvie until Garmon left at dawn. They'd follow him home and teach him a lesson. For what, Travis refused to specify. It was hard for Cory to say no to Travis and, besides, he had long felt that every single one of the fucking guards deserved a solid beating.

Cory was surprised there wasn't a big search going on after their prison escape, but Travis just kept telling him the last place they'd look for escapees was right outside the door. At dawn they were rewarded for their daring by spotting Garmon stroll out to his car and drive away. They followed in their stolen car and were surprised when he went to a park at dawn, rather than right home.

As they followed him into the park, Cory was startled to see a couple in the shadows kissing. Then even more surprised to see it was two men. Travis dragged him along to keep him from gawking, as he began to realize this was a gay cruising area. Almost before he caught sight of Garmon up ahead of them, Travis leapt on the man and hit him across the back of the head with a viciousness that shocked Cory. He was enraged and Cory finally began to get it, what had happened those nights Travis had been in the infirmary. He was incensed for his friend and instantly felt ashamed he hadn't protected him better.

Out of his scrubs and with terror in his eyes, Garmon looked pathetic as he was pummeled. Cory soon stepped in and pulled his friend aside. Travis was delighted to step back and let Cory do what he did best. It had always been hard for him to stop after a couple swings and, once he started in on Garmon, everything inside him wanted to keep going. He had not protected his one friend and now he had to make up for that failure. In the past, someone had always pulled him off, but as the sun began to rise on September 12th, Travis didn't pull Cory away. He eventually stopped because he was spent.

They drove away in silence and were out of town before the sun was fully up. When Cory wanted to talk about it, Travis shut him down. They agreed never to talk about this, about Garmon, juvie or the infirmary. None of that had happened and would never be acknowledged between them.

A couple days later, Cory read in the paper about a hate crime in a gay cruising area of a local park – a man had been beaten to death. He showed the article to Travis and they knew they needed to be on the run. The government would not forgive a prison escape or a hate crime. They were high value targets and had to go underground.

———

JOE WAS WRAPPED around Kat and dead to the world, but she was sleeping lightly. She'd been so unnerved by the shooting, she felt anxious, even with his comforting arms around her and hourly police cruisers driving by. She woke up yet again and contemplated going around the apartment to check all the windows once more, but knew it was absurd. She heard the ding on her cell phone and couldn't imagine who was sending her a text in the middle of the night.

She slipped out from his arms, pulled on a robe and went into the living room in search of her phone. There was a text, but who the hell was 'Anne' she wondered. When she opened it, she saw it was addressed to Joe and went to rouse him. No mean feat. He was deep into his much-needed sleep, but the text seemed important.

"You got a text from Anne," she said to Joe as he started to realize she was waking him.

"Who?"

"It's about Travis Devins," she said handing him her phone. "You must have given the computer expert my number."

She crawled back into her spot that was still warm, but now Joe was sitting up and reading the text.

"Jesus," he said as he slid out of bed.

"What's happened?"

"Anne set up a search bot or something to dig into ownership records and shell companies. It discovered that Devins owns more than the Fluff and Fold."

"So?"

"So we have surveillance on only his home and the laundry," Joe said as he dressed. "Her program woke her up when it found some other properties. A couple other laundries, a locksmith, a few other shops...and a farm."

"A diversified drug dealer."

"Seems to me an isolated farm would be a good place for Trammell to hide with his wife and daughter."

She watched him pulling on the rest of his clothes and knew it was too late to talk him out of going. "You're taking Byron, right? Don't go alone."

"Right. Good thinking."

Suddenly she flung back the covers, got up and strode naked out into the living room. As Joe tied his shoes, she returned with the pistol Enright had given her and held it out insistently. "If you're lucky and find either of these guys or the whole fugitive family..."

Finally Joe took the gun and didn't look at it as he watched her climb naked back into the bed. Once she was snuggled up under the covers, she slipped the pepper spray she'd also grabbed from her purse under the pillow. Before he turned to go, she pointed at the gun.

"The safety is the lever on the side."

"Gotcha," he said and he leaned down to kiss her. "I'll call you."

"How?"

"What do you mean?"

"You're going to take my phone to navigate, right?" Kat said. "If I'm not at home when you call, try Marlo, I'll be with her in the morning."

"Go back to sleep," Joe said, taking the phone and the gun with him. As he walked down to his car, he typed the address of the farm into the phone's map, then called Enright. "You once told me to call you, day or night."

"I didn't mean it," Enright said groggily.

———

SIMON PICKED up a functioning junker from Cushing Avenue and drove toward the garage. As always, he parked a couple blocks away and made his way through the shadows to his workshop. It was a good thing he did, because half a block from the garage he spotted a car he didn't like. There were two people in it just sitting. 'So what are they doing?' he thought as he reached in the jacket for his gun and silencer. He was certain they were cops and it distressed him to think anyone was this close to him.

He twisted the silencer on and backtracked to approach the car unseen. He figured he'd give them each two pops, head and heart, and the loudest sound would be the breaking of the glass from the first bullet. He didn't like it – killing two cops on the street so close to an operation – but nothing was going to stop him now. After he did them, he'd have to pull their car into the other bay of the garage, but it wouldn't matter if they were discovered later. By then everything would be over.

As he crept up in their blind spot, he saw one guy was asleep leaning on the passenger window and the man behind the wheel was chewing on an electronic cigarette. They were oblivious that Simon was fifteen feet away, gun at his side. It would be so easy, but he realized the car was oriented straight at the laundry. There was no clear sight line from them to his garage and a hedge blocked some of their view. There were better spots to watch his garage. They were staking out Twitch, who'd probably been careless, so local narcs had identified the laundry for a stakeout.

Nevertheless they presented a problem for him and he had to revise his plan. He still needed time to fill his three hundred and thirty gallon tank at the gas pump beside the garage. These narcs were bound to notice, it would be notable after the bombing and could potentially lead the inevitable investigation to him. Having to get rid of the surveillance team without implicating himself was a new wrinkle, but not insurmountable. He'd use Twitch to divert them and his plan would go on without interruption.

Joe was driving and Enright was following the directions on Kat's phone to guide them along dark country roads. Thought unhappily awake, Enright had thought that this discovery was too hot to sit on until daylight. He had also agreed a remote farm was the likeliest place for them to check first. A wife and a kid, that would require space.

"Pull over here," Enright said. "Kill the lights."

Joe stopped on the tiny road and shut off the lights but kept the heater going, it was frigid out. "What's up?"

"It's pitch black out here."

"No kidding. Gives me the creeps."

"Our headlights would give us away long before we got near enough to get hold of this guy."

"What do you suggest?"

"Loathe as I am to walking in a freezer..."

Joe parked on the shoulder and they both studied the map on the phone screen, memorizing where they were heading before getting out. Joe pocketed the phone as they pulled their coats tight and headed cautiously up the narrow road.

It was so black they almost walked past the little dirt path that led off to the side. It was a starless night and they were feeling each step ahead with their feet as they inched down that two-track trail. Joe was aware on one level he was frozen, yet he had sweat dripping down his sides as they crept ahead into the unknown. Then they suddenly stopped short when the space in front of them became even denser black. It was a little house and they could barely make it out against the empty field and the stand of trees beyond.

There was no sign of life, no light from inside as they tiptoed around. They could see nothing.

Enright put a hand to Joe's chest indicating that he should stay, then he edged closer to the house. Joe noticed a glint of reflection and realized it was from Enright's gun. He wasn't the only one with his hand on a weapon while his heart thundered in his ears. Maybe they should have called this in. 'And told them what?' he asked himself.

Enright disappeared and Joe felt alone in the abyss. He had his eyes wide open, but there was nothing for them to land on. He shivered and it seemed like ages before suddenly a light came on. And then it seemed blinding.

"Oh Jesus," Enright said from just inside the door where the ceiling light flooded around him.

Joe ran up beside him, the gun in his hand outstretched past Enright and into the empty house.

"Safety's on," Enright said, then looked back inside.

Joe followed Enright's eyes, which led him to a large, dried pool of blood on the floor. And then he spotted a bunch of stuffed yard and garden bags strewn about.

"Kat didn't wound him that bad," Joe said as he watched Enright squatting down to inspect the bloody pool.

"No. Someone was shot right here," Enright said as he pointed at the spatter of blood against the wall.

"Who?"

"Maybe one of them killed the other and took the body," Enright said as he scrolled through his cell phone listings. "Which Anoka County officials do I wake up and piss off?" He pressed an icon to call, then looked at Joe. "This wasn't Cory unless he was on his knees. The shot was going downward..." Then he started talking into the phone.

Joe looked at the blood on the wall and the bullet hole at the center of it. It reminded him of Bitt's friend, but it came from a smaller caliber.

He noticed bags of groceries beside a recently scoured sink, but otherwise the place was a mess. Even a can of bacon grease was splattered on the floor. Joe stepped over the pool of blood and looked into the sordid little back room, where clean sheets were halfway on the bed and he noticed the TV's power cord had been yanked out.

"Anoka's finest are on their way," Enright said, calling out from the front room. "We should get a warrant for Devins' house now. This is plenty of probable cause."

"It's in Anoka County, not Ramsey."

"Find the judge who ordered the surveillance on his house, I think it's time to close any loop we got open."

Joe had thought to bring the court orders for the house and laundry surveillance with him. He looked up the number of the county's night judge and was just calling when Enright said, "You smell something?"

Joe stepped back into the main room and spotted flames crawling out from below the stove right behind Enright. The fire followed a trail of bacon grease across the floor.

"Fire," Joe shouted.

Enright spotted it, looked at the overturned can of bacon fat about to go up and kicked at it. Too late.

Fat and fire leapt onto Enright's pant leg and he frantically swatted at it with his gloved hands. The flames were spreading from the grease, now strewn every which way and taking hold as Joe dragged Enright out the door.

They got the fire on Enright's pants out, but it left a sizable burn on his calf and a hole in his pants leg.

When they turned back to the house, flames were already consuming the ratty curtains and jumping in every direction. In less than a minute, fire was leaping from the roof and they finally had plenty of light in the night.

"Anoka Fire Department now too," Enright said as he dialed. "Shame about the crime scene, huh?"

While Enright told the fire department that a crime scene was going up in flames, Joe contacted the Anoka court and initiated a warrant for the police to search Devins' house. That was not a rapid process at three in the morning. While Joe slowly explained his needs to the Clerk of Anoka Night Court, Enright roused Bittinger from his bed, detailed what was happening and asked him to interface with the Anoka police at the house of Travis Devins.

"I'm getting used to being the cop the locals resent."

"Then you'll feel right at home in Anoka," Enright said. "Whatever it is we got hold of here, it's nasty."

While Bittinger started the long drive and Enright watched the fire consume all the evidence that might have led them to Devins and Trammell, Joe began to dictate into Kat's phone everything he remembered from inside the house. The blood, the bullet trajectory, the bags, speculation of which of the people in Cory Trammell's circle might be dead and, quite importantly, the can of bacon fat which now seemed clearly intentional. Since they were tracking an arsonist, this was certainly not an accidental fire, it had been set to go up when someone entered.

"We're getting closer to this guy," Joe said.

Enright realized his leg burn was third degree and said, "You got a first aid kit in your car or anything?"

Joe ran back up the path to the road as the fire lit his way. In the distance he could hear sirens. Lots of them and all of them too late.

ack in the garage, Simon stashed the mounting board, the Hilti, all the tools he could possibly need and the set of 'caution' barricades in the plumbing truck. Then he ran the whole scenario through his mind – all he had left to do here was send the narcs chasing Twitch, fill the tank at the gas pump and get downtown by the time the parking ramp opened at 7:00.

That left time for a last visit with Travis and Cory. He had to explain the details of the plan as they needed to believe them, but even more importantly, he wanted to make sure they were psyched. If they didn't make him confident they were fully invested and would hold up their end, he'd have to take drastic action. That would be regrettable.

He slipped outside, snuck around to make sure the narcs had stayed put and drove back to Cushing Avenue where he called Travis to come pick him up. Travis hadn't been asleep and Simon suspected he'd been down in his gun range. Without mentioning there was surveillance at the laundry, he cautioned Travis to be extra careful. The last thing he needed was for the dolt to lead cops right to him.

"Good thing you gave me the heads up," Travis said when he arrived in an old car. "Cops were watching outside my place. I had one of the guys sneak me out and then I swapped cars. Got no tail now."

"Damn. Cory's putting everything we've built in jeopardy, isn't he." Simon said. "He's led them way closer than I care for, so we better not go back home until this whole thing is over."

"Yeah, I thought of that," Travis said and indicated the back seat where his sheepskin coat was spread out. It covered all the weapons and ammunition he planned to bring.

"You know we have to do it this way, right?" Simon said. "At least it'll be a blaze of glory for him and after that, everything will cool down for us. Back to business." Travis nodded solemnly and that made Simon go on. "And you know this will play well for you with The Movement."

"Yeah and I know Cory's never joining us. I'm not even sure he's hoping to come out of this."

"Best thing for him," Simon said, faking sympathy. "Sorry, man. I know how close you've been."

"Him and me had fantastic days together until Abby fucked it all up. Truth is...it's been over a long time."

Simon realized that Travis was almost fully extracted from Cory now. Right where he needed to be. As always, Simon could trust the dishonesty in men. Travis had worked out the excuses he needed for why Cory had to go and they all came from taking care of his own needs first, plus possible recognition from The Movement, which he craved.

When they slipped in the back of the locksmith shop Cory was surprised. He'd been stewing, counting bullets and recalling the faces of his two targets. Yet none of that had kept the ghosts of Abby and the kids from haunting him. All he had left now was revenge.

The three men shuffled awkwardly in parallel. Each had his own reasons for joining together and their expectations were extremely different. Only Simon knew precisely what was in store for both of them and was determined to make certain it all came about before either of them figured it out. The wanna-be and the Boy Scout would have their final day together and he'd have a future free of suspicion.

"It's on," Simon announced. Travis brightened and became instantly energized. Cory worried for a bit, but finally started to share the enthusiasm.

As had been their pattern since Simon first met them, Cory had lots of questions about the process and plan while Travis simply got jacked at the prospect of action that carried a low risk of his being hurt.

The three of them sat around the little table in the back as Simon nursed Cory ahead, stage by stage, into believing that he had somehow arranged for Brandt to come looking for Nolan in the lower parking level of the Family Services Building. He employed several facile lies about The Movement and its awareness of Brandt, their assistance in planting an urgent issue and his own genius at getting those two agents to converge in the morning at a specific time. To his credit, Travis was a great help to Simon in selling the idea. His enthusiasm helped Cory make the climb from doubt to certainty.

Cory listened to Simon's story of his mysterious allies, his own genius and the complex movements of Brandt and Nolan and, as usual, much of it just flooded past him. Once he got going, Simon always talked too much. The essential points were that his two targets would be in one location at the same moment, so he could take them both out at once.

Cory made Travis promise he was there just as back-up, that he would be the one to make the kill shots.

Simon was relieved when the pair discussed who should be the killer. It meant his magnificent lies about the plan were now accepted facts. Let them worry about who pulled the trigger. In truth he had no idea where Brandt and Nolan's would be and didn't care. What he needed was Cory and Travis to be in the lower level parking garage at 8:15. All the better if Cory got himself recorded on security cameras, which would then match up with his earlier scouting of the building. The police would believe they had him dead to rights as the bomber and Simon would have him as the perfect fall guy to seal up the investigation.

"You two enter the employee parking level at 8:10...we can't risk you being spotted before we know they're in place. They've never seen me, so I'm lookout and I'll call you when he arrives. That way you can surprise them."

Travis nodded enthusiastically.

"So I do it in front of security cameras?" Cory said.

"Your picture is everywhere, so there's no hiding who's behind this," Simon said with reassurance and a kind of fatalism that appealed to Cory. "Doing it on camera will make your declaration of independence the biggest anyone has made in decades."

"Your revenge is gonna be so sweet," Travis added.

"How come you're helping so much, Simon?" Cory said.

Simon was prepared. "Because I'm a selfish prick."

"He's not saying that, Simon," Travis said.

"No, I'm saying it. It's in my interest to help you."

"How's that work?" Cory said uncertainly.

"Your picture is everywhere. You're my business partner's best friend and he's extremely committed to helping you. I'm very sympathetic to your cause, because I love anything that wreaks havoc with the government. But at the same time, as long as you're big news, my business stops dead. Once I help you through this, you win, plus The Movement pats me on the back and I can get back to business with Travis."

Cory studied him carefully. If Simon had said he was helping out of pure friendship, he'd have slipped out the door to try something on his own. But Simon had delivered – Nolan and Brandt would be in the same place – so he started reloading his clips. "How'm I getting there?"

For the next twenty minutes, they discussed where Travis would park after driving them to the building, where they would enter at exactly 8:10 and where Simon would be watching for the arrival of Brandt. Simon went on about their rendezvous point after the shootings, the back-up getaway car that would be waiting in case it was needed and how they'd both help Cory get out of St. Paul afterwards.

On the way out, Travis said he'd return to pick up Cory at 7:00 to give them time to drive side roads to downtown. When they got into his car behind the shop, Travis finally asked the question he'd been dying to ask, "We're really expecting him to get out of there?"

"No, but he's gotta believe he will," Simon said. "The moment he takes them down, he'll run right to you. You take his gun to dispose of it and pop him with it quick. Then you just walk away in the confusion from the gunshots, I'll pick you up and we're free. He's a lone gunman, the news and cops will focus on him and we're back to business."

Travis stewed in silence a moment. "And you've thought of everything, as always?" he said.

"Of course."

"I drop him and walk off," Travis said. "Good to go."

'Separation complete,' Simon thought.

ENRIGHT SAT on the back of a fire truck with his leg up as an Anoka fireman cut his pants up toward the burns. "Careful with the scissors, I already had my vasectomy," he said and the fireman laughed.

The Anoka police, on the other hand, were not happy. They didn't like having a major crime scene burn down.

Joe was watching the last fire crew making sure the embers were out as an Anoka cop walked up and said, "You don't carry a fire extinguisher in your car?"

"No."

"Well you should. You coulda put the fire out."

"No, I couldn't have."

"Why not?" the cop said with clear irritation.

"This place was consumed in a minute."

"So you say," the cop said.

"So do I," Enright said as he approached them. He was peeved and Joe realized he didn't like seeing Enright upset. He was somehow bigger, thinner, stronger and a-force-to-reckon-with. "We're chasing down an arsonist and he rigged the place to burn down. Seems to me he set it to go up once the door was opened. So now it's gone, the guy erased the evidence and we all have to live with it."

The cop spotted a command car arriving and, wanting to escape, rushed to greet Captain Cubbin, a large, ruddy man already in full dress uniform at dawn. He looked with disdain at the remains of the house.

"We might get out of here by Thanksgiving," Enright said. "They should be grateful we found their crime scene, the marijuana fields they overlooked for an entire summer and the descriptions we've both given six or eight times."

Cubbin took his time making his way toward them.

"He's going to want to take us to the station to make statements in separate rooms," Enright bemoaned.

Joe sidled up behind him and said, "Speaking of being questioned...is this gun registered to you, Byron?"

Enright looked at the little pistol and said, "Yeah, good thinking." He took the gun and slipped it into his coat pocket, his back to the captain. "Now I better go eat some shit."

Enright smiled as he offered a hand to Cubbin.

Joe got a text on Kat's phone and punched in her security code. It was from Anne. 'I found the license plate' was all it said. 'What license plate?' ran through his mind as he called her.

"The plate from the truck Trammell drove when you two had that fight in the plaza," Anne said.

"Really? I would have thought he ditched that truck before I even got to the emergency room."

"Criminals aren't always the smartest people," she said. "Looks like he returned to the scene of the crime."

"What do you mean? Where?"

"It's parked below Family Services. It entered last night at 9:41."

"Jesus, really? He drove the truck back there? What, thinking it's the last place we'd look?"

"I didn't see the truck, but for sure the license entered. The camera aims at the plates, not the vehicles."

"No camera looks at the vehicle?"

"The one aimed from the ticket dispenser shows a blue baseball cap, a big scarf around the person's face and the window area of what might or might not be a pickup."

"We also know when the vehicle left?" Joe asked.

"It didn't."

Joe got very excited to think the license, with or without

the truck, was still there. He looked around for Enright to drag him away and spotted him glad-handing with the cops. He seemed to have made headway.

"Anne, you're a genius."

"Be sure to tell my boss," she said with a laugh.

Joe hurried over to Enright. "We gotta go, Byron. I've got a lead."

Cubbin shook his head. "We need detailed statements. You tell us we have a murder scene, then burn it down."

"We didn't burn it," Joe said.

"I'll give it, cop to cop," Enright said, leading Cubbin away. Behind his back, he waved for Joe to go. "I'm thinking head wound from the blood spray on the wall..."

Joe hurried to his car and drove off in a rush.

Near the garage, the narcs were awake and watching Twitch usher a customer out with a bag of laundry. Simon could tell Twitch was completely unaware of the cops. Everything was set in the garage, but it would take quite some time to pump that much fuel into the tank, so the narcs had to go.

It meant walking about eight blocks to come up on the laundry from the alley. It had been an iron-clad rule of Simon's that the rear door of their sites never be used for transactions. Business through the alley looked suspicious and led to more robberies of their on-site dealers. Now he'd see if Twitch obeyed the rule. He rapped softly on the steel back door and got no response. On the second knock, he heard Twitch say, "You gotta come in the front door."

He just rapped more insistently and saw a movement at the grimy back window set behind a heavy steel security grate. He stepped out of the line of sight and watched as a little spot of filth was wiped away from the inside so Twitch could look out. All he'd see from inside was an empty alley, but it was the opening Simon needed.

With the silencer already on, he spotted through the hole into the interior and fired, never intending to hit Twitch. The man freaked at the sound of shattering glass and the ping of the bullet into the wall. Like an addict, he went to dig out the drugs first, then when the second bullet hit even closer, he grabbed the cash.

From the end of the alley, Simon had a good view of the street in front of the laundry as Twitch bolted like a jack rabbit and headed right toward the unmarked car. The lights and siren came on, Twitch darted away and, with any luck, he'd give them a great chase. Either way, once they caught him, he was bound to be taken for booking. It would be hours before they checked out the laundry. By then he'd have his tank filled with gasoline and be well on his way.

Dawn was just arriving as he capped off the tank.

Everything was ready.

31

One of the two cops who had staked out Travis' house had the guard from the yard in handcuffs. He had already confiscated the man's automatic and discovered there was no one else outside anywhere in the compound. The cop's partner had checked the grounds and was watching the back door of the rambling house, but there was no sign of any activity inside. They'd been ordered to await the warrant and arrival of a tactical team of Anoka Police, who were just now driving up from the gate to the house.

Right behind them was Bittinger in his St. Paul City car. He badged his way through reluctant Anoka cops who were securing the property line and talked to the crime scene lead officer, Lieutenant Phil Mattson. Once it was clear that this site was related to the fugitive in the paper, Bittinger was welcomed. He asked if he could join the first walk-through of the house after it was cleared and Mattson agreed.

Bittinger, the stakeout officers and the support team were backed off to the edge of the property. Mattson and his crew were heavily armed men in Kevlar vests and tactical gear. Not quite a SWAT team – the rural area rarely needed one – but they were the most trained group Anoka had available. They approached the house in well-practiced formation and the young lieutenant was first man to the top stair at the front. Meanwhile others were stationed behind him and several more spread around to the back. Mattson peered in the window in the front door with his hand to the glass so he could see. He suddenly went upright, signaled the men to retreat and barked into the radio on his lapel.

"Fall back, fall back."

"What is it, Lou?" several men asked as they converged with him near the small barn.

"Just inside there's an arsenal of guns, including automatic weapons," Mattson said. "There's a wide open cabinet right inside the front door." He turned to Bittinger, "Is this a militia or something like that?"

"We don't know. Definitely anti-government types," Bitt said. "So, yeah, maybe."

He motioned for everyone to retreat to the street.

As he walked with Bittinger, they spoke privately, "We're not prepared for anything like this. I have to call my captain, but could you check with your people? We're going to need some serious assistance."

"SWAT team, all that?" Bittinger asked as he thought about the prospect of a militia stand-off like Ruby Ridge or any of the other battles between self-declared sovereign citizens and the government they feared and hated.

Bittinger made the call and eventually had his own chief on the line, not a common occurrence for him. The St. Paul Police Chief ordered all the tactical support the city police could offer. Then Bitt called Joe.

"We walked into one helluva hornet's nest," Bitt said,

then he described the arsenal inside the front door of Devins' house and the plans of the police, including the commitment from the city to send everyone available on duty at the time. That left a minimal police presence in town.

Joe was driving toward the city from the farm and said, "I got a lead on the truck Trammell was driving when we had that fight, so I'm going to go look into it. Anoka's out of my jurisdiction. You okay there?"

"Yeah, I'll see this through here," Bitt said. "Is Byron with you?"

"He's been detained by the Anoka police who seem to think we lit their crime scene on fire."

Bittinger didn't like the sound of where this was going. "So you're alone?"

"Yeah. It's just a license plate."

"Maybe, or with a truck attached," Bitt said. "You okay with this? I could see about sending a patrol car."

"They don't know we know it's there, that'd sort of give it away. I really doubt he's stayed with the truck."

Bitt nodded to himself and finally said, "Okay. Check out that lead, but...if you find the truck, don't approach, okay? Just call me."

"Will do."

"I'll get them to bring Byron here," Bitt said. "We need his insights on this. You be careful, these guys are marching to a drummer we can't even begin to hear."

———

THE SUN WAS up and it was going to be a clear day. Simon had been driving the plumbing truck for over an hour, slow and careful and taking an entirely different route than he'd used with Cory's pickup. As he passed the Minnesota state capitol and came into view of St. Paul Plaza, he couldn't take his eyes off the Children's and Family Services Building. He wanted to remember what it looked like even though he was confident the news media would remind the world for years to come. It was nothing special, eight stories of glass, steel and cement with a mundane sense of style. But what a great name – 'Children and Family' – ready-made for the outrage of the press and the horror of the public. All that hatred would boil up and be focused on Cory, while he alone would revel in his incredible accomplishment and unbreakable anonymity.

———————

TRAVIS COULDN'T GO BACK HOME, so he was early to pick up Cory. He let himself in the rear door of the locksmith shop and had the sheepskin wrapped around his weapons.

Cory was alert, armed and ready to go. He'd stewed in his impatience to get on with it. He'd killed before – he accepted that – but now he was wanted by every cop in the state on trumped up charges of arson and murder. They would shoot him on sight, so why shouldn't he shoot first? They'd made it 'kill or be killed' and the only solace left in his shattered life was that he was going to make them pay for everything they'd taken.

Travis started pulling on a shoulder holster for his HK. He preferred the one on his hip but it slung too low and the weapon showed below the lower end of the sheepskin. He needed to look unarmed, so he seated the weapon in the shoulder holster, pulled his lighter jacket back on over it and pocketed an extra clip.

"The bulge shows," Cory said.

Travis nodded, but simply slung an automatic rifle on a strap over his other shoulder, above the first jacket, then pulled on the coat atop all of it. "Show now?"

"No," Cory said. "That's a lot of armament."

"Better to have it and not need it than to need it and not have it," Travis said as he slid a thirty-round clip for the rifle into each cargo pocket of the sheepskin. His theory was he could unload the sheepskin in the escape if he needed to change how he looked.

"Let's get this on the road," Cory said.

"It's early," Travis said. "Simon said..."

"Better to be early and wait than be too late."

Travis grinned and it felt good going into action with Cory again. He didn't let himself think about later and instead just focused on letting the adrenaline drive him into their last mission together. He loved the jolt.

———

LIKE ANY ORDINARY DAY, cars, public transportation and pedestrians started to converge on the plaza from the early morning hours. People scurried to beat the lines at the DMV and to go through the security stations at the public buildings before they got too crowded. Employees headed to work for the last workday of the week and others stopped for coffees to help get them through the morning.

At one side of the plaza, Betsy slipped unseen out of the library with the night cleaning crew as they were clocking out. She looked across the plaza toward the Family Services Building, where her father had made her go inside in hopes of finding news about Patrick Henry. She'd hang around the building and the plaza, hoping her father would come by at last and they would go fetch her brother, find her Mom and get out of town. She was deep into the fantasy, the only hope she had left, when the plumbing truck drove past. She didn't notice the driver and Simon didn't begin to recognize her.

There was already a small line of cars at the entrance to the underground parking ramp below Family Services. While he waited his turn to get a ticket to enter, Simon changed his hat, snugged it down to his dark glasses and wrapped the scarf to cover half his face.

Most of the cars drove to the lower parking level reserved for employees because offices weren't open yet. Simon took the ticket in a gloved hand without looking at the camera and followed the flow to the lower level where his first order of business was checking on Cory's pickup. It sat right where he'd left it, so he drove by and pulled the plumbing truck along the side of the elevator shaft, away from the elevator lobby where all the security cameras were aimed. He parked five feet from the cinderblock wall and the space would form a semi-enclosed work area that was entirely outside the view of the security cameras.

The uniform he wore had embroidery over the pocket saying 'Larry,' and he wore a laminated badge clipped to the coat which read 'All City Plumbing,' the same as the magnetic signs on the doors of the truck. The cap he had snugged down had the logo of a plumbing supply company and even had ear-flaps which helped obscure his face.

———————

JOE WASN'T ACCUSTOMED to driving into downtown from the north, nor was he ready for the traffic snarling its way through too many stoplights and one-car-at-a-time left turns. It was slow, but it gave him time to call Kat. He figured she'd be up by now, but he got voice mail at home. So he tried Marlo's cell, hoping he wasn't waking her up.

"Hey there, Kat Nolan," Marlo said, having seen her name on the caller ID. "How you doing, Joe?"

"Glad she told you I'm using her phone. You know where she is?"

"We're heading into the psych ward to get the boy."

Joe heard the phone change hands and then Kat said, "How'd your emergency turn out?"

"Someone got killed and the house burned down."

"That's not funny, Joe."

"I wish it were a joke. These guys are a whole lot worse than any of us could ever have imagined."

"Damn," she said. "You okay?"

"Yeah. You can't just let the boy out of the psych ward, Kat. His dad and friends are still on the loose."

"The seventy-two hours expired, you couldn't get it renewed and they desperately need the bed," Kat said.

"He'll make a run for it, you know."

"Abraham is helping us," Kat said, then whispered, "I think he and Marlo consider this a date."

"Glad to hear he's okay," Joe said. "Where you taking the boy then? You found another place to keep him?"

"There's the rub. We're taking him to my office where Abraham and Marlo and I will sit on him while we find an alternative."

"I don't like it."

"I'm not exactly thrilled," Kat said. "Marlo made contact with a family that takes difficult kids, but we have to wait for the paperwork."

"Okay. So listen to me carefully," Joe said after a long pause. "Don't park in the building today. You guys will be fine in your office, especially with Abraham there, but don't drive into the parking garage."

"I don't like the sound of this. Why?"

"Cory Trammell's license plate is on some vehicle, somewhere in the parking ramp below your building."

"His license plate?"

"It drove in last night at 9:41 and hasn't left. I just found out and I have no idea what it means. It's probably nothing, just stolen or something. And it's not like he's going to stick around the truck."

"So you and Byron are going to check it out?"

"He's dealing with the burnt down house and Bittinger is possibly looking at an armed stand-off out in Anoka, along with most of the St. Paul Police Department. In all likelihood, that's where Trammell is."

"Where are you?"

"On my way to your building and I'd feel a lot better if you weren't walking through the parking ramp at all."

In the back of his mind, Joe had already decided to ask Enright to send a cop to stay in the waiting room for Kat's office. There must be a few officers they didn't sent to Anoka.

"You're scaring me," Kat said. "Where will you be?"

"Checking security camera recordings, trying to match the plate to the truck. Then I'll come up to see you."

"It's a deal."

———————

AT THE LOWER PARKING LEVEL, the flood of arriving employees was slowing down. Simon had been working steadily and was almost ready to turn on the small portable air compressor he'd brought. He had no need for compressed air but those little oil-driven compressors made an awful racket. The noise would drown out the brief blast he now had ready to trigger. He had mounted a modest directional charge inside a tall, innocent-looking trashcan he'd brought with him. Now filled with sand, it was heavy enough to resist the outward pressure of the explosion that would drive a hole straight through both sections of the hollow cinderblock wall between the garage and the elevator shaft. It would be just like the holes he'd practiced on.

He took a look around to see if anyone was in sight. Most people were up in their offices by now, but he saw a straggler and waited with his hat low as if working. The man glanced past the barricade at the end of the truck and all he saw was a workman and tools – just an ordinary worksite. When Simon heard the elevator doors close, he turned on the small, noisy air compressor, stepped past the work 'Caution' barricade and got behind the truck. Then he pressed the button on the remote for his detonator.

He didn't even feel the exploding charge inside the can and it wasn't any louder than the compressor. He pulled the barricade back in place after him and shut off the compressor. The blast left the trashcan standing upright and a couple inches from the wall. He wrestled it aside with considerable effort, then shined his flashlight through the new hole in the wall. Just as planned, light reached all the way into the elevator shaft. He now had an opening through both walls of the cinderblock.

32

There was no parking or stopping on the street passing the open side of the plaza during rush hour, but Marlo pulled over as far as she could and stopped amid angry honking. Abraham got out first, reached in to take a handful of Patrick Henry's collar. Finally Kat and the boy got out, then Marlo sped off. The boy's second-hand coat was zipped to the neck and the big man had such a firm grip on the collar, he could pick the kid off the ground if he needed. They would go in an calm, deliberate manner and the boy didn't have any say in the matter.

In the crowded plaza, Betsy walked among their kind and looked above most of the heads, hoping to spot her father. Given that his picture was in the paper, she had to look really closely at every man passing, because he would certainly be trying to disguise himself. It wasn't like she was dressed in anything he was familiar with either, so they could practically walk right past each other.

If it weren't for the bandages, she wouldn't have lingered on the big black man for a second, but Abraham's wounds attracted her attention. Then she saw him holding onto the collar of Patrick Henry's coat and, right behind them, was the female agent.

Betsy had had the feeling today was the day. It was all going to get better, the whole family were going to be together at last and get away from these awful people and terrible city. But first she had to show herself to her brother. She discovered she had again unconsciously brought the steak knife into her hand and contemplated using it. If she could get Patrick Henry free, they could run for it and look for Dad together. But seeing the grip the big black man had on her brother, she knew it wouldn't work. It was more likely they'd both end up in the man's grasp.

Instead, she rushed ahead to the door to the building and opened it right ahead of the trio, keeping her head down as she let them go in first. But as Patrick Henry passed her, she kicked him in the shin. It pissed the boy off and he angrily looked back for the attacker and spotted her through the glass door as it closed between them. His sister was the last person on earth he expected to see, but he ventured a tiny wave before he was pulled into the line for security. Betsy watched and tried to think like Dad.

The lines to go through security in the Family Services lobby snaked all the way back to the elevators, which now delivered more people to await their turn. Kat, Abraham and the boy were still waiting when Marlo caught up. She stayed with Abraham and the boy as Kat went ahead to make arrangements for how they would go through the scanner while holding onto Patrick Henry. She talked with a guard she knew to coordinate the handover when they went through security.

Patrick Henry watched the parade of people going through the machines his father had always told him never to go near, they'd kill you. The people on the other side didn't seem to be dying, but Dad had said it was a slow death. He finally turned away and looked out at freedom, hoping to see his father with his sister outside.

Betsy walked back from ditching the steak knife she wouldn't be able to sneak through security and watched her brother disappeared inside the building. She knew exactly where they were heading, but she still didn't know how she'd get Patrick Henry free.

JOE PARKED ON THE UPPER, visitor's level, then looked around for the office of the parking manager. Anne had sent him a GIF of the license plate entering, as well as one of the person fetching the ticket. It was impossible to make out anything from the cell phone screen and he wanted to watch it on the building's video feed to see if he could learn more. A police order had already been given to preserve the recording and the manager was expecting him. It was a tiny, windowless office built of cinderblocks and tucked along-side one of the street-level emergency exit stairways that were at the four corners of the structure.

After five minutes with the manager, going over the recordings, he felt fairly certain it was Trammell's pickup truck. The bumper around the plate was rusty, plus the little bit of the door under the driver's window was the same dirty beige he remembered. Unfortunately, the person taking the ticket was successfully hiding his identity.

The parking manager assured Joe that the truck must still be on the visitor's level since it would have been ticketed if had been on the employee level without a parking pass. There hadn't been any citations, so Joe decided to make a systematic search of the visitor level.

SIMON WAS MAKING disappointing progress inserting his mechanism through the holes blasted into the cinderblocks. The nozzles that would vaporize the gasoline were delicate, so he couldn't just ram the device through. His explosive charge in the trashcan had been so precise, the holes it blew were just a bit narrower than he needed, so now he was chipping the holes wider and it was slow going using a cold chisel and hitting it with a heavy mallet. Not ideal and it sure didn't look like a plumbing, so he'd halted the chiseling whenever anyone passed.

Five stories above him, on the third floor, Kat sat in her office with Patrick Henry and Marlo, while Abraham was on guard in the reception area. That boy would not get by.

ENRIGHT WAS DELIVERED TO TRAVIS' house by Captain Cubbin, who instantly started coordinating virtually every man in his department with the SWAT team and support crews that St. Paul had sent.

Bittinger noticed the sliced-open pants and bandaging on Enright's calf, but his questioning look was waved off. "Today would be a good day to rob a bank in St. Paul," Bitt said as he and Enright looked over the men and women who had assembled on the street outside the farm house. "Everyone we got on duty is out here."

"Any sign of life inside?"

"Not a movement."

Enright's phone rang and it took him a second to register that 'Kat Nolan' meant the call was from Joe. "Bittinger paid my bail," he said.

"So where are you then?" Joe asked.

"From here it looks like Waco, Texas, but at least he's got no propane tank."

"Thank goodness for small favors. So you're with Bitt? Could you ask him to assign an officer to Kat's office in Family Services?"

"I can ask. Why?"

"I think Trammell's truck might be in the parking ramp below her office. She's upstairs right now with Patrick Henry. It's a long story."

"I'll ask Bitt to send one to you and one to her," Enright said, then cupped the phone to talk with Bittinger.

Bitt looked around, spotted a St. Paul Police captain and went to make a request. Enright watched as the officer shook his head sadly and gestured at the crowd.

"We're stretched to the breaking point," Bitt said. "He can't authorize it at the moment, not until there's a better handle on what kind of militia we got here."

"Damn. It's for Joe and Kat," Enright said.

"Oaky, I'll call in a couple buddies who are off-duty today. Tell Joe they'll be there within the hour, just give me the particulars."

Joe was relieved and said he'd be found wandering around the visitor level of the parking ramp. Even as he was telling the details to Enright, his phone reception broke up when he took the stairs down into the cement-encased structure. The call ended before he reached the visitor parking level and opened the fire door to a sea of vehicles. More were driving in as he began his search.

33

Simon had the mounting board with his nozzle rig inserted properly and flat against the cinderblock wall. He wasn't far behind schedule and he'd given himself a buffer anyway, so no problem. He picked up the Hilti that already had a full strip of the .27 caliber blank bullets loaded. He inserted an anchor, which was an adhesive-coated large head nail, looked around to be certain no one was nearby, then drove in the first nail to attach the board. He fumbled in his pocket for another nail, which could only be loaded one at a time, and his shaky hands showed that he was more nervous than he cared to admit. As he secured the corners of the panel, he even dropped a few of the heavy anchors, but he kept nailing – he was so close. Finally with eight nails driven into the cinderblocks, securing the board to the elevator wall, he stepped back to admire his work.

Now visible on the board were just the two-inch coupling he would use to attach the hose from the large gas tank plus a small metal box covering the simple ignition device he'd built. His trigger had two wires threaded through the board and into the chamber of the elevators, right along with the nozzles. He checked the charge of the battery and the backup battery. Everything was good to go.

From the back of the truck, he fetched the reinforced high capacity hose and coupled one end to the tank and locked the metal parts together with super glue dribbled onto the screw threads. Then he coupled the other end to the wall unit and locked it in place exactly the same way. After about ten seconds of setting up, that glue would make it impossible to detach the tank from the elevator shaft. All ten of the scuba tanks had already been joined into one central feed leading into the gas tank. Opening the main air valve from the air tanks would drive up pressure inside the big gas tank to four thousand pounds per square inch.

He could hear the pressurization happening and that compressed air would keep flowing as gasoline escaped into his rig, once he initiated everything. Filled with anticipation, he grasped the valve from the tank to the two-inch hose. He wanted to do a test run before he went through the final checklist. Then it would be time for the fateful moment – locking it on. He turned the lever so it was parallel with the coupling and felt the large hose go rigid as he heard the faint whoosh of the gasoline being atomized on the other side of the block wall, where it was being distributed evenly throughout the eleven story shaft. Thrilled, he shut it off until he had the timer set and had gone through his final protocol. He'd planned every step to the minutest detail.

JOE'S FRUSTRATION was growing because he had looked at every license plate on every vehicle, no matter its size or color. The pickup truck license plate was not on any vehicle in visitor parking. He decided to ignore the parking manager, he was going to check the lower level. This was a solid lead and he wasn't about to quit now, there were too many strangely connected elements for which they had found no common thread, except their association with Trammell. This would, Joe hoped, lead to the man.

At the far corner of the garage, he took the emergency exit stairs down another flight. The lower level was packed with employees' cars and he repeated the exact same routine – license plate, vehicle, move on. It was slow but for once, instead of being four steps behind Cory Trammell, he felt like now he was only one step. The man had been here at 9:41 last night.

Before Joe got to the end of the second row, he was standing at the rear bumper of Cory's pickup. It had a parking permit hanging from the rearview mirror along with an air freshener. The pickup was empty, of course, but he'd found it and his heart was pounding as he glanced around for any sign of Trammell. He tried calling Bittinger, because he needed police here right now.

There was no cell reception and he'd have to go up two flights, then leave the building to make a call. But he didn't want to take his eyes off the truck and possibly miss the killer himself. As he'd searched, he'd spotted a plumbing truck boxed-in with barricades and figured it might have a powerful radio like they used to carry. Hoping to use the plumber's radio to call the police and stay close to the pickup, he headed toward the worksite.

———————

CORY AND TRAVIS parked on the street, just as Simon had instructed, and then walked separately a minute apart into an emergency exit stairway in the corner of the parking ramp. Travis tried to delay Cory because they were ten minutes ahead of schedule, but he had insisted they go in as soon as they arrived. He'd risk being spotted rather than wait around for Simon to call. They went directly to the lower parking level and scoped it out until they saw the lobby outside the bank of elevators. Cory took up a position behind one of the cement support pillars that were spaced throughout the parking ramp and Travis waited behind another, feeling amped up. Thrilled, actually.

Cory had a hard time standing still and his hand was continually going to the gun in his jacket pocket. He was itching to move, but he'd found a good spot where he had a clear view of the elevators. Once the two agents arrived, he could reach them in under five seconds. He contemplated moving closer, but worried it might reveal him to them too soon. After all, these two were obviously trained agents.

Travis felt the weight of the two main guns and the three extra clips of ammunition – along with the heavy sheepskin coat itself – and it made him feel loaded down, but he was also energized by all the adrenaline coursing through his body, it didn't faze him. Having so much ordnance made him feel tough, but he'd much rather walk armed to the teeth than hide, so he stepped over to Cory.

"I'm going to look around, make certain our escape route is clear and that I know every step of it."

Cory nodded. He was so focused on watching for Brandt and Nolan that getting away wasn't on his radar. Still, he wanted Travis to be able to escape. He watched his friend stroll away with surprising calm, but quickly turned his attention back to the well-lit bay outside the elevators. He hadn't expected a plumbing truck to be parked right there, with a workman in a big hat working on something behind the barriers. But his presence wouldn't change anything. Cory just had to wait for his targets; from that moment on, it would be a frenzy until it was all over.

Then he spotted Joe Brandt approaching the plumber.

As HE WALKED up to the truck, Joe thought he caught a whiff of gas. Maybe the old truck had a slow leak. As he stepped up to the caution signs the smell was more intense. Hard to believe this guy didn't notice.

Simon had just set the battery-operated timer that would trigger the spark for the gas in the elevator shaft. He set it for ten minutes and synchronized it with a timer on his own watch. He was using super glue to lock the cover in place so it would hold until it was blown to pieces.

"Hey, buddy," Joe said to Simon, "I think you got a gas leak."

Simon had to keep hand pressure on the glued cover so it would set properly. Though startled by the unexpected approach, he masked his surprise, glanced Joe's direction and said, "That's what I'm here fixing." He looked directly at Joe with a smile and absolute earnestness while he lied.

"But it smells like gasoline, not natural gas."

"It's being taken care of, not to worry," Simon said as he turned back to his work. At least this guy was never going to be a witness, he only had ten minutes to live.

"Good to know. Say, you got a radio in the truck, something that will call out?" Joe said.

"Nah. Not for years," Simon said jovially as he held the cover in place for the last few seconds he needed. His hand was on the gun inside his jacket, but the silencer wasn't on it and he'd really rather not have to use it. A gunshot would bring attention and alter his well-planned escape. He'd shoot if that's what it took, but only if this guy forced him.

Joe looked over the rig stretching from the truck to the wall and something was odd about it, but he had the pickup truck and Cory Trammell on his mind. He turned away to enter the central stairs, but realized they led to the security lines in the lobby. So he headed to the nearest corner exit for the most direct route upstairs. He'd call Bitt, then hurry back to the truck to wait until the police arrived.

———

BETSY PEEKED in the glass door that led to the Psychological Therapy waiting room and saw the big guy with all the bandages sitting there. She spun on her heel, marched down the hallway and stopped at a fire alarm with a fire extinguisher beside it. Ten seconds later, she flung open the door and sprayed Abraham in the face with the extinguisher as she shouted "Patrick Henry."

While the man yelled and wiped at his face, she shouted her brother's name again. The receptionist looked to the back and Betsy went running toward the sounds of a scuffle she heard from behind Kat's office door. She threw that door open and beckoned Patrick Henry, who broke free of Kat and Marlo.

Betsy led her brother on a mad dash out the door just before Kat and Marlo followed. Marlo saw Abraham, grabbed a bottle of water from a horrified client and started helping Abraham wash the stuff off his face. Kat dashed out and caught sight of Betsy and the boy at the end of the hall just as the stairway door closed automatically.

———

AS HE RUSHED to the corner exit stairs, Joe thought about that apparatus the plumber was working on. Something just wasn't right. It didn't seem like plumbing and the workman had to know the difference between the smell of gasoline and natural gas. A week earlier, he may not have thought twice about it, but now his recent experiences had him questioning everything he saw. He headed back for a second look before making his call to Bitt. The pickup wasn't going anywhere.

As he approached the plumbing truck, Joe saw Simon putting continuous pressure on a large valve lever to the hose leading to the wall. He looked about warily, spotted Joe paying way too much attention to him and coming back toward him. Simon suddenly took off running toward the exit stairs in the corner of the ramp.

Alarmed, Joe stepped past the barricades cordoning off the area and studied the truck, the hose and the thing mounted on the wall. There were tools strewn all about and he heard the echoing sound of the exit door closing. He tried to turn the valve lever and it wouldn't budge. He could see hardened super glue that had oozed out around the mechanism, so it was locked open. And now he could hear a whooshing sound that was muted but distinct while the smell of gas just kept getting stronger. The hose was rigid and felt like something was flowing through it, but it wasn't water. There was no plumbing anywhere nearby, not even a water fountain.

The image of the propane tank raced through his brain as he hurried over to the lobby outside the elevators. There was a red fire alarm on the wall, and he hesitated half a second, then he pulled the fire alarm lever.

The alarm resounded throughout the building as he rushed back to the truck. He tried to turn the valve handle and even banged at it with a mallet he found on the floor, but it wouldn't budge. He followed the hose and yanked down the tailgate at the back of the truck to reveal a huge tank and a bunch of scuba tanks. He didn't need to understand the whole thing, all he knew was that this was all wrong.

All valves were glued open, so he inspected the coupling of the hose to the metal which passed through the wall. Nothing would move, including the little metal box which had hardened super glue all around its perimeter. He tried to remember everything Denny had told him about the shotgun shells and wires at the arson fire. He felt certain the box contained a triggering mechanism. The Hilti, which looked like an Uzi, was nearby and much heavier than the mallet, so with the butt of it he smashed at the box.

Cory hit Joe from behind and it sent him flying right into the caution barricade. He careened to the floor and the Hilti skittered out of reach.

———

BETSY AND PATRICK HENRY had raced down the exit stairs. When they heard the fire alarm, they thought it was because of them and darted out the stairway door on the main level right into a mass of panicked people. In the lobby, guards were attempting to direct the mob toward the exit doors. To escape the throng, they ran back into the stairway just as a flood of people began streaming down from upper floors. To escape them they headed farther down.

Among those evacuating were Marlo and Abraham. With his vision blurred, she had to guide him down the increasingly crowded steps. She suspected Patrick Henry had pulled a fire alarm and this was merely a means of escape for them, but they had to get out of the building with everyone else.

***

SIMON STOOD OUTSIDE THE BUILDING, troubled to hear the fire alarm. That wasn't supposed to happen. He figured the smell of gas would leak out in the upper floors and people would step out to investigate – exactly as he'd planned. By the time they grew really alarmed, it would be too late. But somebody, maybe it was that damned busybody down in the garage, had pulled the fire alarm and people were getting out of the building too soon.

He tried for a third time to call Travis, but once again his call went to voice mail. He wondered if Travis was out of range or if he'd chickened out, so he didn't know if they were in place. That guy in the garage had startled him into leaving the truck with all the tools out and he'd failed to glue the truck locks. His slim margin of potential failure was widening.

He checked his watch and knew he had a couple minutes of leeway. This was too important to leave to chance – with or without Cory and Travis. So he dashed back inside, passing more people evacuating as he ran down the stairs to the lower parking level.

34

Travis had hidden behind an SUV when the fire alarm first started blaring, then scanned the area for the nearest exit. This was not part of the plan and, not knowing what was going on, he headed to the corner stairs to get the hell out of Dodge. This wasn't what he'd signed up for, so fuck Cory. Once he opened fire, they'd kill him, likely as not. End of story, end of his worries, back to business. What difference did it make if the plan didn't go exactly as Simon wanted if Cory still died and they both got away?

But then he realized, if Cory lived, it would be a disaster for him and Simon. If they spared his life, the feds would get everything out of Cory eventually and they would be toast. He pulled the HK out of the holster and held it under his sheepskin coat. He had to make sure Cory did not get out of this alive.

On his way back into the heart of the parking ramp, he spotted Cory's pickup. What the hell was it doing here? The last anyone had been anywhere near it, Simon had faked a government tracker device on it to convince Cory about the agents. Simon told them he'd left it where he found it –

outside a big box store. Simon's grand plan was looking more fucked up by the second.

He peered inside the truck, which had a parking pass, and the seat was pushed all the way to the front. Cory drove with it far back for his long legs. Then he spotted the tarp and tools behind the seat and, almost before he'd thought it through, Travis smashed the passenger-side window with the gun butt. He pulled at that tarp behind the seat and saw Abby's legs.

JOE HELD a caution barricade up to fend off Cory's onslaught. Luckily he was faster and there was a truck he could dart around, while he hoped the alarm and evacuation would bring help. 'How long ago had Bitt promised men?' he wondered. Not long enough.

Cory got hold of the barricade and sent it flying. Rather than run, Joe darted ahead. Just like he'd done with large basketball players, he avoided being stopped as he ducked under the hose and looked for a weapon. All he could reach was a mallet that Simon left. It wouldn't do anything against Trammel, but the metal box was still intact. He couldn't just keep running away from this guy, he had to destroy the bomb trigger. The mallet might work.

Cory was getting tired of chasing around and figured that even if a gunshot brought the police, at least he could kill this prick and hope to find the woman later.

"Simon, you fucking bastard," echoed throughout the parking ramp and seemed to come from every direction. It was Travis' voice and it momentarily confused Cory.

The first gunshot reverberated from everywhere at once and neither of them could place the direction. Cory realized the whole plan was falling apart, so he abandoned waiting for the second agent and reached into his pocket for the gun.

The mallet smashed his hand inside the jacket pocket with such power, Cory knew instantly that several bones were broken. As he pulled the damaged hand out, the gun went clattering to the floor and Joe was so fast, he had it before Cory could scream through the first spasms of pain.

Joe flicked the safety off and leveled the gun at Cory, stopping him in his tracks. Joe looked over at his greatest worry, the triggering mechanism, while the big man was stunned into inaction. With the gun in one hand, he used the mallet in the other to pound as hard as he could, but the metal box did not budge.

Sustained automatic weapon fire sounded like it came from all around, as if he and Cory were being shot at by an army. Joe instinctively flinched.

That was when Cory lunged.

No conscious thought moved from mind to finger, but Joe pulled the trigger. The bullet caught Cory in the side and sent him sprawling.

Blood spread out from the man on the floor as more high caliber automatic weapon fire echoed around the garage and then abruptly stopped. After a pause, there were two quick pops from a smaller caliber gun, then silence.

With Cory wounded and down, Joe thought of the box still protecting the bomb trigger, but shooting it seemed like a dangerous idea. He fetched the Hilti, spotted one of the anchors on the floor and inserted it. He carefully aimed it right at the joint between the box and the mounting board, hoping it would dislodge the mechanism.

A bullet slammed into the cinderblock beside his head, peppering him with cement dust.

Joe glanced quickly and saw the plumber sprinting away, then he pulled the Hilti trigger. The nail went in at an angle, loosening the box from the board. He yanked the mechanism away, finding long stiff wires taped together so their bare ends were nearly touching. He remembered what Denny had told him at Cory's house about the electric spark for a detonation.

He slipped a finger between the wires while he tried to separate them. He felt a sudden surge of electricity jolting him and realized that shock would have been the spark meant to ignite the gas in the elevator shaft.

Simon ran out the emergency exit from the building at top speed. He was quite a distance behind a large crowd of people who were still moving away from the building. The fire alarm blared as the wail of many sirens headed toward the scene. In every direction, he saw the lights of fire trucks and police vehicles on site and some just arriving.

He checked his watch and saw its countdown timer had reached zero already. Yet there had been no explosion.

He slowed and looked back at the building, hoping for it, but he knew that his trigger had somehow failed. The gas mist would settle in the bottom of the elevator shaft and his nearly perfect atomization would quickly diminish. The blast potential got smaller with every second of delay.

Joe ripped the batteries out of the detonator and saw that Cory had struggled to his feet, the cold chisel in his good hand. Joe fumbled around with the gun as Cory was straightening up, poised to attack.

"Daddy," Patrick Henry cried as he and Betsy flew out the doorway from the central stairway twenty feet away.

Cory was paralyzed with shock as his son ran up and threw his arms around him. Then Betsy was there, wrapping them both. He was beyond mystified, and remained frozen inside their embrace, as the other agent ran out of the stairs after them.

Kat stopped at the sight of the wounded man, the kids, and Joe with a gun in his hand. She was almost overwhelmed by the reek of gas surrounding them all.

The chisel fell to the floor as Cory held his kids. They were alive and their embrace overcame him.

With an arm around their shoulders, Cory led them toward the stairs the pair had just come down.

"I can't let you go," Joe said, holding the gun.

"You can't stop us," Cory said as Betsy pulled the exit door open for them. His blood trailed behind them.

"We gotta get out of here," Kat said to Joe, her hand on his arm pulling him away. "We gotta get away from the gas." Gasoline mist was now spewing from the hole left by the dismantled triggering mechanism.

"Don't go up those stairs," Joe shouted at Cory, but the automatic door just closed behind him and the kids.

Kat yanked him again and Joe threw down the gun, then raced with her toward a corner stairway. As they neared it, they passed Travis' body. He'd been shot in the head and heart.

The explosion was deafening. It threw Joe and Kat flying against a car near the exit door. Alarms blared and lights flashed in half the cars as they looked back and saw the whole central stairway, as well as the elevator shaft walls, decimated. Cinderblocks tumbled down and the nearest elevator car crashed to the bottom, sending a second shock-wave through the lower level parking area. Cement dust blanketed the flames that had escaped from the demolished walls to the elevator shaft and stairway.

Joe and Kat were picking themselves up from the floor when they heard, "Help!" coming from the central stairs.

ALONG WITH THE crowd of evacuees, Simon watched as the explosion rocked the building. Unlike everyone else, he was neither surprised nor horrified, he was disappointed. The detonation had been substantial, but it was far smaller than he'd planned. The building hadn't come down and wasn't likely to. Most of its windows were even still intact. He guessed the elevator shaft was gone, the elevator doors on each floor had probably flown out, killing anyone in the halls, maybe there was internal collapse.

At least that guy who interfered died in the blast.

He turned away, while all around him people gasped and watched. He couldn't linger and there wasn't much here to savor. This was nothing like he'd envisioned and, judging from the crowds outside, the death toll would be low. Not what it would have been if it had gone off as planned.

THE METAL FIRE door to the stairs had blown off and flown all the way across the driving lane. The hose from the plumbing truck had snapped in the blast and was now spraying the last remnants of the gas onto the floor making mud of the mounds of cement dust.

Kat looked through the opening left by the demolished wall to the central stairs and beckoned Joe. The entire poured cement stairway had collapsed onto itself, but some of the automatic emergency exit lights had survived, leaving individual pools of light.

A fixture lit the wreckage at the base of the stairs – it was a tangle of huge cement fragments, reinforcing bars, hand rails and billowing dust from pulverized cinderblocks.

Together, Joe and Kat ventured past where the wall had once been and threaded cautiously past spikes of rebar sticking up at odd angles out of the rubble. Joe spotted Betsy, who had been calling for help. She was about ten feet over their heads, clinging to a dangling section of stairs with one of Cory's arms wrapped around her. She teetered on the edge of a void that was open all the way down to Joe and Kat who stood among the rising rebar. Behind her, they could make out Patrick Henry and then, sandwiched between them, Cory turned to look their way.

It was miraculous they'd survived a blast that had collapsed the stairs under them. Cory had been wrapped around them, protecting the kids, when they'd been thrown by the explosion. He was now bleeding profusely.

"Help them," Cory pleaded.

Kat held onto Joe from behind, trying to steady him, as he stepped into the crater of the stairs and reached up. He could see the agony in Cory's face as he held on with his broken hand while he lifted his daughter off their tenuous perch and lowered her with one arm into the middle of the abyss below them. Betsy could feel Joe's hands grab her legs.

"I got her," Joe said.

Cory let go and somehow with the help of Kat, he caught the girl and kept her from falling onto the rebar. Kat tried to lead her away, but Betsy refused to go.

"Come on, Patrick Henry," she shouted.

Joe reached up as Cory lowered his son, but he couldn't reach the shorter boy's legs, even when Cory was at full extension.

Joe shouted, "Let go of him," and the boy plummeted down onto him. Kat and Betsy yanked on Joe and, together, they all fell into the garage area, away from the rubble.

Kat helped the kids to their feet and pointed them to one of the corner emergency exits. They looked back up toward Cory, but he frantically waved for them to go. And finally they ran off together.

"We have to go, Joe," Kat shouted to Joe who was looking up at Cory.

"Can you lower yourself down?" Joe said.

Cory shook his head.

"I was wrong," Cory said.

Joe nodded, then followed Kat out of the stairway and discovered there was fire once again in the gas pooled in the bottom of the elevator shaft.

Then Joe and Kat ran for their lives.

35

As Joe and Kat dashed into the exit stairway, they could hear the door two flights up closing behind the kids. They ran up the stairs as fast as they could and were a half flight from street level when the large tank in the plumbing truck exploded. The impact knocked them both to their knees, but they kept crawling upward and were on their feet just before they slammed through the crash bar on the door and out into the bright light of the morning. As they straggled away, they heard and felt the first car gas tank explode.

As they rushed away, Kat strained to look in every direction for Betsy and Patrick Henry, but they were gone. The two kids had just kept right on running.

Surrounding the building were fire engines and crews already working, while police were ushering the evacuees farther away. Kat and Joe had emerged on the side of Family Service where the drive-down entrance to the underground parking was. There was noxious black smoke billowing from the opening as more car gas tanks on the lower level began to explode. They sounded distant and muted, but Joe and Kat knew exactly how powerful each of those blasts really was. The garage was now an inferno.

After they checked each other for signs of injuries and found none, Joe wrapped his overcoat around her. She'd raced after the kids without a coat. Then they made their way toward the plaza side of the building and found what looked like the fire department command center. Joe realized the police presence must be seriously diminished because so many units had been sent out to Anoka. They walked as far from the building as the balustrade above the parking entrance would allow and watched smoke billow out windows that had broken, mostly from the ends of hallways.

"I hope everyone got out," Kat said.

FOR BLOCKS in every direction from St. Paul Plaza, no traffic was getting through on the streets. Many drivers had simply stopped where they were to watch the smoke in the distance and they could hear the explosions. There was a 9/11 feeling among everyone in the city as ash already rained down and each person's fears leapt to the worst imaginable scenarios. What kind of terrorists this time? Who were the crazy people behind it?

Walking past all those bewildered citizens were Betsy and Patrick Henry, who was now wearing one of his sister's two coats. It had warmed up and was sunny, so it wasn't too bad outside. Each of them thought of their father's fate, though neither could say it out loud. So they kept walking until the gridlock on the streets finally diminished.

Betsy was looking in all the cars that had stopped helter skelter in the street, especially the empty ones. At the end of a block she saw what she was looking for – keys in the ignition. There was a briefcase on the seat and a tray of Starbucks coffees. She spotted a man holding a coffee and talking animatedly with a group of onlookers. She quietly slid in behind the wheel and Patrick Henry dove into the back. She started it, backed it up and turned down the side street. No one paid a bit of attention to them.

They drove away, with no destination in mind. All they knew for certain was they couldn't go back anywhere they had ever been in their entire lives. It was just them now.

AT THE FARTHEST edge of the plaza itself, within direct view of the Family Services Building, a young cop stopped Joe and Kat from running to the gathering of fire captains and police brass. They looked like any other pair of the displaced when they reached the cordon around the leaders who were directing the response to the disaster.

"There will be answers to your questions on line as soon as they come up with some answers," the cop said. It was his job to make sure the fire captains were left alone.

Joe was too energized to stand still and looked around in the group until he spotted Russell Filmore.

"Russell!" he shouted as they pushed past the cop and ran. Everyone in command seemed to be simultaneously on radios and cell phones, in the midst of multiple urgent conversations and barking orders.

"Get this man a blanket," Russell shouted to a nearby fireman as he held a hand to the cop to stop him. "Sorry, Joe. I got no time," he said and started to turn away.

"I triggered that fire alarm," Joe said.

The activity all around them stopped as orders and phone calls were put on hold.

"I was in the parking ramp and found a very large bomb," Joe said as a blanket was wrapped around him.

Everyone at the command post crowded closer.

"The bomb had two wires to create the spark," Joe said. "He had a plumbing truck pumping gasoline through a thick hose into a wall. Into the elevator shaft, I think."

"Vaporizing it?" was called out. Joe looked toward the voice and spotted Denny moving closer.

"I think so. Smelled like gas. There was a huge tank and a bunch of scuba tanks for some reason."

"These smaller explosions are car gas tanks?" Denny asked. "Anything else inside we have to worry about?"

"I don't think so. The plumbing truck was his main thing. This is a third guy, somebody we didn't know about."

"He's the arsonist. Cory never felt right for this," Denny said. "You actually saw the bomb maker?"

"I talked to him."

"Jesus, Joe," Kat said with alarm.

"I scared him off, but then he came back while I was trying to disarm it," Joe said, then looked at Kat. "He shot at me, but it was too close to time and he ran again."

"He came back to make sure it went off?" Denny said. "Wow, this guy doesn't like loose ends." She was beginning to see the enormity of what Joe had gone through, but needed to get everything she could from him before he faded. "What was the sequence of explosions inside?"

"The first explosion was the elevator shaft, the second I think was the big tank that was mounted in the back of the plumbing truck."

"And now every car in the parking ramp," Filmore said. "Don't go anywhere, Joe. I'll get back to you."

Filmore and all the fire chiefs spoke together as they got back on their phones and radios.

Denny patted Joe on the back. "Enright is going to be so pleased," she said. "He's been calling every minute or so." Her phone rang and she handed it to him. "That's him."

"Hi," Joe said into the phone. "You still in Anoka?"

"You're alive," Enright said excitedly, then yelled to Bitt, "He's alive. Look, Joe, right now we're sending a SWAT team into this prick's house and then Bitt and I are part of the first walk-through team after it's cleared. It'll be a treasure trove of evidence."

"A SWAT team?" Joe said.

Denny grabbed her phone back and put it on speaker.

"Bryon, this is Denny, what's going on?"

"We're sending a SWAT team into Travis Devins' house."

Joe looked at Denny and said, "I don't like it." To the phone, he added, "There's a third guy. I met him inside before the explosion."

"He's the bomb maker," Denny said.

"Good to know," Enright said, "but I gotta go. The team is ready to storm the house."

"Stop them," Denny said with great authority.

"What?" Enright said through the phone.

"This guy plans well and he's so determined, he runs back toward a fully armed bomb," Denny said. "He's not going to leave a house filled with evidence for us. He's got another bomb up his sleeve."

"How certain are we?"

Denny and Joe exchanged nods. "One hundred percent," she said into the phone.

On the other end they heard Enright shouting, "Stop, stop. Abort! Captain, we have to fall back. The house is rigged to blow." There was more shouting, then rustling and then finally the connection went silent.

Filmore, who had been listening in, went back to the other fire captains while Denny led Joe to the rear of an ambulance parked on the plaza. Kat was sitting on the back bumper, her blood pressure being taken as she cupped a steaming coffee. He was placed beside her and the EMTs started to check him out.

Denny had fetched a cup of coffee from somewhere for Joe, then said, "Tell me everything you remember inside there. What prompted you to pull the fire alarm?"

Joe explained about the plumbing truck, the hose, the attachment to the cinderblock wall, the smell of gasoline and the little metal box he had been certain was the triggering mechanism. He told about the plumber running off, then coming back to shoot at him as he beat on the trigger. Kat stared at him with awe and horror, which only increased when he revealed he'd been shocked by the wires after he'd removed from the triggering device.

"Wow," Denny said. "You're right, that was the trigger, just like he used for the shotgun shells. It's a good thing you didn't realize he might have rigged it to go off if anyone messed with it."

"Glad I didn't know," Joe said. "So if I did stop the trigger, why did it blow up anyway?"

Denny surmised that once the gas vapor filled the elevator shaft, there could have been a spark from just about anywhere in eleven stories of electrical connections. Any spark would have caused that explosion. Once the shaft was filled with vapor it was going to blow sooner or later.

"He had it set to go at the optimal distribution of his gas vapor. Once you delayed that, the gas settled and the delay greatly diminished the power of the explosion."

Filmore stepped up and offered a hand to shake. "And that fire alarm started an evacuation to make us all proud," he said. "It's like a lifetime of fire drills actually kicked in for most people."

"Most people?" Kat asked.

"We won't know for a while if everyone got out," Denny said, then gestured toward the massive crowd gathered outside. "But all <u>these</u> people did. Thanks to you."

SIMON UNLOADED the last packets of cash from the Ford Falcon in the towing yard and found the old flip cell phone he'd left himself at the bottom. It was sealed in a baggie with several loose batteries. It had been there for a long time, but one of the batteries had enough juice to power it up. He only had to make one call, so it was enough.

He loaded the second duffel bag stuffed with cash into the passenger knee space of his crappy Oldsmobile. He got in, ready to leave town for a good long time.

Then he made the call.

WITHIN MINUTES after pulling back the SWAT team on FBI orders, Captain Cubbin had begun to think about ignoring the warning and send the team in anyway, he was tired of losing his crime scenes.

That's when his crime scene exploded.

Enright and Bittinger hit the ground fast for a couple of old guys, as did everyone else. Enright had a picture forever fixed in his mind of the roof lifting straight up, then fragmenting before everything in the house sailed about a quarter mile away in every direction.

The ammunition started popping off faster than machine gun fire and that sent everyone ducking. It didn't last long, despite the number of rounds that exploded.

Even as the deafening sound of the explosion was still reverberating in their ears, and the fear of lingering ammo eruptions plagued everyone, Captain Cubbin, the SWAT team and Bittinger all looked at Enright and nodded their thanks. In his mind he thanked Joe. He and Bitt were supposed to follow on the heels of the SWAT team, but once again Mrs. Enright would not become a widow. 'Good for us,' he thought.

36

K at loved her new office. She had the entire sun porch for her desk and computer and files and reading chair. She was surrounded by windows that she made certain were locked, of course, but that fear would eventually calm down. She could look up and down the boulevard and across at the dense woods along the river which were much as they had been for millennia. It was fantastic and airy and roomy. She felt on top of the world.

Joe carried the last box of his stuff into the second bedroom which was overflowing with his things stacked around his easy chair, ugly thing that it was. He plugged in one of his surviving floor lamps and searched for the least offensive shade, but decided the bulk of the unpacking and settling-in would wait for another day. They were both still recovering and they'd been at it for hours. It had helped them avoid thinking about the events in that parking ramp. They also desperately wanted home to be comfortable for both of them, because for the foreseeable future, she was going to have to work from there. The outlook of her building was still entirely up in the air.

It was already heading toward dusk and though he real- ized that sunset came early this time of year, it was late enough for Joe to pour a couple of bourbons for them. He stopped and stood in the archway from the dining room to the living room and watched Kat happily settling into her office. She was nicely framed by the windows and he was reminded of their many near-misses. They both had minor cuts and bruises and he marveled at how lucky they both were that was the extent of it.

"Come here, I have something to show you," Joe said as he offered her the cut crystal glass.

She took it and ignored that it wasn't quite cocktail hour yet. It was late enough in New York anyway.

"To our home," he said and they clinked glasses.

Joe led her to the door of the second bedroom, the new residence of his familiar and unsightly things. "I live here in this wonderful apartment," he said as he pulled the door shut. "And you don't have to look at it."

"Great invention. What do you call it?"

"Door."

"That might just catch on," she said and opened the door to look. Now that his things weren't clashing with her things, she momentarily thought it wasn't that bad. Then she took another look and realized, yes it was.

"I do love the owner of that stuff," she said, taking his hand and leading him to their living room. "And I love living with him." She sat on the couch, promptly put her feet on the coffee table and patted the seat next to her.

Joe gaped at her in shock. "Really?"

"I'll order a glass for it tomorrow, but for now..."

He kicked off his shoes, sat beside her, put his feet up and leaned back to relax. They both noticed that the hole in the wall from the bullet Kat shot at Cory was directly in their line of sight, but they chose not to mention it at the moment. 'Life can be perfect,' he thought as they clinked glasses again.

Before either of them finished a sip of bourbon, their door flew open and in stormed three heavily armed FBI agents. They darted in every direction with guns raised, as they checked all the rooms, before Denny strode in. She looked at the shocked couple on the couch.

"God, I love your place!" she said, marveling at the vintage elegance. "That must be you," she said to Kat.

Denny nodded at the other agents and sent them away, then gestured for Joe and Kat to sit back. "We picked the locks, so nothing got broken."

"That was sort of the last of my questions," Joe said.

Denny sat down in one of the easy chairs facing the couch and pulled a sheaf of papers from the pocket of her jacket, then handed them to Joe.

"The plumber got away," she said.

Joe glanced at the papers, then back to her. "How are you sure?"

"We've had teams in the building all last night and all day today. We found everything that remains of the things you told us about, the truck and bomb mechanism."

"Cory died, right? And Devins?"

"Yes and yes, but Devins was shot. Executed. And we found a third body in the carcass of Cory's pickup truck. We're guessing it's his wife, but preliminary suggests she didn't die in the building or even at that time."

"She was probably shot in the little farm house that burned down," Joe said. "How'd she get there?"

Denny shook her head. "One thing we got a lot of is questions. Mysteries all around this thing still."

"How about other people in the building?" Kat asked.

"We've got a couple people injured from trampling in the evacuation, but no bombing victims."

Kat happily clinked her glass with Joe at that news.

"And the two kids?" Joe asked.

"Gone," Denny said.

"I wonder if they'll ever surface again," Joe said.

"Not if they have anything to say about it," Kat said. "They have amazing determination."

"And no parents. That's rough," Joe said.

"Back to the adults," Denny said. "So three bodies were found in the building, including the woman, but no third male terrorist...that means the plumber got away."

"Terrorists?" Joe said, "Officially?"

"Kind of goes with attacking the government and having a house filled with munitions, arms and explosives."

"So...you thought he might come here?" Joe said, gesturing toward the FBI agents just outside the door.

"You've seen him and talked to him," Denny said. "You said it yourself, he's not the sort to leave loose ends."

That sunk in, leaving a silence around them. Finally, Joe looked down at the papers she'd given him. It was a variety of tracts, credos and other printed ramblings of white supremacists. He handed a couple to Kat and they both looked through them with alarm.

"You picked some nasty people to piss off, Joe," Denny said with a smile. "The little barn next to Devins' house didn't blow up and we found those and a bunch more tucked into a hiding spot in there. And a lot more guns.

"The plumber must be three states away by now," Kat said with uncertain conviction.

"Maybe. But I'd like to find out for sure and catch him

and whoever helped him with this thing. It seems to be much bigger than we thought. So, in the mean time..."

Joe and Kat looked at each other. "In the mean time?"

"You're kind of sitting ducks," Denny said as she got up and walked to the sun porch. "What a perfect office!"

DENNY LED the parade out of the beautiful brick three story, six-unit building on Mississippi River Boulevard to a pair of black federal SUVs parked outside. Enright would love them, Joe thought.

All six of them carried some of Joe and Kat's hastily packed belongings to put in the back of the cars.

"By the way," Denny said. "The mayor wanted to give you a citation for, you know, saving hundreds of lives."

Joe looked at Kat with a smile. This might make up a bit for being displaced.

"Don't let it go to your head," Kat said.

"Don't worry," Denny said. "We cancelled that."

Joe got into the back of one of the SUVs and found a wide, flat box with a bow. "What's this?"

Denny turned from the front seat and smiled.

Joe opened it and found an elaborate embossed citation with hand calligraphy from the mayor. And Joe's cell phone.

"You should take more pictures," Denny said as the car drove off, taking Joe and Kat away from their perfect home.

Please rate/review this book
on Kindle & Goodreads

WANT MORE JOE BRANDT?
Click: <u>"Recollections of Murder"</u>
Look for the third Joe Brandt Thriller,
"The Bridge"
coming in early 2019

ALSO BY DAVID HOWARD

Joe Brandt novels

"RECOLLECTIONS OF MURDER"

"THE UNRAVELING MAN"

"THE BRIDGE" (coming in 2019)

Non-fiction

"THE TOOLS OF SCREENWRITING"

St. Martin's Press

"HOW TO BUILD A GREAT SCREENPLAY"

St. Martin's Press

Look for David Howard's author page at:

amazon.com/author/david.howard

Contact the author at:

David@davidhowardbooks.com

ABOUT THE AUTHOR

When I was nine I decided to write a novel because I loved stories. Whatever tale I tried to tell in those few pages – which I guarantee were not scrawled in crayon – has been consigned to the ash heap of childhood. But the passion for writing and storytelling has always remained with me.

Once I overcame the widespread Midwestern belief that real people don't make a living by "making stuff up," my desire to tell stories took me to New York and film school at Columbia University. From there I began a career as a screenwriter and now I get paid to invent fictions that take place in worlds of my own creation. I have written over two dozen produced (and award-winning) film and television projects as well as a couple successful books on screen-writing which have been widely adopted and translated. Along the way I became the founder of the graduate screen-writing program at the School of Cinematic Arts at USC where I continue to teach and encourage others to make things up for fun and profit.

And yet with all that, my desire to write novels never truly abated.

So Joe Brandt was born and his fictional life began in my

home town of St. Paul, Minnesota. Joe is a scrappy assistant district attorney with a dark past who obsessively fights for underdogs, which inevitably gets him into hot water (on its way to a full boil). I still write for film and television – I have an international series in active development right now – but I have returned to my first passion. I write legal and crime thrillers, novels that I hope will be too exciting for you to put down.